TRUFFLE TROUBLE

Books by Amanda Flower

The Katharine Wright Mysteries
To Slip the Bonds of Earth
Not They Who Soar

The Amish Candy Shop Mysteries
Assaulted Caramel
Lethal Licorice
Premeditated Peppermint
Criminally Cocoa (ebook novella)
Toxic Toffee
Botched Butterscotch (ebook novella)
Marshmallow Malice
Candy Cane Crime (ebook novella)
Lemon Drop Dead
Peanut Butter Panic
Blueberry Blunder
Gingerbread Danger
Truffle Trouble

The Amish Matchmaker Mystery series
Matchmaking Can Be Murder
Courting Can Be Killer
Marriage Can Be Mischief
Honeymoons Can Be Hazardous
Dating Can Be Deadly
Newlyweds Can Be Knocked Off

TRUFFLE TROUBLE

Amanda Flower

Kensington Publishing Corp.
kensingtonbooks.com

KENSINGTON BOOKS are published by

Kensington Publishing Corp.
900 Third Avenue
New York, NY 10022

First Printing: April 2026

ISBN: 978-1-4967-4377-0

ISBN: 978-1-4967-4378-7 (ebook)

10 9 8 7 6 5 4 3 2 1

Printed in the United States of America

The authorized representative in the EU for product safety and compliance
is eucomply OU, Parnu mnt 139b-14, Apt 123
Tallinn, Berlin 11317, hello@eucompliancepartner.com.

For my husband, David

Acknowledgments

I always love returning to my Amish village of Harvest and am so grateful to my readers who enjoy traveling back there book after book. This series and the Amish Matchmaker Mysteries would not be possible without your love for the characters and their stories.

I want to thank Kensington for their support of my writing for over a decade. I have written well over twenty books for Kensington now. For any author these days, it's rare to have a home in publishing, but I have a home at Kensington. Thank you. And special thanks to my kind editor, Elizabeth Trout, and my hardworking publicist, Larissa Ackerman.

Also, thanks to my amazing agent, Nicole Resciniti, whom I have been with for more than fifteen years. That in and of itself is an accomplishment. I'm so grateful for her partnership and more so for her friendship.

Love and gratitude to my husband, David Seymour, who is my best friend and biggest cheerleader. I love you, David.

Finally, thanks to God for letting Harvest continue to thrive.

Chapter One

"Bailey, you're getting married tomorrow!" My cousin Charlotte squeezed both of my hands and jumped up and down. Her red-gold braid bounced behind her head as she moved. "Finally."

"Finally?" I arched my brow at her. "Why is everyone saying 'finally'? Was there ever any doubt that Aiden and I would marry?" I smiled to take the bite off my words.

"Yes! So much doubt. The two of you dragged your feet. It's been years! Everyone in Harvest—no, in all of Holmes County—has wanted this from the time you and Aiden met. It was love at first sight. You would have to be blind not to see it."

I thought back to the moment I'd met Aiden. I had been standing in my Amish grandparents' candy shop, Swissmen Sweets, cutting up fudge when he came in. I had just popped an extra-large piece of fudge in my mouth when he spoke to me. I was so startled I almost choked. It had not been my finest moment by any means. I wouldn't have called it love at first sight. He had been much closer to giving me the Heimlich maneuver than falling in love with me.

I rolled my eyes. "That might be a bit of an exaggeration."

"Don't kill the fantasy everyone in the village has had about your love story. It's one for the ages and will be passed down from one generation to the next." She dropped my hands and placed hers over her heart.

I snorted.

"Aren't you happy to be getting married?" Charlotte looked stricken. I thought the person who would be most devastated if Aiden and my romance had a bad end was her. Well, her and Aiden's mother, Juliet Brook. I suspected that Juliet had been waiting for Aiden and me to marry before we'd even met.

"I'm very happy," I said, doing my best to put her fears at ease. "I have been waiting for this day for a long time, too. Maybe not as long as the entire village, but I'm ready to start my life with Aiden. There's so much to do, and then there's the Summer Soiree on top of the wedding. Margot said she had a little project for me for the soiree, but she hasn't told me what it is yet. I'm hoping to leave for the honeymoon before she gets a chance."

Margot Rawlings was the community planner for the village of Harvest. She orchestrated all the large events on the square, from the Christmas parade to the farmers' market. Every year, she added more and more events with the hope that Harvest would surpass Berlin as the most-visited Amish town in Holmes County,

Ohio. So far, Berlin was still winning, but Margot was never discouraged.

"Don't you want to know, instead of having her spring it on you?" Charlotte held on to the end of her braid. Even though she was no longer Amish, she still dressed modestly in a SWISSMEN CANDYWORKS T-shirt and long denim skirt. My cousin had left the Amish way over a year ago, when she married Sheriff Deputy Luke Little. Deputy Little was a kind and steady man, and he was a perfect fit for Charlotte's bubbly personality.

I would not say that Deputy Little was her true reason for leaving the faith. She'd had one foot out the door already when she left her very conservative Amish district to live in Harvest and work with my *maami*, Clara King, and me at Swissmen Sweets. Years later, we expanded into our candy factory, Swissmen Candyworks. I couldn't imagine running the business without Charlotte, especially when I was in New York City so often filming my show for Gourmet Television, *Bailey's Amish Sweets.*

I walked around the lobby of Swissmen Candyworks, straightening displays and checking the expiration dates on the packages of candy. We couldn't have anything past due out on the shelves.

"I'd rather not." I tightened the ponytail on the back of my head. At the moment, I was dressed for a workday in a T-shirt and jeans, but soon I would have to get ready for my rehearsal dinner.

I felt like I was moving in a fog. After all the time Aiden and I had been together, through so many ups and downs, we were finally getting married. Charlotte said that she couldn't believe it, but I *really* couldn't believe it.

"My goal is to avoid Margot at all costs. I'll get married and then leave for my honeymoon right after. There won't be any time for her to trap me into one of her projects."

"Have you met Margot?" Charlotte asked.

It was a fair question. Even I doubted the success rate of my plan, but I wasn't going to admit it. I just needed to make it through the next thirty-six hours, and I would be in the clear.

Charlotte put her hands on her hips, and her bright green eyes flashed with irritation. "I can't believe that Margot had the nerve to schedule the Summer Soiree just days after your wedding. Everyone in the village has known the wedding date for months."

"She said that it was the best date for the vineyards that are participating."

Charlotte sniffed. "I don't even know that she should be doing it. I know I'm not Amish any longer, but I still believe in the idea that alcohol leads to trouble. Margot knows how most of the Amish feel about it, and she's just throwing it in their faces."

For the Amish, alcohol consumption was a tricky topic, and it truly depended on the individual district as to whether it was allowed. Some said "absolutely not," and others said it "was all right in moderation." All agreed that getting drunk was wrong. The Amish believed overconsumption of anything was wrong—from alcohol to food to even candy.

Harvest was predominately an Amish village, and the reception Margot had received from the event from the Amish population, and even some of the English community members, had been less than favorable.

I would never admit this to Charlotte, but I, too, wished the soiree wasn't so close to my wedding. Because of the closeness of the dates, the soiree would be a main topic of conversation at the reception. I was confident of that. Most of the village would be at my wedding, and when they all got together, the gossip flew.

I prayed that Margot and Ruth Yoder, the bishop's wife, didn't get into a fistfight over the matter at the wedding reception. Ruth had been the most vocal against the idea of the Summer Soiree. Anyone who knew her wasn't surprised by this. She constantly lamented the fact that Harvest seemed to be turning more English, at least in her eyes. The soiree was the final straw for her. She had even gone so far as talking to the town council about the matter. For an Amish woman to dip her toe in politics in any way was unheard of. If the Amish had an issue with the English powers that be, more often than not they ignored them, or in extreme cases, a male leader of the church would step forward.

It seemed to me that Bishop Yoder, Ruth's husband, had chosen the "ignore" method, and apparently that left her no choice but to go to the council herself to shut the soiree down. Unfortunately for Ruth, it was very much still on. The chance of her and Margot coming to blows over the matter was unlikely, but still a possibility.

"We can worry about the Summer Soiree after the wedding," I said. "I can only handle one giant event at a time."

"Understood." Charlotte clasped her hands together. "You and Aiden make the most beautiful couple, and to think that you are marrying my husband's best friend, and we are cousins! We're all going to be one big family soon."

I smiled. This was true. Aiden was close friends with Charlotte's husband, Deputy Luke Little. Also because Aiden was the Holmes County sheriff, he was Deputy Little's boss. Now that we were about to be family, I would have thought that I would start thinking of Deputy Little as Luke, but in my mind, it just didn't fit him. He was most definitely Deputy Little, and he always would be to me.

"What time is Darcy getting here?" I asked as I looked around the lobby of Swissmen Candyworks, the candy factory that I had built from the ground up. After I took over most of the operations of Swissmen Sweets from my grandmother, it was clear that we were outgrowing the old candy shop, as online orders skyrocketed with the popularity of *Bailey's Amish Sweets*. Moving the candy shop was never even an option as it was also *Maami*'s home. The most obvious choice was to make a second, much-bigger location. I opted for a factory and not a traditional storefront because it would give me the best opportunity to expand our business to large retail stores across the country. We hadn't made that giant leap yet. At the moment, our candies were sold in a number of smaller shops in Holmes County and at the Harvest Market, which shares the parking lot with Swissmen Candyworks.

The candy factory had taken almost two years to become a reality. The process had been full of challenges, some worse than others, but now we were open and overall business was good. I was also grateful for Charlotte, who had become my right-hand woman in the candy business. I didn't know how I could manage both places without her or without *Maami.* For over fifty years, *Maami* had awakened every morning at four to make fresh candies and fudge to hand-sell to the tourists who came in by the busload to Swissmen Sweets. For many coming to Harvest, the candy shop remained the main attraction. It was an authentically Amish candy shop where everything was made by hand.

For the most part, we made all the candies in the factory by hand, too, but we certainly had more equipment to speed up the process and increase efficiency. Visitors could watch us make candy from beginning to end on one of our candy-making tours. However, there would be no tours on my wedding weekend, as the reception was to be in the factory and on the neighboring grounds.

"Darcy should be here any minute," Charlotte said.

As if she'd beckoned her on, the front door to the Candyworks opened, and Darcy Woodin came inside, wheeling a large wagon ladened down with containers and dishes.

She held the door for her grandmother, Lois Henry, who pulled an equally large wagon.

"Good heavens, it has to be a hundred degrees out there. It's not supposed to be this warm in June. This is August weather, if you ask me. The world must be really heating up. When I was young, it was cool and rainy in June." Lois delicately touched her brow. "I think my makeup is running. I hate going through my day with a bare face. Can someone powder my nose before I run into a potential husband?"

I smiled. Lois was always on the lookout for a potential husband. She had had several over her life, and she'd told me more than once that I was "behind the eight ball" just having my first marriage in my thirties.

"Your makeup looks perfect," I said.

"You're sure? It must be my new setting spray that is holding it together. I got the kind that could freeze an elephant in his tracks." Lois wore a flowy, floral caftan. Her spiky, red-purple hair was perfectly in its upright and locked position. There was so much product in Lois's hair that nothing short of a hurricane would move it. She finished the look with a full face of makeup, including false lashes and enough costume jewelry to open her own shop. Everything from her clothes to her makeup to her hair was bright and vibrant. And this was her day look. I couldn't wait to see what she wore to the wedding. There was a good chance that she would outshine me, and I was completely fine with that. No one could compete with Lois Henry when it came to fashion.

Lois dropped the handle to her wagon. "Seriously. I should at least powder my nose. I know that some of the young folks find the dewy look appealing, but at my age it does not work."

"Grandma, you look fine," Darcy said and quietly set down the wagon handle.

Darcy was a reserved young woman and could not be more opposite from her boisterous and outspoken grandmother. Even so, their bond reminded me so much of my *maami* and me. There was nothing like a close bond between grandmother and granddaughter.

Darcy pushed her long blond curls out of her face and gave me a hug. "Bailey, I can't tell you how happy we are to be part of your big day. I'm honored that you asked Sunbeam Catering to be part of this. This is our first big event, and you are really taking a chance on us. I wish I could repay you."

"Don't be silly. There is nothing to repay. Aiden and I love your food. You know that we eat at the café way more times than we do at home because of our busy schedules. You were always going to be our choice."

Darcy blushed.

She might be embarrassed by the praise, but what I said was true. Sunbeam Café was always our first choice. Darcy had opened Sunbeam Café a few years ago, and since day one, the café on the square had become a staple in Harvest. Her food, which included soups, sandwiches, and salads of all kinds, was a nice respite from the heavy Amish food that most people came to expect in Holmes County. It was especially popular with locals. One could only eat so much Amish fried chicken or ham steak before the doctor started muttering about cholesterol numbers.

There'd been some pushback when she'd opened the café. Harvest was primarily an Amish town in the middle of Holmes County. Not everyone—mainly Ruth Yoder again—was happy with the idea of a non-Amish business being on the square, which up to that point had all been Amish-owned.

"I'm so glad we have this extra time to set up. I hope

it didn't hurt your factory too much to have it closed two days for the wedding. It certainly makes everything easier."

I smiled. "I thought so, too. My main goal for this wedding is *easy*. I don't know if I will achieve that on all fronts, but at least I know the reception and the food will go that way." I bit my lip. "The ceremony might be another issue."

"Why's that?" Lois asked. "Isn't Aiden's stepfather officiating?"

I nodded. "Reverend Brook is officiating. I'm more worried about what Margot Rawlings has up her sleeve. She is decorating the square, so it could be"—I paused—"memorable."

Lois chuckled. "I bet it will be. Millie's husband, Uriah, takes care of the square grounds for Margot. I'm sure he knows her plan by now. I'll see what intel I can find out."

Millie Fisher Schrock was Lois's best friend, and she and her husband, Uriah, were just about the sweetest couple in Harvest. Uriah would be able to put my mind at ease, and I felt better knowing he would be involved. He was Amish and would understand my desire for something simple. Yes, it was my wedding, but I wanted my Amish grandmother and Amish friends to feel comfortable at the ceremony and the reception.

I grinned. "If you could, I would be grateful. I'm on pins and needles over it. I asked for simple."

"Margot doesn't do simple," Lois said.

How well I knew.

Darcy wrapped her hands around her waist. "Bailey, I'm just so impressed with how you are able to juggle everything—the candy shop, the factory, your show, and now the wedding. I can barely keep it together since I added catering to my repertoire."

"You're doing just fine, but I'm happy to talk to you any time."

"But not today." Charlotte looped her arm through Darcy's. "There is too much to do. Darcy, let me show you where to set up the buffet. You'll be bringing the food tomorrow, correct?"

"We have some of it in the van," Darcy said. "Bailey said we could store it in the refrigerator here."

"Absolutely," Charlotte said and started to pull her away when the door opened again. I expected it to be a member of my staff or perhaps Jean Pierre, my mentor from JP Chocolates in New York. Jean Pierre had insisted on making my wedding cake, and he was flying it from the city to Harvest today. He was set to land any time. I wanted a simple, picnic-style wedding, but I knew there would be nothing simple about Jean Pierre's cake. I hoped I had a table big enough to hold it.

But Jean Pierre was not at the door. It was none other than Margot Rawlings, followed by a small group of people I didn't know.

Across the lobby, Darcy gasped.

Chapter Two

I glanced at Darcy. She was as white as a sheet, making the freckles that danced across the bridge of her nose look that much brighter.

"Won't this work beautifully?" Margot asked the group behind her.

"It's perfect," a tall, thin woman in a sundress said. "There's so much potential."

"Exactly. It will be the perfect place for people to come and cool down during the soiree. It promises to be a hot night, and we have to have some place for people to rest. I think one of the wine stations could go in here as well."

"It should be mine," a very handsome man close to my age said. The man looked around the room as if he was assessing everything. His hair was dark brown and on the longer side, and he wore dark sunglasses over his eyes. His clothes were pressed, and I noted that he wasn't wearing socks with his leather loafers. This was not the typical clientele to wander into Swissmen

Candyworks. "My vineyard is the oldest at the soiree and should have the best spot."

One of the two women in the group folded her arms across her chest. "And does that mean that I should have the worst place because I have the newest winery?"

He narrowed his eyes. "I don't care where they put you, Carly, as long as you're as far away from me possible."

She glared back at him.

Margot clapped her hands. "Now, let's not argue about placement. I will have it all sorted out. This will simply be a place to refresh and escape the summer heat that evening. All four vineyards will be on the square. We must remember that the square is the focal point of Harvest."

"Margot, did you need something?" I asked.

"Oh, Bailey, there you are!" she said as if I hadn't been standing in the middle of the room the entire time. Margot wore her typical summer uniform of jean shorts and a Harvest T-shirt, and her brown–going gray, short hair bouncing on the top of her head like a collection of springs. "I'm so glad I caught you before all the craziness of the wedding. I realize you must have so much to do, but I do have to ask one little favor. It's small and should take no time at all."

I was in for it.

"What's the favor, Margot?"

"We need a cooling venue for the Summer Soiree on Thursday evening. There promises to be a terrible heat wave coming in. The temperatures are set to be close to ninety. We need a place to go where people can cool off and enjoy their wine in some air-conditioning. The Candyworks is the perfect spot."

I bet it was.

"I don't know if I can do that, Margot. I don't want to upset my grandmother's Amish district. Bishop Yoder does not approve of the Summer Soiree because of the alcohol." I shot an apologetic look at the group with her. "No offense."

"Bishop Yoder?" Margot yelped. "Does anyone even believe it's Bishop Yoder and not that *woman*? She has been trying to bring down the entertainment I bring to Harvest for years, and now she's kicking up a fuss over the soiree. It's not like I'm throwing a frat party."

"Nobody thinks that, Margot," Lois said.

"I still should talk to my grandmother before I agree to anything," I said. "I don't want her to be uncomfortable."

"Do you want people to faint from the heat? No one will come back to Harvest if tourists drop dead from heatstroke. I don't think you want that on your conscience, do you?"

"I don't know how it would be on my conscience when I won't even be here."

She nodded. "Exactly. You won't be here, so how can your grandmother be offended?"

"I can't ask my Amish staff to be here."

"What about Charlotte? She can do it."

Charlotte looked at me in panic.

I sighed. "I will have to think about it, Margot. I'm getting married tomorrow, and you're not giving me much time to think it over." As I said this, I guessed that was exactly why she was asking me the day before my wedding—so I wouldn't have the time to address it. Margot could be sneaky when she thought it would benefit Harvest. Planning the next big event on the square was always on the top of her mind.

She placed a hand on her chest. "It's not my fault that the weather report changed. I'm just trying to think of solutions that will protect the many visitors who will be coming to Harvest for the soiree. The Amish business, including yours, should be grateful for it. The inn is booked solid, and so are many of the surrounding hotels as well. It will be the premier event in Harvest this summer." She paused as if she realized what she was saying. "Your wedding is important, too."

"Thanks," I said. "You haven't introduced us to your friends."

"Oh, I'm so sorry. I was just in such a rush to find out if you would be willing to support us, considering how much this village has supported you over the years."

I made a face.

"These are the owners of the four wineries who will be sharing samples of their wines at the Summer Soiree. Because this was our first event like this, I didn't want to overbook the wineries. There are so many in Holmes County, but these are the best of the best." She cleared her throat. "Bailey King, may I introduce to you Angel Stark from Celestial Vineyard, Jon Michael Grimes from Country Vintage Wines, Carly Crestwood from Hackney Family Winery, and Jason Hackney from Swiss Valley Winery."

"Jason Hackney!" Lois cried. "This is Jason Hackney? *Your* Jason Hackney?" She directed her question to her granddaughter.

Darcy clamped her mouth shut and nodded.

Lois reached into her purse. "Why can't I ever find my brick when I need it? I hope I didn't leave it at home."

I put my hand on her arm. "A brick? Why do you need a brick?"

Jason smiled smoothly. "Darcy, it's so nice to see you again. I wondered if I would run into you when I came to Harvest."

Darcy shot a glance at her grandmother, as if to make sure Lois wasn't about to hurl a brick or any other heavy object at Jason's head.

Margot looked from Jason to Darcy and back again. "The two of you know each other."

"Yes, of course. Holmes County isn't that large, and many of the business owners know each other."

I would agree that this was true on principle, but I had never met Jason Hackney before, and I was a business owner. In fact, I didn't know any of people in front of me. I had always meant to visit the vineyards that were scattered throughout the county, but it was just one of those things that I never got around to doing. It was difficult to be a tourist in the place where you lived.

"Hmm," Margot said as if she wasn't so sure that this was good news.

"That's hogwash," Lois interjected. "This spineless weasel broke my granddaughter's heart. What do you have to say for yourself for doing that?"

The other vintners took a big step back from Jason. It was clear to me that they didn't want to be in the line of fire in case Lois hurled a brick—or something worse—at him. I didn't even want to think what in her purse might be worse than a brick. There were times when ignorance really was for the best.

Darcy's face, which had been stone-white a moment ago, now flushed bright red. The poor girl was going through all the stages of shock.

"Oh," Jason said, not missing a beat. "We were just friends for a time, weren't we, Darcy? I think your grandmother might have misunderstood what we meant to each other."

"I don't misunderstand anything," Lois snapped. "You—"

"Yes," Darcy said loudly. "We were friends. Just friends." She glanced at her grandmother with pleading eyes. "I told you that, Grams. Remember?"

Lois pressed her lips together and zipped her massive purse closed with a jerk. "I suppose you did."

"Well, now that we have that settled," Margot said. "Bailey, I just thought of another thing that you can do for the soiree. I don't think it's too much to ask."

She never thought anything was too much to ask. Sometimes I envied Margot for her confidence that everyone would say yes to her. Then again, she didn't take no for an answer that often . . . or ever.

"I'm hoping you can create a signature candy pairing for each of the wineries, to go with one of their wines. It will add so much value to the event."

"Margot, I'm getting married tomorrow, and my family is arriving soon, as well as my friends from New

York. I have the rehearsal and rehearsal dinner tonight. I just can't do that. I'm happy to donate chocolate and candy to the event. I don't think my grandmother would have any issue with that, but I can't make all new recipes in less than twelve hours."

Margot scowled. "It would be better if you made something special and new."

"Then you should have asked me weeks ago."

"I can handle it, Margot," Charlotte said. "I know everything that we have in stock. I'm sure something we have ready-made will work."

Margot gave a great sigh. "I suppose the two of you leave me with no other choice."

"This lovely young lady looks like she will have everything well in hand," Jason said.

Charlotte frowned at the compliment. Even though she was no longer Amish, she still had an Amish sensibility. Amish women did not welcome such compliments from men other than their husbands, and Charlotte was married.

The doors to the Candyworks opened again, and this time my future mother-in-law, Juliet Brook, came inside, walking her pig on a leash. I looked up at the lobby's oak-beamed ceiling. The best part of getting married tomorrow would be getting out of town and going on a real vacation with my new husband, because at least then no one could ask me to do something for them.

"Oh, Bailey," Juliet said. "I didn't know you would have so many people here today. Isn't the factory closed?" She wore overalls over a pink-and-white polka-dotted

T-shirt. In one hand she held a basket full of mushrooms, and in the other she held the end of the leash. At the end of the leash was Jethro, her black-and-white polka-dotted support pig. He had dirt on his snout, and I could have been wrong, but it looked like Juliet also had dirt on her overalls. Their physical appearance was the most shocking thing about them. Juliet and her pig Jethro were always pristine, and I was certain this was the first time I had ever seen Juliet in pants. She was known for dresses, preferably ones with polka dots because they went best with her pig.

She smiled. "Darcy, you and Bailey are just the people I wanted to see. Look what Jethro has collected for you." She walked over to Darcy and placed the basket of mushrooms in her hand. "We were foraging today, and he found a stash of mushrooms that will be perfect for the mushroom tarts that you and your cook, Enoch, are making for the reception! Isn't that wonderful?"

Darcy stared down at the basket as if she wasn't sure to make of it. "Thank you. These are chanterelles."

"That's right," Juliet said with a beaming smile. "Jethro found a stash of them in Harvest Woods."

"You should be careful with those," Jon Michael said. "If you're not careful, a wild mushroom could kill you."

Juliet huffed. "I will have you know that Jethro went through all the required training to be a mushroom-hunting pig. There is no chance that he would pick the wrong mushroom. Our instructor said that he had the nose for foraging."

"Don't pigs hunt truffles, not mushrooms?" Angel

asked, speaking for the first time. She was a tall, thin woman with black hair, and she wore glasses on the tip of her nose.

"They can find both," Juliet said as if she was offended Angel would question her pig's fungi-finding skills. "Jethro is particularly talented at finding any of them."

Jon Michael rolled his eyes. "If the instructor said it, it must be true."

Juliet frowned. "My son is marrying Bailey tomorrow, and I would never do anything that might upset the wedding."

"That's true," Margot piped up. "She has been waiting for this wedding for ages."

Darcy looked through the basket. "I actually took a course in mushroom foraging. From what I see, these are all chanterelles, and they are safe to eat. Thank you, Juliet, it was very thoughtful of you to collect these for me. Enoch is well versed in foraging, too. He will know for certain if these are all safe to cook with."

Juliet gave Jon Michael a look, then smiled at Darcy. "I'm so glad. Now I must be off. There is so much to do before tomorrow. I don't think I was even this excited for my own wedding to the reverend, and that was the best day of my life!" She scooped Jethro off the floor. "Oh, Bailey, Jethro is so tired after foraging for hours and hours, can he stay here with you for a little while so I can go check on the reverend at the church?"

I sighed. "Sure, why not?"

She put the pig in my arms and walked out the door.

"I can see you have your hands full, Bailey," Margot

said. "We should continue the tour of the square." Her tone was mock-regretful. "So that everyone knows where to set up before the soiree." She shook her head. "Such a shame that you will miss such an important event."

I wasn't regretting it in the least. I told the vintners that I was happy to meet them and said goodbye, but my eye was on Jason. I couldn't suppress my curiosity over his relationship with Darcy. Were they really "just friends"? She and Lois had had a very big reaction to him, much bigger than "just a friend" would warrant.

Margot and the winery owners left, and still holding Jethro, I gave a sigh of relief.

After they were gone, Lois muttered, "Scoundrel" under her breath.

I wanted to ask her what she meant by that, but Charlotte waved her phone at me. "Jean Pierre just landed. The cake is on the ground."

By the time I turned back to speak to Lois, she and Darcy had left the room.

As much as I wanted to run after them to find out what was going on, I shook my head. Those were questions for another day. I was getting married tomorrow. I didn't have the time to take on anyone else's problems.

In hindsight, I wished that I had.

Chapter Three

"Easy does it! Easy does it! That cake has some of the most expensive chocolate in the world baked into it. You don't want to be the one to lose it," Jean Pierre said as five Amish men carefully wheeled my wedding cake into Swissmen Candyworks on a custom-made dolly.

The cake wobbled as the dolly's wheels rocked over the threshold.

"Careful! Don't touch it, but be careful!" Jean Pierre cried in his heavy French accent.

Sweat gathered on the men's brows as they wheeled the cart to a stop in the middle of the candy factory's lobby.

Jean Pierre, an angular man in his seventies, floated around the cake like he was performing some kind of ballet. He inspected every inch of the cake, then stepped back. "She is perfect. Not a mark on her. As it should be. She is my finest creation."

I stepped forward. “Jean Pierre, you have outdone yourself this time.”

He grabbed my hand and squeezed it in both of his own. “Yes, I have, because it was for you, *ma chérie*. You know how I feel about you. You are the daughter I never had. I had to make something spectacular.”

And spectacular it was. The cake was seven tiers high and constructed from every kind of chocolate there was. If anyone coming to the wedding didn’t like chocolate, this cake was going to be a massive disappointment. Thankfully, we would also have a candy bar that should keep anyone else happy. It had plenty of sugar-free options, too.

Each layer of the cake was decorated with cascading flowers and truffles of every kind. To be honest, I had never seen so many chocolate truffles on a cake in all my life, and that was saying something, considering Jean Pierre had been my mentor. He’d never met a truffle that he didn’t like.

“It’s not completely done yet,” Jean Pierre said. “I will make all the final tweaks on the day of the wedding. Do you like it, *ma chérie*? We have been working around the clock at JP Chocolates to make sure you have the perfect cake.”

“It is perfect. I honestly don’t know what else you could have done to make it better.”

“Everything and anything can be made better,” Jean Pierre said. “You will be dazzled on the day of your wedding.”

“Should we put it away so that it stays perfect for tomorrow?” my best friend, Cass Calbera, asked. I had known Cass since I was a teen and went to pastry school in New York City. She was a student at the same school. When I got the job at JP Chocolates, I encouraged her to apply there, too. She did, and for nearly a decade we worked together and became even better friends.

If Jean Pierre looked like he didn't fit in Amish Country, Cass appeared to be from Mars. She wore her signature black: black pants, and a long-sleeved, sheer black top over a black tank top. In this heat, the outfit looked terribly uncomfortable to me. She was also my maid of honor, and I had told her that she could pick her own dress. All I knew for sure was that it was black.

"You can move it right into the walking fridge," Charlotte said. "We cleared a place for it." She bit her lip. "It should be big enough." She waved to the Amish men. "Here, let me show you."

With a cacophony of grunts, the men began to move the cake again.

"Be careful," Jean Pierre warned, as if he hadn't been giving them the same warning just moments ago.

Charlotte led the men and the cake into the kitchen, and Jean Pierre watched them go with a forlorn look on his face. "It is my greatest work, and tomorrow it will be eaten." He threw up his hand. "*C'est la vie.* Such is the life of a chocolatier."

Darcy came into the lobby from the direction of the kitchen. She smiled at Jean Pierre, then said to me, "We have everything set for tomorrow. I'll be here bright and early to start the prep work. Will there be someone to let Enoch and me in? He would have loved to have been here today to see where everything would be going, but someone had to stay back and run the café. Iris can't do it herself."

I nodded. Iris Young was an Amish woman who worked part-time as a waitress for Darcy at the café. She could be a bit high-strung at times, so she wasn't the person whom Darcy would want to leave in charge on a bustling Friday in June.

"My staff will be here as early as five. They are making fresh candies for the wedding, too." I reached into my pocket and pulled out a key on a pig key chain. The key chain had been a gift from Juliet, of course. "But just in case they have to step out and aren't here when you arrive, here is a key." I dropped the key in her hand.

She tucked it in her pocket. "Perfect."

I turned to Jean Pierre. "Jean Pierre, this is my friend Darcy. She is catering the wedding."

He bent at the waist and kissed her hand. "It is a pleasure to meet one of Bailey's friends. She has spoken so highly of the people here in Ohio. It's my first time visiting the state. It's very rural. On the drive from the airport, I saw chickens, goats, cows, sheep, and ducks just frolicking about like Noah had just freed them from the ark." He released her hand.

I laughed. "Holmes County is rural, Jean Pierre. Ohio has big cities."

"It's hard to view any place as a big city after a lifetime in New York."

"I would love to see New York City someday," Darcy said. "I've never been."

Jean Pierre turned to me. "You have to bring her to your next taping. She is a chef, is she not? She would be a wonderful addition to the show. Perhaps you could do a sweet and savory episode."

Darcy shook her head. "I'm not a chef. I'm a cook and baker. I never went to school to learn to cook."

"Self-taught is nothing to ignore," Jean Pierre declared. "Many of the best at their crafts are self-taught. It does not matter how much formal education you have if you don't have the talent and determination. What are you making for tomorrow?"

"I would call it 'elevated picnic fare,'" she said.

"That sounds enchanting. A Frenchman loves a good picnic. There is nothing like a good, aged piece of cheese, a fresh baguette, dark chocolate, and nice bottle of wine."

"I'm sorry to disappoint, Jean Pierre, but there won't be any wine or alcohol at the wedding," I said. "I don't want to put my grandmother in an uncomfortable situation with her Amish district."

He shook his head in mock despair. "Yes, you have already told me this. Thankfully, I have brought enough on my private jet to sustain me over the next few days."

"If you stay for a few more days, you could attend the Summer Soiree on the square. It's set to be lovely," Lois said, coming into the room. "And there will be wineries from Holmes County there sharing the best vinos they have to offer."

Jean Pierre placed a hand on his chest when he saw Lois. "Who is this vision?"

Lois looked behind her to make sure he was talking about her and not someone else.

I suppressed a smile. "Jean Pierre, this is my friend

Lois Henry. She's Darcy's grandmother. She will be helping Darcy tomorrow."

"*Enchanté.*" Jean Pierre gave a slight bow. "Are you the mastermind behind this delightful wedding menu I have been hearing about?"

Lois chuckled. "I can't cook a thing. I have no idea where Darcy got her talent, but I do make a mighty fine waitress."

Jean Pierre removed a handkerchief from the inside pocket of his suit jacket. "I'm sure you are the very best. The colors you have chosen for your ensemble this afternoon are striking. They make your beautiful eyes just pop."

Darcy and I shared a smirk.

Lois looked down at her caftan. "Oh, this, I've had it for decades. You can never go wrong in a summer caftan."

"Yes, I can see that." He pulled at his collar. "You said that there is a soiree in a few days."

"Thursday evening," Lois said as she adjusted her giant patchwork purse on her shoulder.

"It sounds intriguing. I will definitely want to stay for that."

"Jean Pierre, we will have to go back to New York for work. Remember JP Chocolates? Your pride and joy?" Cass asked.

He waved his hand. "You can go back on my jet as planned, Cass. You have taken over the day-by-day operations, and all can agree that you run the place much better than I ever did." Jean Pierre straightened his shoulders. "I believe that it would be a good experience for me to see what an Amish Country Summer Soiree is all about."

"You won't regret it," Lois said.

"I don't doubt that," he said and held out his arm to her. "If you won't mind, I would love to be guided around the village by a local. Bailey is far too busy to take me about, and I would never ask her to do such a task just hours before she is to walk down the aisle. I hope it's no trouble for you?"

"It's no trouble at all." Lois looped her arm through his, and the pair walked to the door together.

Lois wiggled her fingers at us before stepping over the threshold. "Darcy, sweetheart, don't wait up for me."

Cass stood in the middle of the lobby with her mouth hanging open. "What just happened here?"

"Looks to me that Lois might just have found husband number five," I said.

Darcy groaned.

Chapter Four

I looked in the floor-length mirror that had been set up in the corner of the room as my mother buzzed around me and fussed with my dress. We were standing in the front room of Swissmen Sweets, across from the square where I was to marry Aiden. I couldn't believe this day had finally come. Now that it was here, I couldn't wait to walk down the aisle to meet my groom. Despite my mother's nerves, I was at peace. I had never been surer about a decision in my life. Aiden was the man for me. He always had been since the day we'd met.

White twinkle lights wrapped around every tree trunk and hung from the branches. The gazebo where the wedding was to take place was decked out in pale pink ribbons and bunting. Margot had decorated the square simply, as I had asked. Part of me wondered if she'd followed my request because she was trying to butter me up so I'd help her more with the Summer Soiree, but there wasn't much more I could do. *Maami* had agreed to have the factory open as a cooling station for the evening, and Charlotte and some of my non-Amish staff would be there to keep the building open. Charlotte already had a list of candies to donate to the Summer Soiree. For anything beyond that, I was out of time. I was leaving for my honeymoon that night after the wedding. Not even Margot would corner me at my own wedding to ask for another favor, so I felt like I was in the clear.

White wooden folding chairs covered the square with just enough room for a center aisle for me to walk down with my father, along with a few paths, so guests could move about. To be honest, I didn't even know how many people would be at the wedding that afternoon. Juliet had insisted that the wedding had to be open to her whole church, and *Maami* had insisted that it had to be open to her whole Amish district. Between the two, I was already looking at four hundred people. Then there was Aiden's sheriff's department and our own family and friends.

I shook my head, feeling grateful that we'd decided to do a picnic reception at the Candyworks instead of a sit-down meal. There was no way we could accommodate so many people if we had made a more formal choice.

"Oh, Bailey, I wish you had followed my suggestion and gone with a more form-fitting dress. You have a lovely figure, and you should show it off. You are all covered up. You won't always have a body to wear a dress like that."

I glanced down at my white lace dress with the high collar and cap sleeves. There was no train, but there was a bit of a fishtail in the back that I particularly liked. It was modest. I didn't disagree with my mother on that point, but this was the perfect dress for me. It was what I wanted to wear.

I let my mother's criticism roll off my back. I had learned a long time ago that our tastes were not aligned and likely never would be.

I peeked out the large front window again, curious about each person who came.

"Bailey," my mother chastised. "Get away from the window. Someone will see you."

I glanced over my shoulder at her. "They will all see me in a matter of minutes."

"It's bad luck." My mother sniffed and pulled at her form-fitting designer dress, which I knew for certain cost more than my entire look, from the top of my head to the tips of my toes. She looked beautiful, though. After leaving Holmes County, my mother had successfully transformed herself into a refined New England wife. I knew that deep down she wished I had followed in her footsteps rather than returning to the village she and my father had fled all those years ago.

"I thought it was bad luck for the groom to see the bride before the wedding, not everyone else," I said.

The shop's door opened, and my father popped his head inside. "They just seated my mother. It's your turn, my dear."

Mom nodded. "All right. Let's get this done."

Dad winked at me over her head as they went back out the door.

When they were gone, I gave a great sigh of relief, and Jethro came out of hiding from behind the counter. He knew my mother wasn't his biggest fan.

Nutmeg, our orange shop cat, followed closely behind him. The little ginger tabby jumped onto the windowsill so he could watch all the proceedings.

Jethro grunted in dismay because he couldn't jump onto the windowsill.

I held out my hand to the little pig and scratched him between his ears. "We will be out there soon enough, buddy, and Nutmeg will be stuck watching from the window."

The cat flicked his tail at me for that comment.

I stood beside Nutmeg at the window and looked out. Charlotte and Cass, my bridesmaids, were already waiting at their posts at the edge of the square to walk. Charlotte wore light pink that matched the ribbon on her bouquet. Cass wore black, of course—I would never have asked her to wear anything else. Because there were only the two bridesmaids, I had let them pick their own dresses, and they each picked a gown that suited them perfectly.

I smiled as I watched my two closest friends chat. They were from two very different worlds, but they'd come together on this day for me.

I was itching to get out there, but I knew I needed to wait there until my father came back to get me.

I closed my eyes and was grateful I had a few moments alone to center myself. I looked down at my feet, and Jethro stared back at me.

His snout was turned up as if he smelled the reception goods in the air. I wouldn't doubt it if he did. Jethro had a nose for sweets.

He wore a little black bow tie and jacket with tails. His leash, which was in my hand, had black-and-white polka dots. I knew there were polka dots on his outfit somewhere if Juliet had had any say in it.

He was the ring bearer, but at that moment the rings were in Cass's possession until just before the little bacon bundle walked down the aisle.

He would walk down with Cass. At present, he was with me until showtime, because for whatever reason, I had the best luck for keeping him calm, and the last thing I needed today was an anxious pig running amok through the square.

"Are you ready for this?" I asked Jethro. "I'm about to be your sister-in-law."

He grunted in return. I took that to mean yes.

Ignoring my mother's earlier warning, I looked out the front window again. I saw my father hurrying back to the candy shop, but that wasn't all I saw. To the right of my father, on the corner of the square, I could see Darcy and the vintner Jason involved in a heated argument. Whatever they were tensely discussing didn't seem to be going well, and Darcy pushed him away from her when he took a step too close. A young woman stood a few feet from them. She had short blond hair and wore a sundress. She had her arms wrapped around her waist.

Jason said something else to Darcy, and she turned her back to him.

He made a rude gesture in return, snapped his fingers at the blond woman, and stomped away.

The young woman glanced at Darcy before running after Jason.

My father opened the door. "Bailey, are you ready?"

I glanced back at the window in the direction where

I had seen Darcy and Jason arguing, but now they were both gone. I hoped Darcy was all right, and I did my best to shake the unease from my mind as I smiled at my father. "I'm ready."

He held out his arm to me, and I took it.

Uriah Schrock had parked a large buggy on the other side of Main Street that blocked the view of Swissmen Sweets from the gazebo.

Charlotte, Jethro, and Cass stepped around the buggy when it was their time to walk down the aisle, but when the music played to indicate it was my turn to enter on my father's arm, the buggy pulled away, revealing us to the guests and to Aiden.

From the top step of the gazebo, Aiden grinned from ear to ear, and all the nerves that had been fluttering inside of me all morning flew away.

The small church band played as I walked down the aisle. I knew there were other people around me, but the only person I could see was Aiden. He looked so happy—no, he was radiant. I guessed I looked much the same.

The walk down the aisle seemed to take a thousand years, but when we finally reached the gazebo steps, Aiden came down them, and my father put my hand into his.

I kissed my dad's cheek before I then walked up the steps with Aiden to stand with Reverend Brook.

"Bailey, Aiden," Reverend Brook asked, "are you ready for this?"

"I've never been more ready for anything in my life," Aiden said.

"Me either," I whispered back.

Jethro yanked his leash from Cass's hand and bolted up the steps to stand with us. The little bacon bundle must have thought the question had been posed to him, as he gave a loud *oink* in agreement, too.

The assembly laughed. Jethro had stolen the show, and it seemed that much more fitting.

"Then let us begin," Reverend Brook said to the congregation.

"One more picture!" my mother cried forty minutes later.

Aiden and I shared a look. Both of our mothers had taken over the photography session after the wedding.

"We got it," the photographer declared.

"Thank goodness," Cass said. "I'm not used to smiling this much."

I raised my brow at her. "You smiled in every picture?"

"Not every one. I'm not a robot." She tossed her black hair over her shoulder.

I laughed, not too concerned about it. Cass always looked beautiful, even when she was scowling. "Everyone should be at the reception by now," I said. "Let's head over. I told Darcy to go ahead and let people eat as soon as they arrived. There's no reason they should have to wait for us. It's supposed to be a casual picnic."

My mother shook her head in disapproval. "I hope there is some food left for the rest of us."

"There will be," *Maami* said as she stood up from one of the folding chairs. She grabbed onto the back of it for support.

I noticed that more and more often, she was leaning on walls and pieces of furniture when she tried to get up. I had asked her to see a doctor about it, but she claimed she was just stiff from old age.

I went over to her and held her arm. "I'll walk over with you, *maami*."

"Don't be silly. You need to be with your groom. Your father will walk me over."

I bit my lip. "I just want to thank you again for taking a photograph with me today. I know that it's not the Amish way, but it meant so much to me."

She touched my cheek. "I just wish your *daadi* was here to see this day. He loved you and Aiden so dearly, and to see you two so happy together would have made his heart sing."

Tears came to my eyes. "I wish that, too. I would give anything for that."

"*Gotte*'s plans are always right. We may not see the truth in it here on earth, but all will be known on the other side, in heaven. Remember that, and take it into your marriage." She placed a gentle hand on my cheek.

I nodded and watched in dismay as my grandmother shuffled over to my father. She was slowing down. Why hadn't I seen it more clearly before? How was I going to get her to settle down and not work day and night in the candy shop?

Aiden grabbed my hand. "You all go on over. I just want a minute with my bride."

Reluctantly, the wedding party and photographer left, Jethro looking over Juliet's shoulder as if he was saying goodbye. So far, so good. He had been an excellent ring bearer, and if I was honest, in his little bow tie and jacket, he'd outshone even me during the ceremony. I didn't take it personally. Who could really compete with an adorable pig?

Aiden held up my left hand and looked at the ring that I now wore. "I like seeing that there."

I smiled. "Me, too. I think everything went pretty well."

He laughed. "'Pretty well'? What went wrong? We've gotten through the hard part, right? Now it's just a big picnic and then vacation. I can't wait to get away from the department for a few days and spend time with you."

I smiled. "I'm surprised you're willing to take the time off at the height of tourist season, when the department is the busiest."

He grinned. "I could say the same to you."

"That's fair." I took his hand and pulled him in the direction of the reception. "We will have plenty of time alone soon enough. I'm worried about Jethro and the enormous cake that Jean Pierre made. Don't forget what he did to your mother's wedding cake." I shivered when I thought of marshmallow icing all over the reception tent.

He hugged me. "I know you thought of everything. Nothing can go wrong."

I pulled away from him and wished he hadn't said that. It felt like a jinx in some way.

"Maybe you should knock on the gazebo. It's wood, right?"

He laughed and playfully knocked on the nearest post. "I pulled you away from the group, but I wanted to tell you privately how much I love you. I am so honored to be your husband, and I plan to make you proud every day of our life together."

"I love you, and I want to make you proud, too."

"You do. You always have." He held me close and kissed the top of my head.

I was tempted in that moment to tell Aiden that we should just jump in his car and drive away, right then and there. There was too great a chance of one or both of us getting sidetracked by someone asking for help. Darcy Woodin, who had been visibly upset before the ceremony, came to mind. I couldn't help but be curious as to what her argument with Jason was about.

As if he could read my mind, Aiden said, "Let's go face it. Maybe we can slip away right after the cake. We can always count on Jethro to cause a distraction."

I grinned. "That's what I was thinking."

Chapter Five

Aiden and I walked hand in hand to the factory. Uriah and Millie sat on the front seat of their buggy. The older man grinned. "Can I give you a lift to your reception?"

"It's not that far," I said. "We can walk."

"And miss this chance to have a grand entrance? Never. You only get married once." He laughed. "Maybe not in our case." He smiled at Millie. "You don't want to get married more than twice, then."

"Not in my case," Lois said as she poked her head out of the buggy.

"Okay, these examples are horrible," Uriah said. "I give up."

Lois opened the door and got out. "Millie and I will walk back to the reception so the two of you can make your grand entrance."

"It won't offend some of the Amish there if we arrive by buggy? I don't want it to look like we are mocking anything."

"You'll offend Ruth Yoder," Lois said. "But she's the only one, and you were going to offend her anyway. You might as well have fun doing it."

"I didn't know Ruth came to the wedding," I said.

Millie smiled. She was a petite Amish woman with stark white hair pulled back in an Amish bun, and she wore a plain lavender dress in honor of the wedding. "I don't think she would have missed it for the world. It's the biggest event in Harvest this year, and she wanted to be there so she could talk all about it."

"Critique it, you mean," Lois said. "She wants to take everything in and give her two cents on it. Don't doubt for a moment that she's not going to march up to you and tell you what you did wrong and how you could have made it better."

I laughed. "That is something to look forward to, at least."

Uriah helped his wife down from the buggy.

"Are you sure you want to walk? There's enough room in the buggy for all of us."

"Pish," Lois said. "You are the one making an entrance. Besides, I have to fill Millie in on my chat with Jean Pierre."

My eyes went wide. "You like him?"

She stared at me. "Do I like him? He's a dreamboat with a French accent who makes chocolate for a living. He's like a gift from heaven."

Millie pursed her lips. "I don't want you jumping into anything too quick."

"Too quick? Millie Fisher Schrock, I'm seventy years old. How long do you want me to wait, until I'm on my deathbed?"

"Now, Lois," Millie began.

"We'd all better get into the buggy," Uriah said. "The two of them could bicker about this topic until sunset."

Aiden helped me into the back of the buggy, then climbed in himself.

Uriah shook the reins, and we were off.

We waved at Millie and Lois as they walked at a much more leisurely pace toward Swissmen Candyworks.

Aiden leaned over, gave me a kiss, and then laughed. "It's not a horse-drawn carriage, but it's the closest we can get around here."

As the factory came into view, I was happy to see so many people eating at the outdoor tables that had been set up in the parking lot. They looked like they were enjoying themselves. Both English and Amish children ran around the parking lot with no fear of cars or buggies, with both the Harvest Market and the candy factory closed for the wedding. I was so grateful that the market had agreed to close for the day. When I asked the owner if he was sure he was willing to lose a Saturday of business at the height of the summer, he had said, "Are you kidding? I should be thanking *you*. Your factory has brought so much more attention and business to my market. Tourists are coming in by the droves. Closing for one Saturday after everything Swissmen Candyworks has done for our business is the least we can do."

Other businesses in Harvest had expressed the same feelings, and I was so thankful that the village and its businesses had been so accepting of Swissmen Candyworks. I had expected some pushback, like complaints about traffic and noise, but there had been none of that. At least there had been none of that from anyone but Ruth Yoder. Like Lois had said, complaints were to be expected from Ruth.

The wedding reception appeared to be going seamlessly—and I could see this might be a chance for me to grow my business even more. I could create another revenue stream by renting out the candy factory for events. It certainly had the space, and it wouldn't take much from the staff to prep the place. The industrial kitchen would also be a perfect option for any caterer.

I shook my head. What was I thinking? It was my wedding day, and my mind had traveled to business. I was just hardwired that way. I had spent too many years building my brand to let it take a back seat in my mind, even on the most important day of my life.

Once you've become business-minded, it was hard to turn it off.

Aiden and I climbed out of the buggy to cheers, and we greeted individual guests as we made our way to the factory doors. I was smiling so widely my cheeks hurt, and I could understand Cass's complaint about having to smile so much.

Charlotte and our friends had transformed the parking lot with both long and round tables for seating. Pink linen tablecloths covered each table, and matching chair covers had been placed over the chairs. Summer wildflowers made up the centerpieces, and beautifully wrapped candies from Swissmen Sweets adorned the tables as edible décor and gifts for the guests.

Everyone was laughing and smiling, and my heart ached as I took it all in. It was exactly what I had wanted, an elevated picnic for the people whom I cared about the most.

Aiden and I made our way through the tables, greeting and thanking each guest for being there. It took longer than expected to make our way through the crowd. By the time we did, Lois and Millie had arrived on foot.

Finally, Aiden reached over to pry me away from one of the deacons from his stepfather's church and lead me toward the factory door. "I am on strict orders from *Maami* to get something for you to eat."

I laughed. "That sounds like *Maami*, but isn't it customary for the bride not to eat much on her wedding day?"

"Not in Amish Country, it isn't." He grinned.

"That's good, because I'm starving. I didn't eat before the ceremony. I was too nervous."

"I didn't eat for the same reason," he said.

"You were nervous about marrying me?" I arched my brow.

"No. Were you nervous about marrying me?" he asked.

"I wasn't, but I *was* worried that Jethro was going to trip me in the aisle."

"That's a reasonable fear," he said as we finally reached the reception doors.

Juliet stood at the door, holding Jethro in her arms. She kissed my cheek. "You are my daughter now. I couldn't be happier."

I smiled. "Neither could I." I patted Jethro's head.

Aiden wrapped his arm around my shoulders. "I am under strict orders to get her something to eat."

"Yes, yes." Juliet stepped aside.

In the air-conditioned lobby, the twelve-foot-long buffet of picnic fare that Darby and her cook had made dominated the room. The tables stretched from one end of the room to the other. There were crepes, salads, finger sandwiches, and tarts, including the mushroom tart, with what I had to assume were Juliet's foraged mushrooms. Everything was beautifully displayed on crystal and China plates.

Darcy stood near the table.

I hugged her. "It's beautiful. Everyone outside is raving about the food."

"I'm glad," she said, but she didn't look me in the eye as she spoke.

"Are you all right?"

She blinked and looked at me then. "Yes, I'm fine." She gave me a bright smile. "Bailey, you had the most wonderful ceremony."

I frowned and was about to call her out for not telling me the truth, when Aiden was at my side again and handed me a China plate. "Eat. Please, before you grandmother hunts me down for starving you."

I took the plate from him, and when I turned to speak to Darcy again, she was gone.

Aiden and I loaded our plates and took them out to the reception area, where a head table waited for us.

A little while later, Jean Pierre clapped his hands. "Bring out the cake!"

Three Amish men rolled the giant truffle wedding

cake into the middle of the parking lot and the center of the reception to claps and cheers. The photographer took dozens of pictures of the cake from every angle.

"That's the biggest cake I have ever seen," I overheard someone say.

"It's the biggest cake that anyone has ever seen," another person replied.

When the cake was in place, Jean Pierre admired it. "This is my finest work."

I noticed at the top of the cake were Jean Pierre's finishing touches. They were exact replicas of Aiden and me made from chocolate. I got out of my seat and walked over to the cake for a closer look. "Is that Jethro?"

Sure enough, Jethro was at my little chocolate feet at the top of the cake. He even had a bow tie.

Juliet squealed and held the actual little pig close to her chest. "It's just what I imagined it would be! Jean Pierre, you caught the image of Jethro perfectly."

Jean Pierre bowed, and all I could do was laugh. Somehow it felt right to have the little bacon bundle on the cake.

Juliet held Jethro up to his likeness, so that he could have a better look. Not one to miss the chance for a tasty morsel, Jethro bit into the cake, smearing chocolate all over his face.

Juliet screamed. "Jethro! Are you all right?"

"That pig is a menace."

I looked over my shoulder to see who had said that, and I wasn't the least bit surprised to see Ruth Yoder. Ruth in her gray plain dress, sensible shoes, steel-gray hair, and white prayer cap stood next to her husband,

Bishop Yoder, who had a long white beard and was a good twenty years older than her.

She caught my eye and frowned.

I didn't take it personally.

While this was going on, Jean Pierre was swearing up and down in French. I was grateful that most of the people there had no idea what he was saying. I didn't know myself, but I caught the gist of it.

"My cake! My cake!" he was screaming.

I clapped my hands to get everyone's attention, but to no avail. Finally, Millie put her fingers in her mouth and let out an earsplitting whistle. The village fell silent.

She nodded. "That whistle works on my goats—I thought it would work in this case, as well. Go ahead, Bailey, and say what you need to say."

"Thank you. Let's not panic. The cake is enormous, and there is plenty of it that Jethro didn't touch. If you ask me, it seems fitting that he took a bite out of the cake. If Jethro had been a perfect gentleman all day, I would be alarmed."

There was a lighthearted chuckle, and the mood lifted, much to my relief. Jean Pierre threw up his hands and laughed, as well. I just might have saved Jethro from being the main ingredient in Jean Pierre's next recipe.

The only person who didn't find my comment amusing was Juliet. "What?" Juliet said. "Jethro never does anything wrong. He's an angel."

I thought it was best to ignore her comment. I took Aiden's hand. "Let's cut the cake, husband."

He grinned. "I thought you would never ask."

The photographer hurried into place as Aiden and I cut the cake and fed each other a piece.

"Are you ready to get out of here?" Aiden whispered into my ear.

"I'm so ready," I whispered back.

After a few more photos, I slipped away. Before leaving, I wanted to grab my laptop computer from the office. Even though Aiden and I would be going on our honeymoon, there was bound to be some downtime, when I could get a little bit of work done. If anyone would understand my need to work, it was my new husband.

I walked into the candy factory and gave a sigh of relief. All the staff and guests were outside enjoying the reception. I was finally alone. I stopped myself from picking up abandoned paper plates and napkins and throwing them away. My staff would take care of everything. If someone caught me cleaning up in my wedding dress, I would never hear the end of it.

I walked down the hallway in the direction of my office, and I was almost there when I heard a scream.

It wasn't the same scream that Juliet had let out when Jethro bit into the cake. This one was full of horror.

I spun around and headed in the direction of the noise. I pushed the door open to the kitchen.

Darcy Woodin, wearing her all-black catering uniform, stood in the middle of the room. Her mouth hung open, and tears streamed down her face. She looked at me. "He's dead."

Jason Hackney lay at her feet.

Chapter Six

I hurried over to her. "Darcy, are you all right?"

She grabbed my forearms. "Bailey, I didn't do this. I swear to you."

I glanced down at Jason's body. He lay on his side. He was in a suit but no tie, and he wasn't wearing socks. I don't know why it was important that he wasn't wearing socks, but it seemed like it was to me. He could have been asleep. It had been a long day for us all.

"Are you sure he's dead?"

She nodded. "I—I took his pulse. There was nothing there."

Not that I doubted her, but it was better to be safe than sorry.

I bent over the best I could in my wedding dress and reached for his wrist. It was cold, and I felt no movement. "I need to get Aiden."

She looked me in the eye. "They're going to say it

was me," she whispered. "It wasn't me. I swear to you that it wasn't."

The kitchen door opened, and Enoch Unger walked in with a tray of dishes. I had always thought Enoch was built like a telephone pole. He was well over six feet and always walked ramrod-straight, like he had a brace under his Amish shirt. He had a short Amish beard indicating that he had been married, but I knew he'd been widowed a long while ago. It wasn't something that we talked about. I guessed that he was in his forties, as his beard was just starting to show signs of graying.

He'd only started working for Darcy as cook three months ago, but Darcy said in that time, her kitchen began to run like clockwork, and she had so much more time to dedicate to the new catering business.

He pulled up short. "What has happened?"

"It wasn't me," Darcy said.

I had a feeling she would be repeating that line a few times more.

The kitchen door opened again. "Bailey, did you find your computer?" Aiden asked. "Maybe it's at home." He stopped dead in his tracks when he saw now both Darcy and me standing over Jason's body.

Enoch remained in the corner with his tray of empty dishes.

"Aiden, I was just going to come get you," I said.

"What happened?"

"I—I don't know," Darcy said. "After the cake was taken out, I came into the kitchen to start cleaning up. I assumed the reception would begin to wind down."

She pointed to Jason's body on the floor. "And he was like that. He's dead."

"I can see that." Aiden removed his cell phone from his tuxedo pocket, then glanced at Enoch. "Were you with Darcy when she found the body?"

"*Nee*," Enoch said.

"He just walked in," I said, answering for him. "He stepped into the kitchen just seconds before you did."

Darcy stood up. "Can she take my knives with her? I can't lose them. They cost more than a car." She picked up the knife case that was in the middle of the island.

"What are you doing?" Aiden asked. "Don't touch anything."

But it was too late. Darcy had already picked up the knife case. Unfortunately, the case was open, and the knives fell to the floor, along with what looked like part of a white sponge.

Darcy bent to pick up the knives.

"Don't touch them!" Aiden repeated.

Darcy froze.

"Step back from the knives," he told her.

Darcy straightened up and took one big step back.

"Everything in this room is evidence right now."

"You think he was murdered?" I asked.

Aiden shot me a glance. And I knew he wouldn't answer my question—at least at the moment.

"What's that?" I pointed at the piece of white sponge.

"It looks like part of a mushroom," Darcy said. "I have no idea how it would have gotten in there, or how my knife case would have even been open. I'm very careful with it, and I always keep it clean and organized and zipped up tight."

Aiden glanced back at Jason's dead body on the floor and then again at the pile of fallen knives.

"I made the mushroom tarts, but that was last night in my kitchen in the café. I didn't make anything with mushrooms here. That is a raw mushroom. It's not even cooked."

"Bailey, does the candy staff here use any mushrooms in the recipes?" Aiden asked.

I blinked at him. "Mushrooms? In candy? No. Never."

"So, there is no real reason for it being here in the Candyworks."

Darcy and I nodded.

Aiden tapped on the screen of his phone, and it took a matter of seconds for five deputies to be on the scene, since they were all attending the wedding.

To give them room, I pulled Darcy out of the kitchen and into the break room down the hall. I had the room set up with comfy chairs and couches so that my staff could really rest when they weren't working. A large, Amish-made oak table and chairs were in the middle of the room. I sat Darcy in one of the chairs.

"We just left Enoch in there," Darcy said.

"He will be all right," I said. "I'm more worried about you right now."

"Can you find my grandma?" Darcy asked.

I bit my lip. I knew Aiden would want me to keep Darcy alone for the time being until he had a chance to question her, but at the same time, she was my friend, and she looked so young and alone in that moment. I didn't criticize her for wanting her grandmother at her side. I certainly would have wanted *Maami* with me at that moment.

However, logic and years in a relationship with a cop prevailed. "Not yet. I'm not sure how Aiden wants to handle telling the guests, and we can't risk rumors flying through the village."

She nodded, resigned. "That makes sense. Grams isn't great at keeping a secret."

That was one way to put it.

I glanced over my shoulder at the closed door. I knew Aiden wouldn't be happy with me for asking questions as much as he wouldn't want Lois in the room, but I couldn't help myself in that regard.

"Can you tell me what happened?"

"I already told Aiden. You were there."

I reached for her hand. "Darcy, you have to be straight with me. I want to help you if I can."

"There is nothing to tell." She wouldn't meet my eyes.

"I saw you and Jason arguing just off the square before the wedding. You both appeared to be very upset."

"How did you see that? We were on the corner, away from the ceremony."

"I was in Swissmen Sweets, waiting to walk down the aisle, and I could see the two of you standing on the corner together."

She let out a breath. "It was just a stupid argument. I wanted him to stay away from me, and he insisted on following me around all morning. I was tired of it."

"Why did you want him to stay away from you?"

She wouldn't look me in the eyes.

"Darcy, please, I am trying to help."

She looked up at me. "Can you help? You're married to the sheriff now. Won't anything that I say go straight to him?"

I shivered but said nothing, because I realized what she said was right. I would be likely to go to Aiden, especially if another person was in danger and it was a race against time to help them. Darcy knew me well enough to know that.

"Were you afraid of Jason?" I asked in a hushed tone.

She looked me in the eye, and I saw fear.

Before she could answer, the door opened, and Aiden and Deputy Little stepped inside.

"Bailey, can you step out for a moment so I can talk to Darcy? Deputy Little will go with you back to the reception and share the news and plans with the guests."

I stood up.

Darcy stared at me with pleading eyes. I knew she didn't want me to leave the room, but I could tell by the set to Aiden's jaw that staying was not an option.

Deputy Little held the door for me to walk out. I couldn't help but note the absurdity of the situation. Here I was, in my wedding dress, walking past a murder scene in my factory's kitchen, escorted by a deputy in a tuxedo.

I glanced into the kitchen as we walked by and saw the other deputies, all in their wedding finery, moving around the room looking for evidence.

When Deputy Little and I reached the lobby, I asked, "Do the guests have any idea?"

"Not really," he said. "They know something is up

because all the deputies present rushed into the Candyworks after I got Aiden's text."

"How are you going to tell them?" I asked.

"I was hoping you would," he said.

I should have expected that.

As soon as we stepped outside, Charlotte was at our side. "Luke, Bailey, what's going on?"

I glanced at Deputy Little.

He pulled at his collar and said, "There's been an accident in the kitchen."

Charlotte narrowed her eyes at her husband. "An 'accident'? Six deputies ran in there like their tails were on fire. I know it's much more than an 'accident.'"

Deputy Little shifted back and forth.

"We're calling it an accident at the moment," I said, then lowered my voice. "Jason Hackney is dead in the Candyworks kitchen."

Charlotte covered her mouth. "What? What happened?"

"That's what we are trying to find out," Deputy Little said.

"Before we do that, we have to wrap up the reception," I said.

Charlotte nodded. "It was coming to an end anyway. Several people asked me to say goodbye to you on their behalf because they had to go and you were in the Candyworks for so long." She wrapped her arms around her waist. "But now I know why you were in there so long. This is just awful. Does Darcy know? She was friends with him at one point."

"She knows," Deputy Little said and added nothing further.

Charlotte's mouth made an O shape, as if she knew it wasn't something that simple. Charlotte had been married to Deputy Little for years. She knew when something was amiss and when her husband was purposely leaving information out.

Lois and Millie walked over to us. Millie held Jethro in her arms. His white chin was still stained with chocolate from his attack on the wedding cake. If only that had been the only mishap at the wedding. I would have been very happy with that.

"Bailey King, I want you to tell us what is going on. Everyone is on edge. Half the guests have left, and we haven't even give you your big send-off yet."

I shifted back and forth on my feet. "I don't think there is going to be a big send-off. Aiden is going to be here at the Candyworks for a long time yet."

The remaining wedding guests gathered around us at that point.

Deputy Little nudged me.

"What do you want me to say?" I whispered.

"Just what I did, that there was an accident."

I gave him a look. I really thought he should be the one doing this, since he was a deputy and had some semblance of authority. My only authority came from making candy.

I cleared my throat. "Aiden and I are so happy that you could be here today to celebrate with us. It was wonderful to have both of our families here." I smiled at Jean Pierre and Cass. "And my dear friends from

New York. And all of our beloved Harvest friends." As I spoke, the crowd quieted. I kept my expression calm, but I pitched my voice louder because I didn't want to have to say this twice. "I do have some news. Aiden and I won't have a send-off tonight. There was an accident inside the factory, and Aiden and his deputies are taking care of it. It might take some time, so we have to end the reception early. I know Aiden wanted to be here standing with me to thank you all himself."

Lois stamped her foot. "I don't like this. I don't like being in the dark of what is really going on, and where is my granddaughter? I haven't seen her in hours." Lois put a hand on her cheek. "Is she the one who had the accident inside? Is she okay? I need to get to her!"

Deputy Little stepped between Lois and the front door. "You can't go in there, Lois."

Lois wagged her finger at him. "Don't tell me what I can and cannot do when my granddaughter might be in trouble." She stomped into the building, and I wasn't the least bit surprised when Millie went in after her.

An ambulance turned into the parking lot and parked close to the market. Two EMTs got out and walked toward Swissmen Candyworks. A moment later, another car parked next to the ambulance, and an elderly man got out.

"The coroner? Why is the coroner here?" one of the guests asked.

"Someone must be dead," another said.

That was enough to make the guests scatter, especially the Amish. The last thing most Amish wanted was to be involved with law enforcement. Or a murder.

Deputy Little glanced at me. "You have a guest list, right? If we need to talk to any people."

"Sure. The guest list is all of Harvest."

He groaned, and I went back into the Candyworks. When I was back inside, I was happy to see that Darcy was no longer in the staff room being interrogated by my new husband. She stood in the corner of the lobby, whispering with Millie and Lois. I walked over to them.

"He's a snake, so I can't say I'm not glad he's out of your life. I just wish he would have chosen a more subtle method to leave," Lois said.

"If he was murdered," Millie said in a mild tone, "the method wasn't his choice."

"He shouldn't have been here in the first place. He's not from Harvest. He wasn't invited to the wedding." Lois looked over her shoulder at me. "Isn't that right, Bailey? This man wasn't invited to the wedding."

"He wasn't, but with Juliet inviting all of Harvest and my grandmother inviting most of the Amish in the area, I really don't know who was and who was not supposed to be at the wedding."

Darcy wrapped both of her hands around my arm. "Bailey, your wedding . . . It's ruined, and it's my fault."

"It's not your fault."

"Yes, it is. He came here because of me."

Millie and Lois shared a look.

There was a lot more to this story involving Jason Hackney that I didn't know about, and for the first time, I wasn't entirely sure my friends Millie and Lois were going to tell me the truth.

Chapter Seven

Before the sun was even up the next day, Aiden rolled onto his side and looked at me. "Oh, good, you're awake."

"How could I not be awake? My mind has been racing. There was a dead guy at our wedding."

"Good point, but I would say overall everything went well."

"Yeah, it was great up until the whole murder thing," I said.

He barked a laugh. "I'm going to get up and make us some coffee. I have a feeling we're going to need it." He got out of bed, leaned over, and kissed me on the forehead.

At the foot of the bed, my giant white rabbit, Puff, kicked her legs in distaste, as if to make it known that she wasn't happy to be awake this early. I had rescued Puff when her original owner had passed away a few years ago. She was enormous—much larger than Jethro—

demanding, and a bit dramatic, but I loved her all the same.

"Can you bring Puff a piece of broccoli? She's looking a little peckish, if you ask me. I still feel bad she was stuck at home all day when Jethro got to be at the wedding."

"I think a pig was all we could handle when it came to animals at the wedding, and even in that case, he still got a bite out of the cake," he said. "By the way, there's a huge hunk of the cake in the freezer."

I propped myself up. "Why?"

"Don't you know the old tradition for a bride and groom to freeze part of their cake and eat it on their one-year anniversary?"

I wrinkled my nose. "No, it sounds disgusting."

He laughed. "Well, my mother wasn't going to let me leave the Candyworks without it, so it's in the freezer."

"How big of a 'huge hunk' are we talking?" I asked.

"Bigger than Jethro, smaller than Puff," he said.

I groaned and flopped back on the bed. "I guess it's good we had nothing else in the freezer since we *were* leaving on a trip."

Aiden's face fell. "I'm so sorry we had to postpone our honeymoon. I know you were looking forward to it. We both were."

I sat up again. "It's not your fault. I wouldn't be comfortable going, either. Jason did die in my building. I need to be here if there are any repercussions from that. I wouldn't want to leave Darcy right now, either."

Aiden frowned.

I pushed myself up against the headboard. “You don’t think she did it, do you?”

“Several wedding guests saw her arguing with Jason before the wedding ceremony. That’s not a good sign.”

I had seen the argument, too, but hadn’t said anything. “Did the coroner confirm he was murdered? You got home so late last night I was already asleep.”

Aiden frowned. “He’s still making that determination. We will know more when the toxicology report comes back.”

“But what do you think?”

“Could have been something he ate. Darcy said she saw him during the reception, and he appeared to be ill. He was sweating and stumbling around. She saw him rush to the restroom more than once. If I didn’t know better, I would have said by her description that he was drunk, but there was no alcohol at our wedding.”

Aiden and I hadn’t served any alcohol at our wedding out of respect for our Amish family and friends. With all the controversy over the wine being served at the Summer Soiree, we didn’t want to add to the already-heated debate going on in the village.

“It doesn’t mean that he or someone else couldn’t have snuck some in.”

“True.”

“What does your gut tell you happened?” I asked.

“I’m waiting to make a judgment until I get the results.” He turned to walk out of the room. “I’ll be back with coffee and broccoli.” He shook his head. “Now, that’s not a food combination that I ever expected to say.”

After Aiden left the room, I flopped back on the bed a second time.

Puff wiggled her long ears at me, as if to remind me that she didn't appreciate being bounced around when she was trying to get her beauty rest.

Aiden left for the sheriff's department shortly after handing me my coffee. I hadn't expected anything less. Aiden took crime in Holmes County very seriously, and when it came to murder, he would not give up until the killer was brought to justice.

Even though we had meant to leave for our honeymoon that morning, I planned to stop by the Village Inn and say goodbye to my family and friends who were going back East after the wedding.

The Village Inn was an old, converted farmhouse that was behind the candy factory. Widow Lillian Coblentz owned and lived in the inn with her eleven-year-old son, Adrien.

Lillian, who was in her forties, had been widowed young, and to make ends meet, she'd opened the inn. As far as places tourists could stay in Holmes County, it was the only accommodations in downtown Harvest. It might not have as many amenities as the larger hotel chains in the county that catered to big tour groups, but it was quaint and within walking distance of everything Harvest had to offer.

Between my wedding and the upcoming Summer Soiree later in the week, the inn was booked.

I stepped into the main lobby and found Adrien standing behind the desk. He was so much taller than the last time I had seen him. He was at the gawky stage that seemed to plague so many boys, when he was all arms and legs.

"Bailey," he said with a smile. "My *maam* said to tell you that everyone is in the dining room."

I thanked him and went into the dining room—my favorite room in the inn. It was plain, but it was set up like an old country teahouse. There were large windows that looked out over the full garden, and a potbellied stove was in the corner of the room. As it was June, the windows were open, allowing the summer breeze inside, and the stove was off.

Lillian had talked about expanding her dining area into an outside space, so that guests could eat in the garden. She'd even asked me if I would be interested in partnering with her on it. I thought it was a terrific idea, but I declined her offer. I already had more business than I could handle. I couldn't take on anything else. But I was going to suggest that she speak to Darcy about it. The café might be a better fit for Lillian. That was before Jason's murder, though.

"Bailey!" Jean Pierre waved at me. "There you are!"

He was sitting at a breakfast table with Cass and my parents. He pointed at the empty chair at the table. "We saved you a seat."

I sat in the empty chair next to him.

My father smiled. "When are you and Aiden leaving for your trip?"

I wrinkled my nose. "We aren't going now."

"What?" my mother yelped.

We weren't the only ones in the room. Every table was full, and I didn't recognize most of the guests. They must have been visiting Harvest for the Summer

Soiree. Margot would be pleased it had attracted such a crowd.

Margot's goal for the village of Harvest was always bigger and better. She might have the most wonderfully attended and received event, but the next year it had to be twice as big and twice as good. At times, it was exhausting to keep up with her.

I waited until the other diners turned their attention back to their own conversations, but I didn't doubt for a moment that they were hoping to listen in on what I had to say.

"Aiden has to stay for work," I said.

My mother wrung her cloth napkin in her hands. "This is no way to start off a marriage. Bailey, I know that work is very important to you and Aiden, but what will happen when you have children?"

Not my own mother jumping on the kids wagon, too. I had expected it from Juliet, but not my mother.

"These are very unique circumstances. I've already called the travel agency, and they are making arrangements to switch our dates. We won't be out too much money. I paid for all the travel insurance that was available just in case."

My mother shook her head. "I don't like the precedent he is setting for your married life."

"Mom, we will still go on a honeymoon. It just can't be right now. It's not a good time."

"Because of the dead guy," Cass said in her all-knowing voice.

I shot my best friend a look. She didn't need to add to this.

"There always seems to be a dead guy around here," my father said. "That shouldn't be the reason."

"It's not just Aiden. I want to stay home, too. The man died in my candy factory. I need to stay here in case there are any issues."

"Being sued by the man's family, for one," Dad said.

My stomach tightened. I hadn't thought of that. Certainly, the idea would have come to mind to me at some point, but with all the flurry of wedding activities, I hadn't considered it yet. Now it hit me like a lead anvil. I could very well be sued by his family if they thought either the factory or I were somehow to blame for his death.

Cass must have seen the panic racing across my face. "You're not going to be sued. He was probably murdered, right? It's the killer's fault."

"Murder!" Jean Pierre cried.

At that, every last person in the room turned and looked at our table. I groaned inwardly.

Lillian, a stocky woman with blond hair and pink cheeks, stood in the doorway to the kitchen with a tray of scones and tea. Her mouth fell open when Jean Pierre made his declaration.

This whole conversation was going to be on the streets of Harvest in no time at all.

"We don't know if it's a murder yet."

"But it will go in your favor, suing-wise, if it is," Cass said.

I hated that she had put it like that, but yes, she was right.

Mom tapped the napkin to the corners of her mouth. "I still think it would be best if you and Aiden spent some alone time together, but I can see from the look on your face that your mind is already made up."

"It is," I said.

Dad checked his watch. "We had better get going. Our flight leaves in an hour. Are you all packed, Cass?"

Cass nodded. "I'm ready to go." She reached across the table and took my hand. "I wish I could stay longer, but there is chocolate that has to be made."

I knew about that very well. In the lives we'd chosen, there was always chocolate to be made.

"You all are flying home together?"

"I will be staying here," Jean Pierre said. "Since I will be staying in Harvest through the Summer Soiree, I offered for your parents to fly back to New York on my private jet with Cass."

This caught me by surprise. I knew that Jean Pierre had voiced before that he planned to stay for the Summer Soiree and to spend more time with Lois, but I hadn't really take him seriously on that idea.

Jean Pierre was the type who loved to spout off things that he might do, but not many of them unrelated to his chocolate shop came to fruition. It seemed that Lois had really caught his eye.

"Cass will do an excellent job minding JP Chocolates while I am away." He winked at her.

Cass wrinkled her nose. It was a well-known fact that Cass ran JP Chocolates when Jean Pierre was in the shop, as well. Jean Pierre knew that, too, and was only teasing her.

My father stood. "It's time for us to head to the airport, then."

The rest of the table stood, as well.

My parents hugged me goodbye, and Jean Pierre kissed both of my cheeks before leaving the dining room. "I will be around the village, of course. I just might even stop by Swissmen Sweets to help out."

"I would love that, and *Maami* would, too. She thinks you're a riot."

He smoothed the collar of his dress shirt. "I hope Lois will agree with her. I'm headed out now to see her."

"Oh," I said, a bit surprised. I thought under the circumstances that she would be with Darcy.

"Yes, she is very upset about everything that happened yesterday, and I will be there to lend moral support."

Cass raised her brow behind Jean Pierre's head.

Jean Pierre gave a bow and left the dining room.

Cass hugged me. "I wish I could stay longer and help you find this killer person, but I really have to get back if Jean Pierre plans to stay. Now I'm worried that he's so smitten with Lois that he will never come back."

"I can't imagine Jean Pierre in Harvest permanently."

"I can't, either." She looked me right in the eye. "Ignore what your mom was saying. You and Aiden will be fine. You have been through a lot worse stuff over the years, and postponing the honeymoon will have no impact on your relationship."

A few of those "worse" things came to my mind, and I knew she was right. "Thank you."

"And there was something else I wanted to tell you."

I wrinkled my brow. "What?"

"That Jason guy . . . I have met him before."

"What? When you were in Harvest last?"

"No. I met him in New York. He came to JP Chocolates years ago, wanting to collaborate with us on an event that was to have a wine and chocolate theme. Ultimately, JP Chocolates was already booked on the weekend he wanted to have it, so I didn't even entertain his proposal. He emailed me later with more details, wanting to reschedule. Things got busy, and I forgot about it. I never replied. It wasn't until I heard his name at the wedding that it sparked a memory."

"The event was with his own winery?" I asked.

"Yes. I couldn't remember what the winery was, so I searched through my emails last night and found his proposal. The winery was called Winter Ridge, and it's in upstate New York. Here's the thing. I looked up Winter Ridge then."

"And?"

"It went under three years ago and filed for bankruptcy. Then the owner, Jason Hackney, disappeared."

I stared at her. "What do you mean 'disappeared'?"

She shrugged. "Just that. After the bankruptcy was filed, no one knew where he went."

"And now he's ended up here, in Holmes County?"

"Yep."

"He ended up in Holmes County—dead."

She nodded. "Bingo."

Chapter Eight

It was Sunday in Harvest, meaning all the businesses, including mine, were closed. However, that didn't stop me from going to Swissmen Candyworks to see the state of the factory after the wedding reception and the murder.

The back door to the factory was just a few yards from the Village Inn. I used my key to let myself inside, and I found myself in the back of the factory, where the candy was packaged and boxed up for shipment.

I inhaled deeply. A faint scent of chocolate and vanilla lingered in the air. The smell changed from time to time depending on what kind of candy was packaged up last. I knew our last shipment had been predominately fudge, a very popular treat, especially in the summer in Holmes County.

I never tired of the smell. I knew that when I no longer liked the smell of sweets, it would be my signal to give up this lifetime career of candy. I prayed it wouldn't ever come to that, because I really loved what I did.

I walked through the packaging room and down the hallway, which had windows on one side overlooking the factory floor. From that spot, guests on our popular factory tours could watch our candies being made.

The factory floor was empty, and a trickle of ambient light glowed on the stainless-steel surfaces. I knew I shouldn't be in the factory too long. Aiden wouldn't be pleased that I was there at all the day after Jason's body had been found in the kitchen. However, I still needed my laptop, which I had forgotten in all the chaos at the end of the reception.

I also couldn't fight my curiosity. Instead of walking to my office, I went into the kitchen.

The lights were off, but two skylights overhead, and one large window on the far end of the room, allowed in natural light. Most of the space needed to be used for cooking equipment, but having natural light in all the rooms of Swissmen Candyworks had been a top priority for me. I didn't want my staff to feel like they worked in a dungeon all day, unable even to know what the weather was outside until their shifts ended.

I had my hand hovering at the light switch when I heard a scuttling sound on the floor. I groaned. If I found a mouse or worse in there, I would lose my mind. It was a constant worry with having a food-based business out in the country.

It was no mouse. I turned on the overhead lights and found Darcy on the floor crawling around on her hands and knees.

"Bailey!" Darcy cried and jumped to her feet.

"Darcy, what are you doing here?" I yelped.

"I—I still had the key that you gave me so I could go in and out of the factory yesterday. I'm sorry. I should have given it to you before I left yesterday."

"Okay," I said. "That explains how you got in here, but it doesn't tell me *why* you're in here or why you're crawling around on the kitchen floor."

Her face turned beet red. "No, I suppose it doesn't." She looked around the kitchen, which was still frozen in time from the reception. Pans and trays needed to be washed and put away. Boxes of produce sat on the large island. Aiden had allowed us to put away anything that needed to be refrigerated, but nothing more than that. The room stood still from the time I'd found Darcy standing over Jason Hackney's body.

I prayed Aiden would let my staff and me clean it tomorrow. We had a kitchen to run. Thankfully, the candies we sold were made on the factory floor, so production wouldn't be impacted. I could keep this side of the building closed if need be.

I cocked my head to one side. "So, are you going to tell me why you are crawling around on the floor?"

"I will," she said, not meeting my eyes. "But I don't think you will like the answer."

"I still want to hear it."

She nodded and sat on one of the work stools around the giant, stainless-steel island in the middle of the room. I'd had the island custom-made to look just like the one in the kitchen at Swissmen Sweets, although it was twice the size. Every time I saw it, it reminded me of the Candyworks' roots.

I sat on another of the stools and waited.

"I was looking for a ring." She clasped her hands together in her lap.

"A ring?" I asked. "Was it yours?"

"Kind of."

"What does 'kind of' mean?"

"It had been given to me, but I gave it back."

"Who gave it to you?" I asked, even though I had a good idea who might have.

"Jason." She wouldn't meet my eyes.

I leaned forward onto the island. "Was it an engagement ring?"

"No."

If it had been, it would have come as a shock to me. Darcy was my friend, and I didn't even know she'd had been dating anyone, but in truth, I was closer to Lois than I was to her granddaughter. I knew for a fact that if Darcy ever became engaged, Lois would shout it to anyone who would listen. Lois loved love, and she loved the idea of anyone being in love. I thought that is what had led her to being married so many times.

Then I remembered Lois's reaction to Jason when she'd seen him at the Candyworks on Friday. She was not pleased. In fact, she had been downright hostile. Was this the reason? Had Jason proposed and then broken it off with Darcy? That would certainly have given Lois a reason to dislike him.

She waved her hands in the air as if the very suggestion that the missing ring was an engagement ring was utterly ridiculous. "We weren't engaged. It was a promise ring of sorts. It had an emerald in it. My birthday is in May, and that's my birthstone."

"A promise ring? Isn't that a little junior high–ish?"

I asked, and then blushed. "I'm sorry—that came out wrong. I didn't mean it like that. I've just never heard of anyone being given one after the seventh grade."

She pushed her blond curls out of her face. While she had been crawling around on the kitchen floor, they had flown in all directions. She really had the most beautiful hair.

"It's not wrong. It's very seventh grade. I realize that now. It was just a way to keep me on the hook."

"But I thought you were just friends," I said. "That's what you told us all on Friday."

"That wasn't completely true. I was working on getting to a place where we could just be friends. I wasn't there yet."

"You were dating him."

"I was." She played with the bracelet on her wrist. "Before. We broke up about a month ago."

"When did he give the ring to you?"

"Three or four months ago. We had been dating for a little while at that point, and he said he wanted to make a promise to me to be faithful."

"And did he keep that promise?"

She looked down at her hands. "As far as I know, but sometimes I wondered. I have no proof he did anything wrong in that way." She shook her head. "Anyway, we broke up for other reasons, and I gave him the ring back."

"Why did you break up?"

"I don't think it's important."

"Darcy, you're a murder suspect. It's very important. If you're not open and honest, you could be in a lot of trouble."

She blinked back tears. "I was the one who convinced Margot to bring his cousin's winery into the Summer Soiree."

"Who is his cousin?"

"Carly Crestwood. You met her Friday. She owns the Hackney Family Winery."

So much had happened since Friday, I had to think hard to remember. "Wait, was she the one Jason was bickering with a little bit?"

"Yes, they don't get along. Like I said, she owns the Hackney Family Winery."

"Hackney? That's Jason's last name."

She nodded. "Yes, they have the same late grandfather. He was a winemaker, too. Hackney is her maiden name."

I nodded. I had thought it was odd that Carly had a business with the name of Hackney when that was Jason's last name, but I really hadn't dwelled on it long. I was too stressed over the wedding and the long list of things Margot had been asking me to do for the Summer Soiree.

"If you broke up over a month ago, how did the ring end up in the Candyworks kitchen?" I asked.

"Jason came in here during the reception and tried to give it back to me. He said he was sorry and wanted to be with me again. I didn't want to hear it. He took my hand, put the ring into my palm, and asked me to think about it." She closed her eyes as if she was trying to both see the memory and forget it. "I said that I didn't need to think about it, and I threw it at him. It bounced off his shoulder, and I saw it skitter under the oven."

And that was why she'd been on the floor. She'd

been trying to retrieve the ring, but I wondered if she was trying to retrieve the ring because she wanted it back to remember Jason by, or if she was trying to retrieve it so the deputies wouldn't find it and tie it back to her.

"I didn't even know you were dating someone," I said.

"No one knew. My last relationship was such a nightmare that I wanted to keep my dating life secret until I was sure I'd found the one."

I remembered that. If I wasn't mistaken, that relationship had involved a murder, too—although Darcy hadn't been a serious suspect at the time. Not like she was now. It was clear to me that Darcy had a problem when it came to picking men.

I can't say I had done a much better job before meeting Aiden, though. I'd had a lot of disastrous relationships in New York that I wished I could erase from my memory. I also reminded myself that Darcy was still in her twenties, a time when the bad relationships seemed to hit the hardest.

"On Friday, Lois seemed to know who he was. She didn't like him. That was clear."

"That was because she caught me crying in the café that morning, and I confessed the whole thing. Up and until that point, she didn't know about him. I knew very well Grams would have wanted to know every detail of my relationship, and I just wasn't ready to share it with her. I didn't want every time I left the café to lead to questions of where I was going and who I was seeing."

"I can understand." I paused. "But you know your grandmother means well, right?"

Her eyes went wide. "Of course I do. She's my biggest champion, but I also know she carries a brick in her purse. I don't want her to get arrested for throwing it at one of my ex-boyfriends."

That was fair.

I hated that the thought even crossed my mind, but I knew how protective Lois was of Darcy. If Jason had hurt Darcy, then Lois was a suspect, too.

"Someone said Jason looked ill yesterday." I didn't mention that Darcy had been the one who'd said this to Aiden and he'd told me.

"He did. It was almost like he had the flu. He was sweating and very pale. After he tried to give the ring back, I told him to go home. If he was really sick, I didn't want him to be around you or any of your guests. Before I saw him in the kitchen again, I thought he'd left. I feel awful that I didn't try to help him more. I should have taken him to the hospital right then and there, but I was just so frazzled. I wanted to get away from him. If he wanted to talk about our relationship, right in the middle of the first wedding reception I was catering wasn't the time."

She made a good point. Why had Jason tried to talk to her during the reception? He could have spoken to her at any other time. She lived and worked at the Sunbeam Café. It wasn't like she was hard to track down.

"When you were looking for the ring, did you see it?"

She nodded. "I used the flashlight on my phone, and

I spotted it under the oven, but it was too far back for me to reach."

I stood up. "You're in luck. I have a lot of experience fetching things out from under stoves and ovens. Nutmeg is constantly knocking cat toys under the stoves and appliances in Swissmen Sweets. He's not even supposed to be in the kitchen, but I know he goes in there at night."

I went to the utility closet and removed a broom. I unscrewed the top of the broom from the handle. Then I went to one of the drawers and removed a spatula and a roll of tape. I taped the spatula to the end of the broom handle.

"Can you shine your light under the oven again?" I asked.

"I don't want you to go to this much trouble."

"It's no trouble. I already made the stick," I said.

She knelt on the floor next to the oven and shone her flashlight under it. I lay on my belly and peeked under the oven. Right away, I saw the glisten of a gold ring, but she was right—it was very far back under the oven. I tucked my contraption under the oven and tried to knock it closer to me.

It took three attempts, but finally the ring came flying out from under the oven, along with dozens of dust bunnies.

"I can't believe there is so much dust under there! The factory isn't even that old," I said, sitting up.

She grabbed the ring and held it in her hand. "Thank you, Bailey! This means so much to me. I never would have thought to use a broom handle like that."

"It comes from years of experience of having a cat,"

I said, then I stood up, took the spatula off the broom handle, and screwed the top of the broom back into place. “What are you going to do with the ring now?”

“I—I don’t know. It’s not technically mine, since I gave it back to him.” She opened her palm and looked down at the ring. There was a large emerald set in the middle of it. Even if it wasn’t an engagement ring, it still looked expensive.

“If you threw the ring at Jason and left the kitchen, how did you end up back in the kitchen with his body?”

She closed her hand around the ring again. “After I threw the ring at him, I stomped out of the kitchen. But I came back an hour later to start cleaning up, just like I told you and Chief Brody. I didn’t for a second think he would still be here, and I certainly didn’t think he had died. From what I knew of Jason, he was in perfect health. Yesterday was the only time I had ever seen him not feeling well—and the one time he’s sick, he ends up dead.”

Chapter Nine

Before Darcy left the Swissmen Candyworks, I asked for the key to the factory.

She looked down at the ring in her hand. "You should take this, too. I don't want it, and it reminds me of a difficult time. Maybe it can go to his heir, whoever that might be."

"Did he have any family around here?"

"Other than Carly? I don't know of any. Like I said, their grandfather passed. Carly and Mr. Hackney were the only family he ever spoke of." She dropped the ring into my hand.

"I'm going to have to give this to Aiden," I said. "He's going to ask you about it."

"I understand. He's just doing his job." She walked to the door, then turned back. "Bailey, I know we are friends, and I know you want to help me."

"I do."

"Just know that I don't want to cause any problems between you and Aiden because I was in a relationship with the wrong guy. Your loyalty is to Aiden and should be. I just want you to remember that."

I smiled at her. "I appreciate that, but Aiden knows who he married."

She frowned, then left the factory.

I tucked the emerald ring into my pocket. I would give it to Aiden and tell him how I'd gotten it. However, at the same time, I believed I could protect Darcy, too, or at the very least, buy her a bit more time so we could find out who really had killed Jason Hackney, assuming he was killed and wasn't just ill. How he died was still in question. I would never lie to Aiden if he asked me outright what I knew, but for now, I would keep my friend's confidence until I no longer could.

I collected my laptop computer from my office and left the factory. I walked through the empty parking lot the factory shared with Harvest Market, and then onto the square, with the intention of going to the Swissmen Sweets.

I knew my grandmother wasn't there because it was a church Sunday for her district. Unbeknownst to most Englishers, the Amish only had church services every other week. The off Sundays were meant to reinforce the individual family units with devotions and time spent together.

When they did have a church service, however, it was an all-day affair. I knew my *maami* wouldn't be home until dinnertime, if not after that, if a friend invited her to their home for a meal. I loved *Maami* dearly, but I was happy to have the candy shop to myself for a few hours. There were a few new candy recipes that I wanted to test for my candy show and for the factory.

At Swissmen Candyworks, I had a huge, state-of-the-art kitchen that was light-years ahead of the antiquated kitchen in Swissmen Sweets, but I was still most comfortable testing recipes where my *grossdaadi* taught me to make candy and fudge in the first place. In the small kitchen with the old mixers and ovens, I felt the most creative and the most connected to *Daadi*. How many times over the last several years had I wondered what he would have thought of the life I had today? I wasn't sure he would believe it, but I know he would have been proud, even if pride was a cardinal sin in the Amish Way.

The church bell rang high in the bell tour, announcing the eleven o'clock hour—time for the second church service for Reverend Brook's congregation. I knew Juliet and Jethro would be in the pews proudly looking on as the reverend gave his sermon.

Parishioners in their Sunday best hurried up the church steps to make it to the service in time. While they were running up the steps, Margot Rawlings, in a purple choir robe, was running down them—and she had her eyes fixed directly on me.

I thought it was best to pretend I didn't see her, so I continued on my way to the square. The finery from the wedding just the day before had all been whisked away, and the square was in the process of being transformed again for the Summer Soiree in a few days.

"Bailey! Bailey King! Stop! I know you saw me."

I had made it as far as the gazebo in the middle of the square before I was caught. Considering how good

Margot was at hunting me down, I was happy I'd made it that far.

I turned around. "Margot! How are you today?"

She narrowed her eyes at me. "I saw you running away from me, Bailey."

"I wouldn't call it running."

She sniffed. "In any case, I'm glad I caught you. We have a lot to discuss."

"Oh?" There were times when I tried very hard to play dumb, especially when Margot was involved. It was best to pretend I didn't know what was coming. I did realize it was an act of futility, but somehow it made me feel like I'd tried.

"You and Aiden aren't going on your honeymoon because of the murder." She panted.

I wrinkled my nose. Word traveled fast in Harvest, but at the same time, it would make logical sense that the sheriff wouldn't want to leave the county when there had just been a murder. There was no point in lying to Margot on the matter. "Yes, we are staying home. Aiden is going to do his very best to find out what happened to Jason Hackney."

"It was a hot topic at Sunday School this morning." She sounded unnecessarily cheerful about it.

I bet it was.

"Since you are going to be in town, I could really use your help with the Summer Soiree."

"Oh, Margot, I'm flattered you have asked me, because I know how much the event means to you, but—"

"Do I have to remind you that the man who was helping me organize it is now dead?"

She didn't.

"I'm sorry for your loss. Were you and Jason close?"

"I knew next to nothing about him except that he had a winery and was willing to help me with the event, but I bet you want to know more about him."

I waited.

"What better way is there for you to stick your nose into what happened than to be a part of putting on the Summer Soiree? It would give you plenty of opportunities to talk to all the other wineries and vintners. I'm sure they know Jason well, and one of them just might know who would want him out of the picture—outside of young Darcy Woodin, of course."

She had a point, and I hated that. Margot was going for the hard sell, as usual. She knew just what buttons to push on me to get me to agree. Helping Darcy was at the very top of the list. I couldn't believe my friend would hurt anyone. She just didn't have it in her.

My shoulders sagged, and Margot grinned from ear to ear. She knew she had me.

"What do you need me to do?" I asked.

She slapped me on the shoulder. "That's the spirit! I have to get back to church. I'm singing in the choir today and will already have to sneak in the back. Let's meet here on the square tomorrow at ten o'clock sharp, and we will go over it all." She jogged back to the church, her robe dancing around her as she went.

I sighed. It had been bound to happen. There was no doubt in my mind that as soon as Margot heard that Aiden and I were postponing our honeymoon, she would draft me to help. She took conscription very seriously.

I continued the rest of the way to Swissmen Sweets. I didn't even want to think about what Margot had in store for me. With Margot, providing the sweets and candies was never enough. However, nothing could be as bad as the time she'd made me play Mary in the Christmas parade. I guessed I should be grateful that the Summer Soiree didn't have a costume requirement.

When I unlocked the front door to Swissmen Sweets, Nutmeg, the shop's orange tabby cat, met me at the door and yowled for all he was worth.

I bent down to pet him, but he hissed at me. I jerked my hand back. Nutmeg loved to be greeted by everyone who came into the shop. In fact, he demanded it.

"Nutmeg, are you okay?"

He yowled again, and it was a noise I had never heard him make before.

"Are you sick?" I squatted to be at eye level with the little tabby.

I tentatively reached for him again, and he hissed a second time. This time when he hissed, though, he turned and ran to the counter toward the back of the room.

I stood up and turned on the lights, and the glass-domed counter where we displayed our truffles, fudge, and other sweet treats stood clean and empty. It was Sunday, after all. Nothing happened in Harvest on Sundays.

Nutmeg hissed again, and I followed him to the counter. I lifted the piece of wood that separated the staff area from the rest of the shop.

As soon as I did, I saw the reason Nutmeg was so agitated. *Maami* lay on her side behind the counter, holding her chest. Her eyes were half closed.

I dropped to my knees. "*Maami!*"

Nutmeg lay down by her head and started to purr.

CHAPTER TEN

She was breathing. It was shallow and labored, but I could see her chest moving up and down, even if every breath took its good old time.

I checked her pulse, and it was present, but it seemed off. I touched her cheek, and it felt clammy. Tears itched at the corners of my eyes. I did my best to hold them back. There was no time for crying. *Maami* needed my help.

I dug my cell phone out of my pocket, and with shaky hands, I called 911. Then I called Aiden.

I could barely get the words out about what I had found, but he must have gotten the gist, because he said he would be there right away.

I folded my hands together and bent over my grandmother. I placed my forehead lightly on her shoulder and prayed harder than I ever had in all my life. I couldn't lose her—not now, not ever. I couldn't hold back the tears any longer, and they slowly cascaded down my cheeks.

The sound of an ambulance brought me back to the present.

Nutmeg yowled that terrible sound again and ran to the door.

I double-checked to make sure *Maami* was still breathing and then ran to the door. I opened it wide, and two EMTs came inside. From the many times when I'd had to call for help over the last few years, I recognized them both, but there was no time for small talk.

"She's behind the counter." I wiped at my tears.

The EMTs didn't hesitate, and they jumped into action. I wanted to watch everything they were doing, but there wasn't enough room behind the counter for all of us. Instead I walked to the large window in the front of the shop. Nutmeg shivered in his cat bed. I scooped the little cat up. Now that help had arrived, he allowed me to pick him up. He buried his face into my neck as if he couldn't watch. His tiny pink nose felt cold and damp against my skin.

The door to the candy shop opened again, and this time Aiden came inside. He took one look at me, and I burst into tears. He enveloped Nutmeg and me into a hug.

When he pulled away, he said, "Why don't you wait outside? The fresh air will help. I'll go find out what's going on."

I nodded dumbly and gave Nutmeg a kiss on the top of his head. "You did good. You saved her." I set the orange tabby back in his cat bed.

He looked up at me as if he knew everything that I was saying. He curled up, covered his face with his tail, and immediately went to sleep. It was as if he were asking me to wake him when it was over. I wished that was something I could request.

I heard Aiden speaking to the EMTs over the counter, but my brain was too fogged to understand what they were saying. I stumbled outside into the bright summer day and wrapped my bare arms around myself as if there was a chill in the air.

"Bailey!" Charlotte cried as she ran across the square. Her long red-gold hair was held in place by a floral headband that was an exact match to her flowing Sunday dress.

I held my arms open, and Charlotte dove into them for a hug.

When she pulled back, she looked at my face. "We were in the church service and heard the sirens, and when I looked out the window and saw the ambulance was outside of the candy shop, I just got up and left. What happened?"

"It's *Maami*."

Charlotte's many freckles seemed to pop out of her face when her complexion lost all its color. "Is she . . ."

"She's alive. I came into the candy shop this morning, and she was on the floor behind the counter. Nutmeg was losing his mind. I have no idea how long she was on the floor like that with the poor cat yowling for help." I wiped away tears that hovered in the corners of my eyes. "I went to the Candyworks first. I feel awful. I should have come here first. Who knows how long she was lying on the floor like that . . ."

She placed a hand on her chest. "Oh, Bailey. There was no way for you to know. Didn't you think Cousin

Clara was at church? This is a church Sunday for the district, is it not? You didn't think she was home."

"But still . . ." I trailed off.

"We will pray. Prayer helps more than we can ever understand," Charlotte whispered. She loved *Maami* just as much as I did. After her very strict Amish district had kicked her out because she loved music and wanted to play instruments in church—something that many Amish districts allowed except the strictest of the strict—*Maami*, who was her cousin, took her in, no questions asked. *Maami* even supported her when she decided to completely leave the Amish faith to marry Deputy Little. *Maami* was as much Charlotte's grandmother as she was mine.

"I shouldn't even be here today," I said. "Aiden and I were set to leave for our honeymoon last night. We only canceled because Jason Hackney was murdered. I don't know what would have happened if I hadn't come to the candy shop this morning. Is it horrible to think that Jason's death might have saved her life?"

She held my hands. "You can't think of that. Remember, God works for the good of all those who love Him. Yes, it's horrible what happened to Jason Hackney, but his death has nothing to do with this."

The door to the candy shop opened, and the EMTs rolled *Maami* out on a stretcher. She had an oxygen mask on her face, and her eyes were closed.

"We are going to take her to the hospital. Do you want to ride in the ambulance?" the taller of the two EMTs asked.

"Yes!" I gave Charlotte one more hug.

"I'll go back to the church and tell everyone what is going on. I will get word to her district, too. She will be covered in prayer," Charlotte said.

I thanked her.

Aiden came out of the candy shop and locked the door after himself. "I'll follow in my car."

I nodded and took the EMT's hand as he helped me into the bay.

The door shut behind us, and as we pulled away, I watched Swissmen Sweets, my cousin, and my new husband grow smaller and smaller through the tiny back window.

Chapter Eleven

A doctor came into the waiting room where Aiden and I had been sitting for well over an hour. "Are you Clara King's family?"

I jumped to my feet. "I'm her granddaughter. This is my fia—husband, Aiden."

Aiden squeezed my hand.

She gave us both a kind smile and pulled one of the waiting room chairs in front of us. "Have a seat, and let's talk."

This didn't sound good at all.

"Your grandmother had a heart attack. One of her arteries is completely blocked, and it looks like it had likely been causing her discomfort and shortness of breath for some time. Had she ever complained of chest pains or difficulty breathing?"

"No." I shook my head. "But I don't know if she would tell me that she wasn't feeling well. She keeps those things to herself most of the time."

The doctor nodded. "That's what I suspected. She's

stable now, but she is going to need a stent put into her artery or a coronary angioplasty," she said. "It's a very common procedure, and her overall health is good. I'm confident she will make a good recovery." She paused. "However, some lifestyle changes will have to be made, namely her diet. I'm well aware that the Amish diet is high in fat and cholesterol. She won't be able to eat like that anymore."

I nodded and thought of all the calories that were in the candies we sold. Would *Maami* still enjoy making candy if she wasn't allowed to eat it? I shook the thought away. It didn't matter whether she did or didn't. She could retire from candy making. She had more than earned it. She just had never been willing to give it up in the past. She said it kept her connected to my *gross-daadi.*

"I think she would be fine with the procedure, but she would want me to consult with her bishop. He's an understanding man. I doubt he would argue with the idea. I'm sure others in the district must have had it, too."

"Good. I'm glad to hear that." The doctor stood up. "You can go back and see her now."

Aiden and I stood, as well. He squeezed my hand. "You go first."

As quietly as I could, I pushed open the door to my grandmother's hospital room. There was a curtain around her bed. I peeked around the side and saw her lying in the bed. She had an IV in her arm and an oxygen cannula in her nose. She looked so small and frail, but her prayer cap was still on top of her white hair.

That made me smile, and I was grateful the hospital had let her keep it on. It meant so much to her.

She opened her eyes. "Bailey, my girl."

I rushed to her bedside and sat in the uncomfortable chair next to her. It was like sitting on a concrete paver, but I didn't care. I was just so happy that she was awake and knew who I was.

"*Maami*, how are you feeling?" I gently wrapped my hands around her forearm. I just had to touch her to convince myself that she would be okay.

She gave me a wan smile. "I'm so sorry I gave you such a scare. It was not my intention to cause any trouble."

"*Maami*, you are never any trouble. Ever." I gently rubbed her arm, taking care not to touch her IV. "What happened this morning? Did you fall when you were on the way to church?"

She shook her head and then winced. I wondered if she might have a headache. "*Nee*, I was downstairs early in the morning to leave a message on Millie's shed phone. I wanted to tell her not to have Uriah come and fetch me for church. I wasn't feeling well and thought it would be best if I stayed home and rested."

I nodded. It had just been a development in the last few weeks that my grandmother didn't drive herself to church and on errands in her own buggy.

In the last months, she had become unsure of herself with her horse—to the point that she finally agreed when I said it was time to sell her horse and buggy. I knew *Maami* hated the idea of giving up her independence, but it just wasn't safe any longer for her to drive. Thankfully, Millie and Uriah had stepped in to take her anywhere she needed to go if I wasn't available, and they always picked her up on church Sundays since they were all from the same district.

I was also grateful she'd been able to sell her buggy and horse to Emily Keim and her husband. Emily worked for us part-time at the candy shop, and she and her husband ran a Christmas tree farm with her husband's grandmother and their two young daughters. They were just the most adorable little family. I really couldn't imagine the buggy and horse going to anyone better.

And this way, *Maami* could still see her horse from time to time. I knew it was hard for her to say goodbye to him. A buggy horse was like family to the Amish.

"I left the message on Millie's phone, but I don't remember much after that until I heard your voice. I'm sorry I couldn't say anything back to you. I was not feeling well."

Tears came to my eyes. "Don't worry about me. *Maami*, you have to think about yourself right now. I'm just so grateful that I found you. I can't imagine . . ." I was unable to finish the thought. I licked my lips. "Have you been feeling sick for a while?"

"A little while. I would be short of breath or need to sit down when making candies more often than I used to. I just thought it was old age. I'm not young anymore. I'll be eighty this year."

My stomach sank, and my heart hurt. It was hard to swallow past the guilt. If I had been at Swissmen Sweets every day as I used to be, I would have noticed she was slowing up, but between the wedding, my candy television show, and the extra demands of the factory, I was being pulled in so many directions, I rarely made candies with my grandmother anymore. When I did get over to Swissmen Sweets, it was only to pop in for a minute or two before I ran off to the next thing. *Maami* had been unwell, and I'd had no idea because I hadn't taken the time to notice.

But that was going to change. If I had to completely alter my schedule to keep an eagle eye on *Maami*, then that was just what would have to happen.

"Why didn't you tell me you had been having pain?" I asked. "I would have taken you to the doctor and had you looked at."

"You were so busy, and I didn't want to put a damper on your wedding. I truly thought it was just old aches and twinges from my age. I didn't realize it was anything to worry about." She took a breath, and the oxygen tank buzzed. "I thought I would tell you when you got back from your honeymoon. I didn't want to ruin anything for you. This is such a special time."

"Please. If you are ever feeling unwell or like something just isn't right again, tell me. You're more important than any plans I might have."

She closed her eyes. "All right."

"*Danki*," I said with a smile in my voice. I rarely spoke Pennsylvania Dutch, and when I did, my grandmother found it to be amusing.

She smiled with her eyes closed, and I wondered if she might be falling asleep. I had more to tell her before she dozed off.

"You are going to have to have a minor surgery. You will need to have a stent put into your heart. Will Bishop Yoder be okay with that?"

"Oh my, *ya*. I believe the bishop himself has had multiple stents put in." Her eyes were still closed as she spoke.

That was good to hear. Not that the bishop also had concerns with his heart, but that the stents wouldn't be a matter of debate in the district.

"Mom and Dad left for home this morning, but I know they would come right back if I asked."

"*Nee*. I know they have a big trip coming up, and I don't want them to miss it on my account. I will be fine. *Gott* has always protected me, and He will this time, as well. If it is my time, it is His providence."

I squeezed her hand. "Please don't talk like that."

She opened her eyes. "I'm not wishing to leave you, Bailey, my dear, but I must face the reality of old age. My time will come, as it does for us all, but I don't fear it. I will be with my husband again. It's a reunion that I have dreamed of a hundred times over."

"You're too young yet," I said.

This made her chuckle. "I don't know about that." Her face fell. "It makes me think of the young man who passed at your wedding yesterday. Now, he was too young to die, and yet he is gone. It's a terrible shame."

"We don't have to talk about that now," I said. "It can wait."

"*Nee*. You have questions, I'm sure, and you have taught me that time is of the essence when it comes to such things. I might know something about that poor young man."

I opened my mouth to protest again.

"Please let me tell you," she said.

I nodded. What other choice did I have?

"Jason Hackney cared for Darcy very much. I know Lois wants Darcy to find someone and be happy." She smiled at me. "What I have learned from you is that grandmothers can't rush such things."

"How did you know about Jason's relationship with Darcy?" I asked.

"I had a nice long conversation with him at the reception. He was standing alone, and I wanted to make him feel welcome, like I wanted all your guests to feel welcome. He appeared to be feeling poorly, so I went over and spoke with him to make sure he was all right."

The catch to that was that Jason *wasn't* a guest, but *Maami* didn't know that. She might have believed he was just one of Aiden's friends.

"What did he say?" I asked.

"Just how much he loved and cared for Darcy. He said they had been courting for a short amount of time, but that she had broken up with him over a misunderstanding."

I raised my brow. Darcy had said the "misunderstanding" had been Darcy's suggestion that his cousin's winery join the Summer Soiree.

"What did he plan to say to Darcy?" I asked.

"I don't know. He didn't tell me what he was going to say, but he did repeat at least three times that he planned to win her back, no matter what it took. It was a very romantic sentiment, I thought. I'm sorry he passed before he could succeed."

What *Maami* was telling me wasn't helping Darcy's case in the least. Maybe Jason's advances had made her angry, and just maybe she'd killed him over it.

I shook my head. I would not let myself believe, even in theory, that my friend Darcy Woodin could have killed anyone. I just wouldn't do it.

"You said he appeared to be feeling poorly. How so?"

"He looked very warm, and he was perspiring. He also said his stomach was bothering him. He believed it was food poisoning from something that he ate."

"Did he say what he ate?"

She shook her head. "*Nee.*" *Maami* closed her eyes again. "I'm feeling a bit tired." She placed her hands on her chest. "I think I will rest my eyes for a moment." She closed her eyes, and it seemed that just as soon as they were closed, she was asleep.

Guilt ate at me for asking my grandmother about Jason Hackney when she was so unwell, even if she'd insisted herself that we have the conversation. There were times when I wished that my curiosity didn't get the best of me.

Even so, I was left with more questions.

Chapter Twelve

I spent the night in the hospital. My grandmother was scheduled to have the stent put into her heart at seven the next morning. I couldn't bear the idea of her spending the night before the procedure alone, with all the noise and smells that she didn't know.

There was a recliner in the room covered in plastic that stuck to my skin, but at least it was better than the concrete-hard chair that I'd sat on when I'd first entered her room.

I knew Emily and Charlotte would handle everything that needed to be done with Swissmen Sweets and Swissmen Candyworks. Charlotte had already planned to handle everything with the Candyworks while I was supposed to be on my honeymoon.

I couldn't have been more grateful that the trip had been canceled.

After *Maami*'s procedure, they brought her back into the room, and I sat with her as she woke up.

When she was more alert, she turned to me. "You go

home. You need to rest yourself. I know you didn't sleep at all last night. I heard you tossing, turning, and sighing every few minutes."

"I'm so sorry. Did I keep you up?"

"You did not keep me up. I was awake, too. The hospital is not a place where one goes for rest. Please go and see Aiden. I feel awful that I have taken his bride away from him so soon after the wedding."

"You haven't taken me away from anyone, and I wouldn't want to be anywhere else if you were in the hospital."

"And I appreciate it. You were a great comfort to me last night. Just knowing you were next to me gave me peace, but now it's time for you to go take care of yourself."

"I could use a shower and a change of clothes." I sniffed my T-shirt. It wasn't a pleasant experience. "I could really use a shower."

Maami smiled. "It's settled, then."

"The doctor said that if all goes well, you will be let out as soon as this afternoon. I have already talked to Aiden, and you are coming home to stay with us until you recover. You can't be alone—for a little while at least. But don't worry, the doctor believes you will make a full recovery. A week or two with us will be just what you need."

She patted my hand. "We will talk about it when you get back."

I frowned. I didn't like the sound of that.

I left the hospital and was grateful that I could simply drive myself home, as one of Aiden's deputies had dropped my car off in the parking lot during the night.

After I got home, showered, and apologized to Puff for being an absent bunny mom, I went over to Swissmen Sweets. Emily Keim was working at the candy shop all day. Usually she only worked a few hours at a time because she was so busy caring for her young family.

I opened the door to the candy shop. Emily smiled at me as she cashed out a customer.

Her youngest daughter, Olive, toddled around the dinette tables after Nutmeg. She reached over and over again for his tail. The tabby knew what she was up to and would even tease the little girl with his tail.

The little girl squealed every time Nutmeg pulled his orange tail away from her.

Hannah, Emily's older daughter, was sitting at one of the tables coloring. She was the picture of her mother, blond, blue-eyed, with delicate features. I waved at Hannah, and she waved back. She was deaf. I signed to her, *How are you?*

She signed back that she was fine.

That was the extent of what I knew of American Sign Language. I really should learn more.

The customer thanked Emily and left the shop.

Emily came around the corner and gave me a big hug. "Oh, Bailey, how are you? How is Clara?"

"I'm not sure how I am. I think I'm still in shock, but *Maami* is going to be fine. She came through her procedure fine and might even be allowed to come home as early as this afternoon."

Emily gave a sigh of relief. "I'm so glad. When I heard the news, my heart just dropped. We all love Clara so much."

Olive toddled over to her and held her arms up into the air to be picked up. Emily scooped up her daughter and held her close to her chest. She kissed the little girl's cheek.

After such a rough start for Emily, I was so grateful to see how happy she now was. When I had first moved to Ohio, she'd been living and working with her older siblings, Esther and Abel. It was a strained relationship, made worse by Abel's questionable behavior, which included a stint in jail for a short time.

I hired her to work in the candy shop so that she could get away from the situation, which, to be honest, wasn't that far of a move, since Esh Family Pretzels, where her siblings worked, was right next door to the candy shop. I guessed I couldn't say that Abel worked there. I had never witnessed Abel making an honest living a day in his life.

"I'm sorry the girls are here," she said. "We just got a new shipment of seedling Christmas trees that my husband has to get into the ground before it's too hot out, and Grandma Leah is just not up to watching the girls for me any longer."

Grandma Leah was the grandmother of Emily's husband, Daniel, and she was close to one hundred years old. Up until recently, she had always been in good health. She'd told me once she had no plans to die until after her hundredth birthday. She was determined to make that milestone, and if anyone could, it was her.

"The girls are always welcome in the shop."

She smiled. "*Danki*. I can be here all day if you need me to be. My husband understands."

"Thank you, Emily. That means a lot to me. I think I will need you all day today. But if *Maami* is able to come home today, I can open the shop tomorrow."

The door to Swissmen Sweets opened, and I was expecting to see a customer or two come inside. Instead, Esther Esh walked through the door.

Olive saw her aunt and ran to her.

The cold expression that was ever-present on Esther's face softened as she gave her niece a hug. Things had been tense between Esther and Emily since Emily had left the pretzel shop, but the girls brought them together.

Esther patted the girl on the head, then said, "I came over to see how Clara is doing. Everyone in the village is worried."

"She's much better, and we hope she will come home today. I know it will warm her heart to know about the community's concern."

"I thought for a moment that whatever befell that man who died at your wedding, got her, too. Perhaps food poisoning?" Esther sniffed. "I would be worried if I were Darcy and my food was making so many people ill."

"It was nothing like that. *Maami* had a heart attack."

Esther covered her mouth with her hand, then took a breath. "I'm glad to hear that it wasn't the food. I wouldn't want Darcy Woodin to be blamed for killing your *grossmaami* as well as that young man."

"Why would anyone think Darcy had anything to do with either incident?"

"It makes the most sense. Everyone knew Darcy and Jason weren't getting along."

"Just because they weren't getting along doesn't mean she killed him. I imagine there were many people who didn't get along with Jason."

"Or I suppose it could have been his ex-wife. She's never had anything *gut* to say about him."

"Who is his ex-wife, and how do you know her?"

"She has a coffee cart and orders pretzels from me once a week to sell in her shop. She said they are very popular in the summer with lemonade or iced tea. When she comes in, we chat. Many times, she just wanted to talk about how much she disliked Jason Hackney. I don't think she liked the fact that he was involved with anyone else, either. She wasn't happy when I told her about Darcy, which was for sure and certain."

"You told her that Darcy was dating her ex?" I asked.

She pursed her lips together. "I didn't say it in so many words, but I thought she should know, in case she wanted to warn Darcy about who she was becoming involved with. We all know Darcy has not done the best job in finding a match. You would think it would be easier, since Millie Fisher Schrock is her *grossmaami*'s best friend. I would think that she would get some free matchmaking advice from that. Maybe with *Englischers*, it's just too different."

It seemed to me that the ex-wife was just the person I needed to talk to get to the bottom of the murder. "What's her name?"

"Pearl Gleib," she said and cocked her head. "You are going to talk to her, aren't you?" She scowled again. In my experience, Esther could only be pleasant for so long. We had reached the limit.

"I—I don't know," I said.

"Please, Bailey." Esther sniffed. "Everyone knows you are going to stick your nose into this. Let's not pretend."

"I'm not pretending. I don't know if there is a reason to speak to her. I don't know when they were together or when they broke up. Besides, she wasn't at the wedding. And that's where he died."

Esther laughed. "Yes, she was there. She was the florist."

I blinked. "The florist? I thought she owned a coffee cart."

"She does. She does the flowers on the side." Esther rolled her eyes as if she couldn't believe I wasn't keeping up.

I didn't remember hiring anyone by the name of Pearl Gleib. Then again, the only florist I had worked with handled the reception flower arrangements and bouquet. Margot was the one who had handled the ceremony flowers. She had insisted on doing that as her wedding gift to us. The flowers had been gorgeous.

As all these thoughts played across my mind, they must have shown on my face, because Esther leaned back and tapped her plain black sneaker on the wide plank floor. "See, you do remember."

"I don't remember her, but Margot Rawlings likely does."

Esther wrinkled her nose at this. She liked Margot about as much as Ruth Yoder did. Esther and Ruth were on the same page when it came to not wanting so many English events taking place on the square.

Esther had to know that it brought more customers to her pretzel shop, but she hated it on principle.

Emily set Olive in a playpen in the corner of the room, where she could play with a set of plain blocks and a stuffed cat that looked very much like Nutmeg. Nutmeg jumped into the playpen with the toddler and sat on the stuffed animal as if he were making a point.

Olive clapped her hands in excitement, and Nutmeg purred. If it had been a normal day, Puff would have been there, too. I knew the girls would love to see my giant bunny, and Puff always wanted to get out of the house. She was a social rabbit at heart.

"Isn't Pearl a sister to Carson Lee Gleib?" Emily asked. "He was just in the shop before you arrived, Bailey, asking for you."

"For me? I don't know anyone by that name."

"I found it to be strange myself. I don't think I've ever seen Carson Lee outside of his home. He barely ever comes to church, and he likes to stick to himself."

"Carson Lee goes to your church? So, he's Amish?"

Emily nodded.

I looked from Esther to Emily and back again. "So Pearl is Amish, too?"

"She was," Esther said. "Until Jason Hackney stole that away from her."

Chapter Thirteen

Esther had been right all along. I would have to talk to Pearl Hackney. Esther left shortly after our conversation because she had to mind her shop. She certainly couldn't rely on her brother, Abel, to do it. No one relied on Abel for anything.

I checked my phone, looking for an update from the hospital, but there was none. I thought it was safe to take a little more time and speak to Margot about Pearl and her flowers. It took hours to be discharged from the hospital, and if I could sneak in a little snooping before that, my *maami* would understand.

There were three large trailers parked around the square. They must have just arrived, because they hadn't been there when I'd gone into the candy shop.

Amish men under Uriah's guidance were unloading the trailers, while another team of young men were putting the large white tents together. Preparations for the Summer Soiree were in full swing.

Margot stood on the gazebo steps, overseeing it all

with a clipboard in one hand and a bullhorn in the other. I winced. It was never a good sign when Margot had her bullhorn out. She only brought it with her to the square when she was particularly anxious about the success of an upcoming event. She must be on edge about this one, which was bad news for us all.

Margot lifted the bullhorn to her mouth. "Bailey King, come to the gazebo please."

I was already on the square when she made this jarring announcement, and I would have heard her without the amplification, but Margot wasn't one to let a good bullhorn opportunity go to waste.

I walked up the steps.

"Right on time!" she said.

I was grateful that she put the bullhorn down, because if she had spoken into it when I reached the gazebo, she would have knocked me into the next county.

"Right on time for what?"

"Our meeting. I have to say, I do appreciate your dedication to the Summer Soiree, Bailey. This is a level of commitment I have not seen from you in the past."

I touched my forehead. Yesterday she had asked me to meet her on the square about the Summer Soiree. I had completely forgotten, which I thought was understandable under the circumstances.

"How is Clara?" she asked in a gentler tone. "When I heard she was in the hospital, I didn't believe for a second you would remember our meeting, but here you are. She must be on the mend, then. Is she back home yet?"

I decided not to correct her and tell her I had forgotten about the meeting and was only there because I wanted to talk to her about the florist. "She's not home yet, but we hope she will be released from the hospital this afternoon."

"Good. The whole village has been praying for her. Myself included."

"Thank you," I murmured.

She cleared her throat. "Since you are here, I suppose we should get down to the Summer Soiree. I would imagine you are eager to get back to Clara."

I was.

"I would like Swissmen Candyworks to do a sweets pairing with all the wineries. I think the collaboration would be great for both businesses. If we could say that Swissmen Candyworks is involved in the Summer Soiree, that will be sure to bring in fans from your television show, as well."

Ahh, she was back to that again. Margot was a bit of a dog with a bone when she got an idea in her head.

"You might recall, there are four participating wineries. I think a signature sweet treat to go with each will be just what we need, and for those who don't drink, it will be a nice offering."

"The soiree is in three days," I said. "That doesn't give me much time."

"I did ask you on Friday, but you turned me down because of your wedding and then honeymoon. However, now you are home, and you might as well make yourself useful."

I stared at her. My grandmother was in the hospital and a man had just been murdered at my wedding reception. I had more than enough to worry about. I didn't need to make myself "useful." I ground my teeth. "I certainly have enough candies already to pair with each winery. I don't think I can create something completely new for all of them. It takes weeks to perfect our recipes before we share them with the public."

She waved her hand as if it was no concern of hers. "I'm sure you will think of something."

I groaned inwardly. This was the Margot Rawlings I was used to.

"Was that all you needed me to do?" I asked and immediately regretted it. I should have run away when I had the chance.

"No. Now that Jason is gone, I need a second person here the day of. Unfortunately, my husband is undergoing medical tests in Cleveland that day. We tried to get another date, but that was all they had. He hates the doctors, so I have to go with him. I won't be back until just before the soiree begins. Jason was going to handle things for me that morning, but now you will have to be my eyes and ears."

"What about Uriah?" I asked.

Uriah was always the second in command when it came to events on the square.

"He's not comfortable doing it because he's Amish and alcohol is involved. He'll help set up, like he is doing now, but he won't be here on the day it takes place. I have to respect that. But I knew that alcohol thing wouldn't be a problem for you."

I sighed. "Was that it?"

She looked down at her clipboard. "Let me see." When she looked up again, a plain white van pulled up on the square. "Oh, there is Pearl. You will want to talk to her about the event."

And about the murder, I thought.

Margot hurried down the gazebo steps toward the van. I followed at a much more sedate pace, going over in my head what I would say to her. "Thanks for the flowers. Did you kill your ex-husband at my wedding reception?" That didn't seem like a great place to start.

Pearl opened the back of the van, and the smell of fragrant, fresh flowers hit me like a wall. I was grateful I didn't have allergies. Had I, I would have been completely bowled over by the smell.

"I brought some samples of the flowers that I want to use for the soiree," Pearl said. "These aren't the actual flowers that will be there. These will fade before the event, but I thought it was important to give you an example."

"These are lovely," Margot gushed. She even dropped her bullhorn in the grass to get a better look at the flowers. "The hydrangeas and dahlias are a perfect choice. They always make a big splash, and the pastel shades are exactly what I was going for. I asked all the vendors to dress in pastels for the evening." She looked over her shoulder at me. "That goes for you, too, Bailey."

Pearl stepped around the van door. "Oh, you're Bailey." She held out her hand to me. "Congratulations on your wedding."

I shook her hand and noted that her fingernails were encrusted with dirt. She caught me looking and pulled her hand away. "Hazard of being a gardener. Dirty fingernails."

"Your flowers were very beautiful at the wedding. I just found out that you did the flowers around the gazebo, or I would have thanked you earlier."

She adjusted her glasses on the tip of her nose. "There is no reason to thank me. It was truly my pleasure. I was just too happy Margot asked." She smiled at Margot. "I hope it leads us to working on a good number of floral arrangements together for various events. Nothing adds to the ambiance of an event like fresh-cut flowers. They just make everything so special, don't you think?"

I nodded. "Do you have a flower shop?"

She shook her head. "This is more of my passion and hobby. I work out of my home and this van. I'm so grateful that Margot gave me the chance, and I know that the Sumer Soiree will be just gorgeous. Margot has impeccable taste," Pearl said. "I own a coffee cart at the Harvest Flea Market. That's my real job." She laughed.

"Esther Esh mentioned your coffee cart to me."

"How nice! I love Esther, and her pretzels sell out fast on the cart in the summer. That reminds me, I will have to stop by and pick up some more while I'm here in Harvest."

I raised my brow. I had never heard anyone say that they *loved* Esther.

I eyed Margot. She seemed surprised by Pearl's comments about Esther, too.

It also seemed odd to me that she was speaking so happily about flowers when her ex-husband had died the day before. Perhaps she was just trying to be upbeat because she wanted to continue to do with business with Margot and the village of Harvest—or perhaps it was because she didn't care that he was gone.

I doubted it was the latter. Pearl seemed to be a sweet

woman who would have sympathy for anyone who passed.

"I'm sorry about Jason."

She blinked at me. "Who?"

"Your ex-husband. He passed away yesterday."

She waved her hand. "That is very kind of you to say, but I haven't seen or spoken to Jason in years. I was sorry to hear what happened."

I glanced at Margot to see if she thought Pearl's reaction was odd, too, but she was too busy studying the flower samples and making notes on her clipboard. If Pearl thought she was leaving the square without a list of suggestions from Margot, she was sadly mistaken.

"Did you run into him at the wedding?" I asked.

Her face turned bright red. "No, not at all. I wasn't even at the wedding. I—I put the flowers up in the early morning. It was cool enough then that I knew they wouldn't wilt before the ceremony, and then I left. I had no reason to stay. I wasn't invited to the wedding."

Margot poked her head out of the van at that point. "That's silly, Pearl. I told you the day before that everyone was welcome to come to the wedding. It was an 'open village' wedding."

Pearl blinked rapidly, and I could almost see her brain buzz through a list of things she could say in reply, but instead she just forced a laugh.

"These flowers will be perfect." Margot ripped a sheet of paper off her clipboard. "I just have a few ideas that will make them even better. The soiree starts at six, so I would like everything in place by four thirty. Will that be a problem?"

"No," Pearl squeaked.

"Unfortunately, I won't be here to answer your questions on the day of, but not to worry. Bailey will be my eyes and ears."

Pearl glanced at me. "Oh."

I could have been mistaken, but I could have sworn that I saw fear in her eyes. Why was she afraid to talk to me? Was it because I was married to the sheriff, and her ex-husband had just been murdered? She had to know there was a possibility that one of the deputies would question her.

Pearl closed the back doors to the van. "Thank you so much for the notes, Margot. I know they really will help, and it will be a wonderful evening. It's just the sort of elevated event that Harvest needs to set it apart from the other Amish town in Holmes County." She glanced at me, but she didn't meet my eyes. "It was so nice to meet you, Bailey. I look forward to working with you, too."

She ran around to the front of the van, jumped into the driver's seat, and pulled away from the curb even before Margot and I could hop back onto the square.

"My goodness," Margot said. "The flower business must be booming if she is in a such a rush to get to her next appointment. Or is it the coffee?"

I didn't believe it was the flower or coffee businesses at all.

Margot dusted off her clipboard. "I have a list of instructions for you, as well, for the soiree."

I bet she did.

A car honked at us, and I saw Lois Henry hanging out of the driver's-side window. Uriah was in the passenger seat.

"Margot, I'm heading out for a little bit. I should be back in a few hours."

Margot consulted her smartwatch as if to note the exact time that I was leaving so she would know the exact time that I would be back.

"Where are you going?" Margot asked.

Lois leaned over Uriah's side of the car so she could see us. "We're off to break Clara out of her cell."

"She's in a hospital room, not a jail cell," Uriah said.

Lois tilted her head to one side. "Sounds the same to me. I wouldn't want to be in either one."

I blinked. "What do you mean?"

"Your grandmother is ready to leave the hospital, and she is going to stay with Millie and me for a few days while she recoups."

"What?" I yelped.

"She didn't tell you?" Uriah asked.

"No, she didn't," I said with a heavy heart.

Chapter Fourteen

"Why didn't *Maami* call me to ask her to pick her up?" I asked.

Lois wrinkled her nose. "We thought she told you."

"She didn't. I want her to stay with Aiden and me."

Uriah stroked his beard. "She said that you asked her to stay with you, but she didn't think it was a good idea because you were newly married. She didn't want to be in the way."

"She would never be in the way. How could she ever be in the way?" I asked.

"Let us go pick her up," Uriah said. "I will have Lois call you when we get to our farm. You can talk to Clara there. I know you don't want to upset her in the hospital."

I didn't. I leaned into the car. "Lois, text me as soon as you all leave the hospital. I just want to know that she is safe and with friends."

Lois reached across Uriah and squeezed my hand. "Of course. You have to remember, Bailey, your grandmother might be old and unwell right now, but she still has a mind of her own. She wants to make her own decisions. It's hard to convince the young folks of that as we age."

Uriah nodded as if he were in full agreement.

I reluctantly nodded and stepped back from the car. I watched them drive away with a pit growing in my stomach.

Was *Maami* uncomfortable coming to my home because I was married or because it was an English home? She knew I would do anything for her. Aiden could stay back at our house, and I would move into the candy shop with her. I would do whatever she needed to make sure she made a full recovery. She had to know that.

I felt queasy at the idea that she thought she could ever be a nuisance to me or to Aiden. He loved her almost as much as I did.

Lois revved the engine. "We shouldn't keep Clara waiting any longer. No one wants to be in the hospital a second longer than they have to be."

I had the urge to jump into the car and go to the hospital with them, but if this was what my grandmother wanted, I would respect her wishes.

I stepped back from the car and watched them drive away with a heavy heart.

Margot slapped me on the shoulder. "We might as well go over your responsibilities for the soiree. It will keep your mind off things."

Leave it to Margot to find *her* silver lining in everything.

Margot consulted her clipboard and walked over to

one of the dozen wooden picnic tables that had been placed all around the square for the soiree. "Now, we have three wineries present. There were four, but I don't think Swiss Village Wines will be here now that Jason is, well, dead."

I winced. Margot never minced words.

"I'm glad you're still here." She sat at the picnic table, then waited for me to sit across from her. "The reps from all the wineries will be here soon. I want you to meet them again, since you will be the one here the day of the event."

My head was still reeling over the fact that *Maami* had asked someone else to pick her up from the hospital—and not only that, but she wanted her friends to care for her as she recuperated, not me. I knew she would never mean to hurt me. She could never hurt anyone intentionally, but it still caused me pain. I wanted to be the one there for her.

Margot rattled off the names. How she expected me to remember them all when I was so preoccupied with my grandmother's health, I would never know. However, Margot wasn't one to stop for another person's health. She was on a mission, and the mission would go on—no matter what.

"Did you get all that?" Margot asked at the end of her speech.

"Uh . . ."

She rolled her eyes. "It's all right here in the clipboard. I'll make a copy for you."

"Thanks. I'm sorry, Margot, I'm just a little preoccupied."

"I can see that, and we all love Clara. She will be in great hands with Millie and Uriah."

"I know she will be."

Margot clapped her clipboard on the picnic table so hard that I almost fell off the bench. "They're here. We will make this quick, I promise, so you can get back to Clara. I'm not a complete tyrant."

That was yet to be proven. I appreciated her sentiment, but I wasn't sure it was a promise she would keep.

Four people walked toward us—three women and one man.

"I'm so glad you all could be here for this meeting," Margot said. "Everyone, take a seat. We haven't much time. You all remember Bailey, right?"

Jon Michael sat across from me. "Yes, of course, the woman from the candy shop."

Carly and Angel sat on the other side of the picnic table.

"How was your wedding?" Angel asked. "I mean, other than Jason dying at it."

Carly wrinkled her nose at Angel's crass words. I wondered how hard it was for her to be at this meeting. Presumably, Carly and Jason Hackney didn't get along, but he had still been her cousin.

I cleared my throat. "I'm sorry about your cousin."

Carly looked me in the eye. "You don't have to be sorry for me."

Oh-kay.

"And who are you?" Margot asked the third woman. She was much younger than Carly and Angel. I guessed she was in her mid-twenties. She was the same young woman whom I'd seen watching Jason and Darcy argue on the square just before my wedding ceremony.

She had a pageboy haircut that made her look more like a little boy than a young woman. Her hair stopped just below her ears, and it seemed to bother her as she tugged on it nonstop. She blinked her large brown eyes and reminded me of a deer frozen in the middle of the road. "I'm from Swiss Valley Winery. I'll be running our tent since . . . well . . . Jason is gone."

Carly stared at her. "You have got to be kidding me. What authority do you have to do that? If anyone should be running Swiss Valley's tent, it should be *me*, since Jason stole it from me in the first place."

"Now, Carly, you can't run both tents," Margot said. "And I think it would be a nice tribute to Jason to have his wine there."

"It's not *his* wine. It was our grandfather's wine that he stole."

I glanced at Angel and Jon Michael to see what they were making of Carly's outburst. Angel was examining her manicure. Jon Michael was resting his eyes. My father had the same talent of taking quick naps anytime and anywhere. It seemed to me that Angel and Jon Michael had heard Carly rant on this topic many times before.

"Now, Carly, you may be right, but what happens to Swiss Valley will not be decided overnight, and we do need four wineries for the soiree. All the others I called in as a replacement are already booked with other events on Thursday. The approximately five hundred people who spent money on tickets whom we expect to be here Thursday evening are expecting to taste wines from four local wineries. We must deliver on that promise. And so, taking that into consideration, I would like this young woman to stay and represent Swiss Valley."

Carly threw up her hands. "This is just an example of *another* time when I am cut out."

Margot ignored that last comment and looked at the young woman. "And what is your name?"

"Dakota Sparrow."

"And you work at Swiss Valley?"

Dakota nodded. "Going on five years."

"Dakota was hired by my grandfather," Carly spoke up again. "But unlike most of the other staff, after my grandfather died, she stayed."

"Oh, you two know each other?" Margot asked.

Dakota looked down at her hands. "Yes."

"Unfortunately," Carly said at the same time.

"Carly, you're intimidating the poor girl," Jon Michael said.

Carly scowled at him. "Stay out of this."

Margot folded her arms. "I don't know what the beef between you is about, and I don't care. What I do know is that this soiree needs to go off without a hitch. Do you think the two of you can be civil for the event?"

"Yes," they said at the same time.

Margot might not have wanted to know what the beef was, but I was interested. To me, it sounded like it was very much connected to Jason Hackney.

Margot tapped the end of her clipboard on the table. "Good. Bailey will be here in my place on the day of the soiree. Unfortunately, I won't be here on the day of until right before the event because my husband has a medical appointment that I need to attend. But rest assured, Bailey can do anything I can." She paused. "For the most part. No one can really be me."

Jon Michael looked skeptical. "Do we really want the woman who had a man die at her wedding in charge?"

"Jon Michael, you don't have to be rude," Angel said. "It wasn't like she killed him. No bride wants to find a dead body on her wedding day."

I could vouch for that.

Jon Michael held up his hands. "Fine. Do whatever you want. I'm just bringing it to your attention. Especially since *her* new husband came to my winery this morning to question me." He looked at all the winemakers in turn. "If the sheriff hasn't talked to you yet, he will."

Carly dabbed at her damp brow with a folded tissue.

"My husband has a job to do," I said. "It is not related to the soiree." As I said this, I realized I didn't know if that was the truth. If I didn't know better, I'd have said I was sitting at a picnic table with a group of murder suspects, and Carly Crestwood, Jason's cousin, was at the very top of my list.

Angel fanned herself with a brochure from her winery. "Ignore Jon Michael. He's still bitter over some bad blood between him and Jason. We are all so saddened over what happened to Jason. I hope this can come to a resolution soon."

"Thank you," I paused.

"I'm from Celestial Wineries," Angel said. "I, for one, am glad you are part of the soiree. I have been meaning to speak to you about selling your chocolates at our winery. It's the busy season at the vineyard, with tourists and harvesting. I just haven't had the time, so I'm especially glad we will be working with you."

"You're such a suck-up, Angel," Jon Michael muttered.

"Enough. Enough," Margot said. "No more bickering. I swear, I thought everyone would be better behaved without Jason here."

Carly sat on the bench like it was a horse that she was riding side-saddle and arranged herself to her best advantage. "Now the two of them can argue over who is the best since Jason is out of the picture."

Angel removed her reading glasses from her face and stuck them on top of her head. "You act like we are happy with what happened. If anyone is happy, it's you."

I blinked and watched the argument ping-pong back and forth. I had come to the square that morning with no suspects other than my friend Darcy, and here I was, sitting at a table with vintners fighting over who was happiest that Jason was dead.

"I'm not happy about it," Carly snapped. "It's not what I wanted, but I do hope our grandfather gives him an earful when he gets to the other side."

"He gave you a spot at a soiree when you didn't even earn it," Jon Michael said.

She narrowed her eyes. "He didn't give me anything."

"That's true," Margot said. "Darcy Woodin suggested her winery. We needed a fourth when another vineyard had to drop out. Carly was a good choice."

"I agree," Dakota said.

Carly narrowed her eyes at Dakota as if she was trying to decide whether she was lying or not.

"That's ridiculous." Carly stood up and flipped her hair over her shoulder. I had a feeling she knew how to use that ponytail as a weapon by the way she threw it around this way and that.

Margot pinched the bridge of her nose as if she had a headache coming on. "Stop fighting. Swiss Village Winery can stay. End of discussion. I think Dakota's presence will bring in even more tourists."

"There are plenty of other wineries in the county. We don't need Jason's to be part of it. It will just bring negative attention to the event. Everyone will be talking about his murder and whatnot."

"Maybe more people will want to come because of the murder," Angel said.

"That's morbid," Carly said.

"Most people are at least curious, if not morbid. I would think Bailey here is curious about all of us, too. Her husband is the sheriff, Jason died at her wedding, and let's not forget her reputation."

"A reputation for what?" Jon Michael asked as he looked me over.

Angel smiled. "I thought everyone knew. She has a reputation for solving murders."

They all looked at me with new eyes. Busted.

Chapter Fifteen

"Are you here because you think one of us killed Jason?" Carly asked.

Jon Michael arched his brow. "No one has a motive as strong as you do, Carly."

"Watch your tongue," she snapped.

"Or what? You will sue me? With what money? Isn't your winery in foreclosure?"

"It won't be as soon as I get Jason's winery back. Then it will be with my family, where it rightfully belongs."

He pointed at her. "There you go, motive."

Dakota watched the exchange, looking as if she was about to burst into tears. Yes, she worked for Jason, but I wondered where she fit into this very odd collection of vintners. She was by far the youngest and the most unsure.

"No one in their right mind would believe you had anything to do with Jason's death, Carly. Your beef with Jason happened years ago," Angel said.

"Revenge," Jon Michael said. "She was waiting for her chance to get revenge. What better time to do it than when he planned this event—which is getting so much attention!"

"You've lost your mind," Carly spat back. "The Summer Soiree is important for my business. Do you really think I would do anything to jeopardize it?"

Jon Michael shrugged as if it was no concern of his. "If there was a bigger prize, maybe."

"What prize? What exactly happened?" I asked.

"This is not up for discussion," Carly snapped.

Angel smoothed the sleeve of her blazer. "It's no secret. When their grandfather died, he left the Swiss Village Winery to Jason. Carly never got over it."

"That's not what happened. He stole it from me. We were the only grandchildren, and I was entitled to half. Like the prodigal child he was, Jason had already taken his half and moved to New York. Everything left was supposed to go to me, the one who stayed behind and worked and helped build Swiss Valley into what it became. But Jason swooped back in and was given it all, even after he'd squandered what he had already been given. Is that fair?"

"That's not what your grandfather's will said."

Through gritted teeth, Carly said, "That was because he got our grandfather to change his will in secret. I didn't know until it was too late. He lied to my grandfather, telling him that I planned to parse up the land and sell it. I would never do that! I grew up there. I worked more on that land than Jason ever did. He was away living his life, and then he came back to take over in the last hour." Her face was bright red at this point. If she didn't calm down, she just might have a heart attack like my grandmother had.

Even though Jason had stolen her vineyard—according to her, at least, and years ago at that—it was clear she was still upset about it. Maybe even upset enough to kill.

"I think that's enough of a history lesson," Margot said. "Now, let's get back to the business of the soiree."

Nothing deterred Margot from planning her events, not even murder. I didn't always like it, but I had to respect her single-mindedness.

As Margot conducted the rest of the meeting, there were no more complaints of murder.

"If I am going to make a candy for each of your tents—" I said when it was my turn to speak.

"You are," Margot said, as if it was up for debate. I knew her mind—it wasn't.

"I would like to meet with all of you tomorrow with your wines at Swissmen Candyworks. We can do a tasting there and pair up the best candy with each of you."

Carly held up her hand. "No."

I blinked.

"No, you will have to come to me," Carly said. "I'm far too busy to come back to Harvest another time this week before the soiree. I have a business to run."

I sighed. "All right, I can come to you." I looked at the other winemakers. "Can you all meet me at the Candyworks?"

To my relief, they all agreed. If Carly's was the only vineyard that I would have to visit on-site, then that was fine, and I wondered if I spoke to her without the other winemakers around, I might just have a better understanding of her relationship with Jason.

Hers wasn't the only winery that I wanted to visit, either.

Margot clapped her hands at the end of the meeting. "Well done. The installation of the booths should be finished tomorrow morning, so I encourage you all to come back to the square at some point tomorrow to look over your space and decide how you want to showcase your wares. This is going to be the best event that Harvest has ever seen!"

I really wondered how many times Margot had claimed that this would be the *best event ever*. It seemed like she'd said that for every last one she planned—the thing was, I thought she believed it, too.

The vintners got up. Jon Michael and Angel walked to their cars together, and Carly followed behind, shooting eye daggers into their backs. Of all the people I'd just met on the square, Carly was my number-one suspect. She certainly had the rage to kill her cousin, but I had to remind myself that Jason was poisoned. That took a lot of premeditation and planning. If Jason had been shot dead in the middle of the street, I would be certain it was Carly, without a shadow of a doubt.

Dakota gathered up her notes and walked in the opposite direction, toward the church.

"Hey," I called and ran after her, leaving Margot alone at the picnic table. I didn't think she minded. She was already on the phone talking to a vendor about linens for the soiree. This would be an elevated event for the square. Most of the time, we just used plastic tablecloths.

Dakota turned and saw me hurrying over to her. Her face paled. She didn't appear to be surprised that someone was following her, but she wasn't happy to find it was me. I really wished Angel hadn't told everyone my history of solving crimes. Besides, I hadn't solved anything alone—Aiden and many of my friends had helped. It wasn't like I was out there by myself chasing down killers . . . at least not too often.

"Are you all right?" I asked when I caught up with her.

"Me?" she squeaked.

"You didn't get the warmest reception from the other wineries."

"No." She looked down at her hands, which were gripping her notes from the meeting. "I should have expected that, but it still came as a bit of a surprise. Jason wasn't everyone's favorite, but he wasn't all bad." She blushed.

For the first time, I wondered if Dakota and Jason had been more than friends, or if she had just had a crush on him. He had been a handsome man in a polished sort of way. Obviously Darcy had liked him at one time, but as Lois said, Darcy wasn't great at picking the right guys.

"I was wondering if I could meet with you for the wine candy pairing at Swiss Valley Vineyards."

She blinked at me. "I thought it was easier for you to meet at the candy factory."

"It would have been if everyone had agreed to do it,

but since I have to go to Carly's winery anyway, I might as well come visit Jason's, too."

"I guess that would be all right. The winery is closed right now. I don't even know if I should be doing this event, but I thought it would be a nice way to honor Jason. He's been good to me. He gave me a chance when I needed work. I will get through the soiree and then see what happens."

"I think it's great that you want to honor him in some way. It doesn't seem like many people do."

"He was good at making enemies," she said.

"Oh?" Now, this was the kind of talk I wanted to hear about. If Jason had enemies, real enemies who wanted him dead, I wanted to hear about it for sure. If I could shine doubt on Darcy's involvement in any way, I would.

She pulled on a strand of bobbed hair.

"You were on the square the day of my wedding, weren't you?"

She shook her head. "No, I wasn't." Her eyes darted this way and that, as if she was afraid someone was going to jump out from behind the gazebo or one of the bushes. The girl was on edge. She was scared. I couldn't help but wonder what she was scared about. Yes, her boss had just been killed. That would be upsetting, but why would it make *her* afraid? The only way it would frighten her was if she knew something.

"I could have sworn I saw you with Jason."

She licked her lips. "It must have been someone who looked like me."

She was lying. I knew it was her.

I changed the subject. "I'm really sorry how rude they were to you. I'm sure everyone is just torn up about Jason's death. They took it out on you, and that wasn't fair."

She shook her head. "It didn't seem to me that anyone is sorry Jason is gone. They seem happy that he is out of the way." She teared up.

"But you cared about him?" I asked as gently as I could.

She wiped at her eyes. "I know what he was really like. No one else tried to get to know the real person. They just knew the tough businessman. He was more than that."

My phone beeped. It was a text message from Lois saying that she and Uriah had picked up *Maami* and were on the way to Millie and Uriah's farm.

There were so many more questions I had for Dakota, but my *grossmaami* had to come first.

When I looked up from my phone, Dakota was running away from me toward the church parking lot.

I might have had questions, but it didn't look like she wanted to answer them.

Chapter Sixteen

My car was parked outside of the Candyworks, and I headed that way. Somehow I had to convince *Maami* to stay with Aiden and me so that I could keep an eye on her. It wasn't that I thought Millie and Uriah wouldn't take excellent care of her, but she was my grandmother and my responsibility. I also needed to see her to have the reassurance that she was all right.

"Bailey," Jean Pierre called to me across the square in his heavily accented voice. "Bailey, *ma chérie*, have you seen Lois anywhere? We were to meet this afternoon so that she could show me around the county. She said there were several places I had to see. Apparently there is a farm where one can even hold a baby goat. I am intrigued." He placed a hand on his face. "But I cannot find her. She was to pick me up at my inn for our little trip, but I can't get ahold of her."

"I'm sure Lois didn't do it on purpose. She is—"

Jean Pierre nodded. "Oh, I see. I know what she is

doing. She is playing hard to get. How enticing! I love a challenge."

"I don't think that is it, Jean Pierre," I said. "She just wanted to help my *maami*."

"Of course she did. She is a selfless woman and would throw herself on a fire for another person."

I didn't know about that. I knew in Lois's case it might depend on who the person was. I thought Lois would even agree with me on that point.

"I don't think she is playing hard to get. It's just been a day full of unexpected events. She went to the hospital to pick up my grandmother."

"What?" Jean Pierre asked. "What has happened?"

I gave him a shortened version of everything that had happened since I'd seen him at breakfast the day before. "I should have told you, but to be honest, I was such a wreck that I'd forgotten you didn't fly home with Cass and my parents."

He took both of my hands in his. "Do not worry about me, *ma chérie*. This is a time when we need to think about you and your grandmother. I know how much you care about her. My goodness, you left me and New York to be with her. If that is not love, I don't know what is. Where is she now?"

"Lois is taking her to Millie and Uriah's home. I'm heading there now."

"And I will come with you."

"You don't have to do that."

"What am I to do, then, wander around the village, worrying about you, with no transport or way to go anywhere other than by foot? No, I need to go with you, not only to support you, but also to show my support to Lois. I know she cares for your grandmother, too. She must be very upset."

"All right," I said, but I didn't really want Jean Pierre to come with me. In truth, I would much rather be alone so I could collect my thoughts over what I was going to say to *Maami* to convince her to come back home with me. I knew it would take all my skills of persuasion to do it, because when *Maami* made up her mind, that was the end of it, most of the time—but not this time. I wouldn't allow it to be.

Jean Pierre walked with me to the parking lot, and we climbed into my SUV.

"My, you have even gotten a country car. How you have changed since your days in the city."

"I don't think an SUV is actually a 'country car.' People have them in the city, too."

"Those are all rentals—I am sure of it. No one would want to pay for the parking for a beast like this in Manhattan, not if you had any sense."

On the drive to Millie and Uriah's farm, Jean Pierre prattled on about how Charlotte and I needed to pick his brain about candies to pair with the wines for the soiree.

"It seems to me that I will need to go to these meetings with you. I have done such tasting with chocolate and wine many times, and there is an art to it. Who better to point you in the right direction than a Frenchman?"

"You're French Canadian," I said.

He placed a hand over his heart. "It is the same in our souls."

"Wouldn't you rather be with Lois?"

"Yes, of course, but two of us can play at the game of hard to get."

"I don't want to take up too much of the time that you want to spend with Lois. I know you will want to go back to the city soon."

"What am I hurrying back to the city for? Cass has everything handled there, and I'm having the time of my life here in your little village, let me tell you."

"I could use your help," I said. "I'm so worried about *Maami*, it's hard to keep my head on straight. I don't know if I can pair the right candy with the right wine."

"Leave that to me. This is my special talent."

When we came up to Millie and Uriah's farm, I was surprised to see more than just Lois's car in the driveway. Four horse-and-buggy pairings were in the yard, as well as Lois's sedan.

I parked the car, and as I stepped outside, Millie's goats, Phillip and Peter, ran to meet us.

Jean Pierre yelped and jumped onto the hood of my car. I didn't even know he could jump that high. "What are those wild creatures doing loose?"

Phillip, the black-and-white goat of the pair, planted his front hooves on the hood and stared at Jean Pierre like they were playing some sort of game.

Jean Pierre backed up against the windshield. "Is it going to bite me? Does it have rabies?"

"Jean Pierre, they are goats, and I wouldn't even call these two 'livestock.' They are more like overgrown lapdogs," I said.

He was still reluctant to climb down off the hood.

"I've heard a person can be knocked out by a goat's hoof."

I guessed that was possible. The goats, if silly creatures, were also very strong, but I wasn't going to tell him that. If I did, he would never leave the hood of my car.

I held out my hand to him. "They're friends of mine," I said. "If you are with me, they will leave you alone."

He scooted to the edge of the hood. "Are you sure? I don't want to get rabies. When I was living on the Lower Westside when I was starting out, I knew a man who was bitten by a bat and got rabies. He died!"

I extended my hand a little closer to him. "That's not going to happen to you."

"I would hope not. I didn't spend my whole life building my chocolate empire just to be undone by a rabid goat."

I had to look down at the dandelion-freckled grass so he wouldn't see I was holding back a laugh.

Finally, after what seemed like an hour, but was likely only a few minutes, Jean Pierre took my hand and let me help him down from the hood.

Phillip and Peter, gratefully, kept a respectful distance from him.

As we walked to the house, Phillip followed us. Jean Pierre gripped my hand tightly and looked left and right for the goats.

I shot Phillip a glance over my shoulder to tell him I meant business. My stern glare was in vain.

As if he could not resist it, the goat gently bopped Jean Pierre on the behind with his horns.

Jean Pierre screamed and ran toward the house. As he disappeared inside, the door slammed closed after him. I gave the goats a look. "You couldn't lay off him? Not even a little?"

Phillip jumped in place and seemed to be quite pleased with his new-found talent of terrifying elderly men from the city.

Before I went into the house, I shook my finger at the goats. "You two behave."

They grinned at me in return. They knew I couldn't tell them what to do. The only person they listened to was Millie, and even with her, they had selective hearing.

I was about to follow Jean Pierre into the house when my phone rang. The call was from Aiden. I picked it up right away.

"How is *Maami*?" he asked.

With everything going on, it warmed my heart that that would be his first question.

"She's fine." I went on to tell him that she was at Millie and Uriah's home.

"She can stay with us," he said. "We will take care of her, and if you need anything at all, I will be there."

"Thank you, Aiden. I want to make sure she is comfortable. I may have to go to her apartment over the candy shop for a few days."

"Of course. I'm in agreement. Her health is our top priority."

"Is that why you called?"

"Yes—and I have news."

"Oh?" I asked.

"The toxicology report came back. Jason Hackney

did die from mushroom poisoning, just as the coroner suspected."

"That was fast," I said.

"It went more quickly because we had a pretty good idea what the source of the poisoning was. It reduced the number of tests that had to be done." He paused. "The same mushroom was in Darcy's knife case."

I grimaced as I remembered Darcy trying to remove the knife case from the Candyworks kitchen. "This makes things worse for Darcy, doesn't it?"

"It doesn't make it better," he agreed.

After I'd said goodbye to Aiden, I opened the screen door and went inside. I found Jean Pierre, needle in hand, sitting at a quilt form with a large star-patterned quilt in the middle of it.

I blinked my eyes and did a double take.

I'd been out on the porch for maybe a minute.

The members of Millie's quilting circle were sitting around the edges of the quilt frame, chattering away. The only one who didn't seem thrilled by the new addition to the quilting circle was Ruth. She sat in the corner of the room, piecing bits of fabric together with a scowl on her face.

Jean Pierre looked up from his stitch. "Bailey, you have to try your hand at this. I never knew I would be so handy at sewing. These ladies taught me how to thread a needle and stitch in no time at all. Had I not loved chocolate so much, I might have been a tailor."

One of the younger women in the quilting circle, Raellen Raber, grinned. "You're a natural. Are there many quilters in New York?"

"I'm sure there must be," Jean Pierre said. "We have everything in the big city."

Lois sighed. "I just love a man who is good with his hands."

I shook my head. "Is my grandmother here?"

"Oh, yes, she is upstairs. Millie is helping her get settled in the guest room."

I thanked her and went upstairs.

I had never been on the second floor of Millie's house before, but it was a small home just the perfect size for Millie, Uriah, and Millie's cat. If the goats had lived indoors, she would have needed something much bigger. She'd also have needed reinforced doors, because the goats would try to barge into every room.

I heard voices coming from the second bedroom. I stepped in the room and found *Maami* lying on the bed, propped up on a surplus of pillows. I could see the bandages on her thin arms where the IVs had been, and she was alarmingly pale.

Millie was at the window, pulling back the curtains to allow the summer breeze inside.

However, what really caught my eye was Jethro, curled up on the corner of her bed.

Chapter Seventeen

"What's Jethro doing here?" I asked.

Millie smiled. "It seems that Juliet was at the hospital visiting with Clara when Uriah and Lois arrived to pick her up. Juliet insisted they take Jethro with them, too, because she knew Jethro could help you with your stress over Clara's illnesses."

I sighed. "She thinks I would feel better if I was pig-sitting?"

Maami smiled. "Juliet has always believed that Jethro can soothe anyone."

I frowned. "I'm not sure he can soothe me at this point. *Maami*, I want to take you home."

Maami's face fell, and I was immediately sorry for speaking so directly.

"I'll give you two a minute." Millie paused at the door. "Should I take Jethro with me?"

The little pig snuffled and buried his snout in my hand. Oddly, he *was* calming me, just as Juliet had promised he would. "He can stay."

Millie nodded and closed the door after herself.

I looked down at Jethro and scratched the top of his head.

When I didn't say anything, *Maami* spoke first. "I can tell you are upset with me."

My heart ached. I hated to admit that I could be upset with *Maami* ever. She had done so much for me over the years, and I knew she loved me. However, in that moment, I felt like a hurt child.

She reached out for me, and after I gave Jethro one more pat on the head, I stepped closer to the head of the bed so she could reach me. She took my hand. "This is the best solution for all of us as I heal. You and Aiden are just married. You don't want your *gross-maami* in your home when you have only been married a few days."

"Aiden doesn't mind. I just spoke to him."

"I know that, and I know that you don't, either. I love you both for that, but this is a time when you need to be together as much as possible. The first few weeks after marriage is when you truly get to know some-one."

"I already know Aiden. I'm worried about you. Besides, Aiden is so focused on Jason Hackney's murder, I have hardly seen him."

"That convinces me that the time that you two *do* have together needs to be even more focused on the two of you."

I was going to argue with her more, when she added, "And I know that you are busy."

"I'm not busy enough that I can't take care of you."

She smiled and reached her other hand out to tap the

mattress. I sat next to her on the bed. "I do love that you want to care for me, but you are just not in a *gut* place to do it. You would be gone for hours at a time, and I would be alone in your home with little to nothing to do."

I wanted to argue with her on that point, but I couldn't. I already knew that for much of the next day, I would be visiting vineyards, trying to find out who killed Jason. Would it be better to give up the investigation to care for my *grossmaami*?

"You have Swissmen Sweets. The Candyworks," *Maami* went on.

I'd set all of it aside. Wasn't that what any loving granddaughter would do?

Maami shook her head. "You have many responsibilities. And so many people—our employees, friends"—she inclined her head, indicating Lois, who could be overheard laughing in the other room—"and family rely on you."

It was true.

"Bailey, Uriah told me that Margot cannot be there for the setup for the Summer Soiree, and that means all of Harvest is relying on you, too. I'm certain she asked you to take her place."

I sighed.

Maami squeezed my hand. "It is hard for me not to be in my own home now, but I'm much more comfortable in an Amish home."

"If you don't want to stay with Aiden and me, I can stay with you at the candy shop until you are better."

"*Nee*." Her voice was gentle yet firm.

"But—"

"My mind is made up, and I am very comfortable here. Millie is a practiced caregiver, and with so many of the ladies coming in and out of her home for the quilting circles and just to visit, I will never be alone.

"I will be well cared for. I don't even know how many ladies from the district are downstairs right now, and every last one of them brought food, flowers, and prayers. I am showered with love. This is the time when our community thrives. Any time one of us is in trouble, everyone else steps up."

I nodded. The sense of community was something I appreciated the most about the Amish Way. It was something I hadn't had or even known I had needed when I was living alone in New York. I had friends, of course, but nothing like a whole group of people who would jump in and help me if I faced any difficulties.

"Is this what you really want?" I asked.

She smiled. "It is what I want and need, and it is what you need, too." Her eyes grew heavy. "I'm feeling a bit tired. I think I will sleep now."

"I'll come see you every day."

With closed eyes, she said, "I know you will."

By the time I tiptoed out of the room with Jethro in my arms, she was already asleep.

I went back downstairs with a heavy heart, not only because *Maami* had refused to come home with me, but because I knew she had made the right choice. I was too busy to give her the proper care. I trusted Millie. She would make sure *Maami* had everything she needed. Even so, it was hard not feeling guilty over it. It was as if I had let her down in some way.

I walked back into the large great room. The first

floor of Millie's house, except for her pantry and a small bathroom, was made up of one big room. The home had been built by an English couple, and Millie had bought the farm from them when she'd moved back to Ohio after years in Michigan spent caring for her elderly sister.

There were telltale signs that the house had once been English. There were solid plastic plates on the wall covering the spots where the outlets had been. Millie had not removed the wiring from the home when she bought it, because she wisely knew the wiring would make the house appealing to an English buyer if she were ever to sell the home. She'd simply made it inaccessible.

Her aloof, cream-colored cat, Peaches, sat on the kitchen stool as I walked down the stairs. The cat looked at me before returning to his grooming. I took it to mean that he wasn't that impressed with me.

"You must all come to New York," Jean Pierre announced from his seat at the quilt frame. "I'm certain that people in the city would love to see the work of so many Amish ladies. The fact that you sew everything so exquisitely by hand will mesmerize so many. Learning crafts like this have really made a resurgence in recent years. You could teach classes. It would be a great way to make money."

"That is the most ridiculous bit of nonsense I have ever heard," Ruth said from her spot on the rocking chair.

"I think it sounds fun," Raellen chirped.

"Of course you would." Ruth set the fabric she was

piecing onto her lap. “If you didn’t have those nine children to care for, you would be off in a second.”

Raellen, who was, in fact, a mother of nine, didn’t appear to take offense at this comment, but then again, I didn’t know whether Raellen took offense to anything at all. Even the reprimands of her strict husband appeared to roll off her back.

“That is very kind of you to invite us, Jean Pierre,” Leah Bontrager, one of the older members of the quilting circle, said. “But I don’t think it would be wise.”

“I think it sounds like a good time,” Lois chimed in. “I would go along for just the fun of it.”

Jean Pierre beamed. “Yes, we would want you there, too.”

“Oh, Bailey,” Millic said, appcaring relieved that she was able to change the subject. “How is Clara?”

“She’s doing well, I think. She’s sleeping. She looks so much better than she did when she was at the hospital. I can’t thank you enough for taking her in. She would like to stay here instead of coming home with me.”

“I do think that is best,” Millie said in a low voice.

I nodded, but I was afraid that if I spoke, I might start crying, so I said nothing.

“That is how it should be,” Ruth chimed in. “The Amish should be cared for by their own.”

“Bailey would take very *gut* care of Clara if it came to that.” Millie gave Ruth a stern look. “I have no doubt in my mind that she would. However, I have the time to give Clara the care she needs. It’s not about being Amish or not—it’s about what Clara needs as she recovers.”

Ruth huffed and rocked back in her chair.

"Jean Pierre, are you ready to go?" I asked.

Jean Pierre looked up from his stitches. "Already? I was just starting to really excel at this. I don't know when I'd last had this much fun. Perhaps it was the time I presented a cake to the president at the White House, but this is so much more relaxing."

"I need to get back to the shop," I said. "Emily has been there all day with her girls, and I need to let her go home. She's already working more hours this week than she usually does."

"Don't you worry about Jean Pierre," Lois said. "I will make sure that he gets back to his inn." She smiled at him, and Jean Pierre beamed back.

At first, I'd found their attraction amusing, because they both could be flirts, but there might be something more to it than I thought.

I nodded. "It was so nice to see you all." I'd just started for the door when Raellen spoke again.

"The wedding was beautiful, Bailey. If it hadn't been for the murder, it would have been a perfect day," Raellen said.

If only, I thought.

"And my cousin did such a wonderful job on the gazebo with the flowers. She always had a special talent for that. She was always growing flowers and arranging them, and she would bring my mother just the prettiest bouquets." Raellen smiled at the memory.

"Your cousin?"

"Pearl. She's my second cousin." She tapped her chin as if she was deep in thought. "Or maybe she is my third cousin." She shrugged. "I have never been *gut* at keeping track of those sorts of things."

"Among other things," Ruth muttered from her spot.

Millie scowled at her, but Ruth seemed undisturbed by the look.

"Pearl the florist is your cousin? Esther Esh told me she was Amish."

Raellen shook her head. "She hasn't been Amish for a long time. I think she left when she was fifteen. She was such a kind and quiet girl that everyone was surprised when she left." She paused. "But it was on *gut* terms. She wasn't shunned or anything like that. She was always bright. I believe she just wanted the chance for more schooling."

Usually, an Amish person was only shunned if they left the faith after they had joined the church through baptism. To accept one's vows and commit to God and the Amish Way and then break that vow was not taken lightly.

"Did you know she'd married Jason Hackney?" I asked.

"I did. The family wasn't happy about it."

"Do you know how she met him?"

She shook her head. "I was busy raising my family, and she was off living the *Englisch* lifestyle. I have nothing against that, but it would have been between my sixth and seventh child. I had my hands full."

I couldn't even imagine, and it wasn't like the Amish hired nannies or extra help when it came to raising children. The fact that every time that I saw Raellen she had a smile on her face was a marvel to me. Some people just had the super-mom gene.

"I did hear about her breakup from her brother, Carson Lee. He's still Amish and works for a tractor company. He helped his sister out the best he could, but since she wasn't Amish, there were limitations."

I wanted to ask what those limitations were, but Ruth jumped into the conversation. "Carson Lee Gleib doesn't have to worry about the situation that his sister found herself in. From what I know, she's doing very well with her coffee business. She should never have married Jason. He was not kind to her."

Raellen wrinkled her nose. "Where did you hear that?"

Ruth folded her arms. "I'm the bishop's wife, and people tell me news as they should. If anyone should know exactly what is going on in this district, it's me. It is my job to know what everyone is up to."

Leah rolled her eyes. "That is your opinion. There is nothing in the church documents that states the bishop's wife should be the biggest busybody in the district."

Ruth scowled at Leah, but she said nothing in reply.

Leah was one of the few women who could talk back to Ruth without any backlash. It made me wonder what Leah had on the bishop's wife, because Ruth certainly didn't accept such disrespect from anyone else. Lois would talk back to her, too, of course, but it never ended as well.

"What were Carson Lee's limitations to helping his sister?" I asked Raellen.

"Oh, I—I don't know, he just he has to take care of his wife and children first. As an Amish man, they are his priority." Raellen stood up suddenly. "I need to run to the bathroom. I've been sitting at this quilt frame for far too long." She chuckled. "It was so nice to see you, Bailey." She rushed to the bathroom, then closed and locked the door behind her.

Ruth shook her head. "I always thought Raellen Raber was an odd bird. With all those children, it's amazing she can string two sentences together."

"Ruth," Millie said. "You know Raellen is a very *gut* mother."

"But not a *gut* liar."

For once, Ruth Yoder and I were in complete agreement.

Chapter Eighteen

When my alarm went off at four the next morning, my eyes shot open, and I turned the blaring noise off with a slap. I glanced over at Aiden, who was in the bed next to me. He didn't even stir. He came home from the office so late the previous night, I'd already fallen asleep. This certainly wasn't how I'd expected our first week of marriage to go.

Aiden might still be asleep, but the other creatures in the bed were awake and ready for breakfast. Puff and Jethro both sat at the end of the bed. The evening before, I had tried to meet up with Juliet to return the pig to her, but she'd insisted that I keep him through the night. She claimed I needed the little bacon bundle to comfort me more than she did at the moment. Maybe she was right. Seeing Puff and Jethro together always made me smile.

"All right, I'll get up," I whispered.

After I'd dressed and gotten ready for my day, Jethro and Puff followed me down the stairs and made a beeline for the kitchen. They were nothing if not single-minded when it came to breakfast.

I fed the animals, then went to the hall closet, where I retrieved Puff's backpack carrier. I had taken the large rabbit back and forth from Swissmen Sweets so many times over the years, but as she grew bigger, it had become increasingly difficult. A traditional carrier with a handle was just too much to manage. Puff was no lightweight, so I had finally invested in the backpack carrier.

"You two are coming to work with me. It's time we get the gang back together."

They both wiggled their short tails in anticipation. I set the carrier on the floor, and Puff jumped inside.

At first, Puff had wanted nothing to do with the backpack, but eventually she understood that when I got it out, it meant she was going to Swissmen Sweets for the day. She was always ready to spend time with her best friends, Jethro and Nutmeg, at the candy shop.

Sometimes I took a beat and wondered how my life had gotten to the place it was. It certainly wasn't what I'd thought my life would be when I'd moved to New York for culinary school when I was just eighteen. Walking a pig on a leash and carrying a giant rabbit in a backpack had never been on the list of possibilities. Even taking that into account, though, I was happy where I'd landed.

Aiden came down the stairs in gym shorts, looking blurry-eyed. "You're leaving?"

"I have to get the candies made for Swissmen Sweets since *Maami* isn't there to do it."

"You don't have someone on your factory staff who can do it?" he asked.

"I will likely have someone else open the shop tomorrow, but I want to get everything organized and ready today. *Maami* had very particular ways that she did things that are different from the factory. It will be less confusing for my staff if I handle this first day without *Maami* there."

"All right," he said and held out his arms, waiting for a hug.

I set Puff's backpack back on the floor and went over to embrace him.

"I'm so sorry about the honeymoon. I'm sorry about all of it."

"Aiden, we already went over this. I can't leave right now, either. *Maami* needs me close by. It's really true now since Margot roped me into the Summer Soiree. Somehow I'm in charge of the whole thing on Thursday."

His chest vibrated against my ear as he laughed. "That sounds about right. In any case, I have an idea of how to make it up to you."

I pulled back from him and looked up. "What's the idea?"

The laugh lines next to his chocolate-brown eyes crinkled. The first thing I had noticed about Aiden was his eyes, since they reminded me so much of chocolate. It seemed right that I would marry a man with chocolate eyes.

"I can't tell you that—it's a surprise."

"Fine," I said with a laugh. "I can wait for a little bit.

By the way, did you learn anything more about Jason's death?"

His mood shifted, and he pulled back from me. "Not a lot," Aiden said. "No more than I told you on the phone yesterday. It was death cap mushroom poisoning. We still don't know where and when he ate it."

"How long does it take for that kind of poison to take effect?"

"It can be anywhere from eight to ten hours. Maybe a bit longer, the coroner said."

"So he didn't eat it at the wedding."

"That's the assumption, but since we don't know where he was eight to ten hours before he fell ill, it makes it that much more difficult to find out who might have been behind it."

I shivered. "Don't more women kill with poison?" I asked, thinking that was another point against Darcy's innocence.

"Statistically, yes, but I'm not ruling anyone out at this point."

"Good, because I know it wasn't Darcy."

He sighed. "Yes, I know. You have made it abundantly clear that you feel that way. I respect your loyalty to your friends, but like I said, I'm not ruling anyone out at this point, including Darcy."

I shivered. "I have something for you." I reached into my pocket and pulled out the emerald ring that Jason had given to Darcy as a promise ring—the one he'd tried to give her again to win her back.

"A ring?" He twisted the gold ring on the ring finger of his left hand. "You've already given me a ring, and it doesn't look to me like this one is going to fit."

"It's not a gift for you. It's Darcy's," I said. "Or it *was* Darcy's. I don't think she makes any claim to it now. It was a gift to her from Jason."

Aiden frowned. "Where did you get this?"

I wrinkled my nose and told him about finding Darcy in the Candyworks the morning before, looking under the oven for the ring.

"Why didn't you tell me about this earlier? She shouldn't have been in the Candyworks kitchen. *You* shouldn't have been in the Candyworks kitchen. It's a crime scene."

"I know."

"And you should have given the ring to me right away."

"I was going to, but I found *Maami* right after that. Everything else went out of my head . . ." My voice wavered.

Aiden grabbed a tissue from a box on the side table and carefully wrapped the ring in it before sticking it in the pocket of his shorts.

I blinked back tears. I knew full well that I'd messed up. "I'm sorry," I whispered.

He wrapped his arms around me and kissed the top of my head. "It's okay. When I heard about *Maami*, I forgot about everything else, too. She has to be our first priority right now."

I looked up at him, blinking back tears. "She is. I just wish that she could be here so I could take care of her. She doesn't like being taken care of."

He smiled. "*Maami* is in good hands with Uriah and Millie. Other than us, I can't think of anyone else I would rather she be staying with. She will do what she wants. She is stubborn—just like another King girl I know."

"Hey," I said as I pulled back from him, but he did make me laugh. I was grateful for that. I was grateful for all the laughs I could get while *Maami* was so sick. I cleared my throat. "This makes Darcy look worse, doesn't it?"

He sighed. "It doesn't make things look better for her."

"There have to be other suspects. You must suspect the winemakers from the soiree, too."

"Why do you say that?"

"Jon Michael said you questioned him at his winery."

"I did, and I will be questioning the others, too." He stepped back. "Don't you have candy to make?"

I squinted my eyes. "Minutes ago, you were trying to convince me to stay home and let my staff handle it."

He grinned. "That was before you started asking me about the murder."

Chapter Nineteen

Aiden went back upstairs, and I put on the bunny backpack and snapped on Jethro's leash. With that, we were out the door.

It had been so long since I'd walked to Swissmen Sweets from my little house in the early morning. For years, it had been a walk I'd made every single day. It was a routine that I had followed, and there had been solace in that. That had all changed when the Candyworks opened. At that point, my television show was doing well, and the factory could barely keep up with the out-of-state demand. Every waking hour was put into the factory.

Now the factory was running smoothly. Charlotte knew as much about the factory business as I did—probably more. She could handle the tours and the orders. There really was nothing she couldn't do when it came to the candy. I was grateful for it. I needed her help now more than ever. With *Maami* at Millie's farm recouping, I needed to be at Swissmen Sweets as much as possible.

When I reached the square, I was hit with the scent of flowers from the planters along the sidewalk, mixed with the smell of freshly baked bread from a neighboring bakery. All was quiet and peaceful. You would never know a man had been murdered in this little village just days ago or that anything at all bad ever happened in Harvest.

I put my key in the lock and was about to turn it when I heard the squeak of a shoe behind me.

I spun around to find Abel Esh leaning on the lamppost outside of Swissmen Sweets. His blond hair was mussed, and his clothes were disheveled, like he might have slept in them.

"I know you must feel horrible you opened that factory now," he said. "Had you been around your *grossmaami* more, you would have recognized the signs of her illness. Do we call it the price of success?"

I had known Abel since we were both children and I would come to Holmes County to spend the summers with my grandparents. He had always been conniving and spiteful.

"Abel, what are you doing skulking around the village at this time of the morning? I know it's not to help your sister open the pretzel shop."

He stumbled toward me, and when he was within four feet, I could smell the liquor on his breath, which surprised me. Abel had been in trouble with the law before for selling illegal moonshine. He'd been released from prison early because of overcrowding in the system. He sold moonshine, and I was sure he drank it, too, but I had never known him to be drunk.

I took a step back, but I couldn't get very far because my hand was still holding on to the key in the lock.

"You should go home and sleep off whatever this is," I said. "You're just going to embarrass your family again."

He took a step even closer to me, and Jethro hid behind my legs. The little pig was terrified of Abel, and for good reason.

"Abel, you need to back off." I held my ground.

Just when I thought he wasn't going to and I would have to resort to kicking him, he slunk back. "You know, Bailey, I wish things could have been different for us. We could have been friends, but you made it clear when we were just kids that wasn't what you wanted." He looked me up and down. "And now you're married."

I blinked at him. "What are you talking about? You never wanted to be friends. We never liked each other."

"Love and hate are on the same coin," he slurred. "You should ask your friend Darcy all about that. She knows." He stumbled away.

I went into the candy shop, ushered Jethro inside, and immediately locked and bolted the door behind me. I wasn't taking any chances with Abel stumbling around the village square in a stupor. I had never known him to be a violent man, but with enough alcohol in him, there was no telling what he could be capable of.

I removed Puff's carrier from my back and let her

out. Nutmeg jumped from his cat bed under the window. He touched noses with his two friends, Puff and Jethro.

I tried to find some happiness in the animals' antics, but I was still disturbed by Abel's visit. I had known he'd had a crush on me when we were younger, but I'd thought that was long over with. Was he implying otherwise? It reminded me that in all the time I had known Abel, I had never seen him courting anyone. It could have been because no Amish family would let their daughter be courted by him due to his reputation.

I reminded myself that he had been drunk on his own moonshine, no doubt, and likely didn't even know what he had been saying. But what had he meant when he'd told me to ask Darcy about love and hate? Was he referring to Jason? I didn't know what else it could be.

How could he know anything about it?

I tried my best to put the incident out of my head. It wasn't the first time Abel had stopped me at the front door of Swissmen Sweets to say something rude, and I doubted it would be the last. He loved a good doomsday proclamation, and they rarely came to fruition. His whole purpose was to get a rise out of me. Which he had, but I wasn't going to let him know that.

I turned on the overhead lights and looked around the shop. I had missed this place. It had been too long since I'd been in the shop alone in the early morning hours just doing what I loved, which was making candy. As my business had grown, I'd spent less time making candy and more time supervising candy making and running the business.

I was happy to be back in the place that felt most like home to me, but I wished it had happened for other reasons, not because of *Maami*'s heart attack.

It was five thirty in the morning and far too early to be calling on even an Amish family, even though I knew from Millie's habits, she was already up and starting her day. Still, I could not wait to see *Maami*. I just had to know she was getting better.

Puff must have felt the same, because she went right over to the small hallway that led to the stairs to *Maami*'s apartment. She waited at the bottom of the stairs as if she was waiting for *Maami* to come down. It broke my heart. She had never been in the candy shop before when my grandmother wasn't there.

"She'll be back soon," I said to reassure the bunny—and myself, too.

I got the animals settled in the front room of the shop. They knew very well that they were not allowed in the kitchen, where the candy was made. There were times when Nutmeg broke that rule, but usually only at night.

The three of them wedged their bodies together in Nutmeg's cat bed. They didn't fit. Half of Puff was on the floor. Nutmeg was on Puff's side, and Jethro sprawled over the bed with his hooves hanging over its edges. I thought it was probably time to get them a larger dog bed if they were determined to sleep together like that.

I went into the kitchen and got right to work. I had four kinds of fudge and two kinds of truffles to make before we opened. We prided ourselves on having fresh fudge every day, and that wasn't going to change.

An hour later, I was slipping the first tray of truffles into the domed counter in the main shop. I noticed the animals were no longer on Nutmeg's bed. I wondered if they might have gone upstairs to *Maami*'s apartment to sleep in her cozy living room as they were prone to do.

I closed the display case and walked around the counter. "Where are you guys?"

I found the animals all cowering together in the hallway that led to the stairs going to the second floor. Puff had her nose buried into Nutmeg's side, and Jethro's hoof covered his snout. Nutmeg stood at attention, as if he was ready to defend his two friends at any cost.

A shiver ran down my spine. I had never seen all three of them act in such a way.

"What's wrong?" I asked.

Nutmeg hissed in reply.

I looked back at their bed, and that's when I saw a face in the window.

I jumped, and the person on the other side of the glass jumped, too.

At first, I thought it was Abel again, but then I saw whoever it was wore a bonnet.

Chapter Twenty

I removed my chocolate-streaked apron and threw it over the counter, then went over to the window for a closer look. It was Iris Young, one of the women from Millie's quilting circle. Immediately when I realized who it was, my heart stopped. Was *Maami* okay? Was Iris here to bring me some bad news?

I opened the door. "Iris, is my *grossmaami* okay?"

She blinked at me and clutched her hands to her chest. "*Ya*, I think so. She is staying with Millie, and there is no better caretaker."

My shoulders sagged, but my relief was short-lived.

"Oh, Bailey, I'm so glad that you are here. I know your *maami* is ill, and I wasn't sure that anyone would be at Swissmen Sweets this early in the morning. I couldn't think of another place where anyone was who could help." She was trembling from head to toe, and she was wearing a jacket and bonnet. It was close to seventy degrees outside, even so early in the morning. I knew it wasn't the cold that was making her shake.

"What's wrong?"

"It's Tuesday, and on Tuesday I do all the baking for the rest of the week at the café. I always arrive at five thirty sharp because Darcy wants me to get it done before the customers start showing up at seven. She always meets me at the door." She took a breath. "She's not there."

"Could she have just slept in?" I asked.

"I thought maybe that was it, but the front door was cracked open. All the lights were out. Call me a chicken, but I was too scared to go in there by myself. Will you go in with me? I know it's a lot to ask. You have so much to do now that Clara is sick."

I grabbed my phone and keys from the counter. "It's not too much to ask, and you did the right thing by not going inside there by yourself. Let's go see."

"Oh, Bailey, thank you. I know it's likely nothing. Maybe she just unlocked the door for me, and it was knocked open, but when I saw all the lights were off, I just could not make myself go inside. I will feel so silly if it turns out to be nothing."

"It's better to feel silly than to put yourself in danger," I said.

We crossed the street and made our way through the square. Uriah was well on the way to setting up for the Summer Soiree, which was just a few days away. How I would have time to make four distinctive candies for each winery was beyond me.

On the square, the trees were wrapped in twinkle lights, and white tents were being erected all over the square. Margot had said my wedding would be the event of the summer in Harvest, but by the looks of it, the soiree had me beat.

I was supportive of most of the events that Margot planned for the village, but I hoped this one, because it involved alcohol, didn't put a permanent rift between the Amish and English communities in the village. Something Harvest prided itself on was how well the English and Amish got along with each other. It had taken decades to kindle such goodwill. I prayed that one wine-tasting soiree didn't ruin it.

When we got to the front door of the café, I half-expected all the lights to be on and Darcy to be bustling around the dining room, getting ready for a long line of hungry customers. That wasn't the case.

Just as Iris had said, all the lights were out, and the door was ajar.

I pushed the door open with my foot. "Hello! Darcy?"

There was no answer.

I stepped inside, and Iris followed close behind me. She was so close that I could feel her breath on the back of my neck.

"Iris, can you turn on the lights? I don't know where the switch is."

A moment later, the café was awash with yellow light.

The main counter was clear, the table and chairs were perfectly in place, and Darcy's collection of teapots sat neatly in rows on a shelf to my left.

As if she was echoing my thoughts, Iris said, "Everything looks okay."

I nodded. "Darcy!" I called. "It's Bailey and Iris."

Again nothing. I stepped farther into the café.

Iris stepped around me. "Maybe she just stepped out for a minute and got sidetracked. Sometimes she will pick up orders of milk and flour from our supplier herself because we can't wait for the deliveryman to start baking."

That didn't explain why the front door was ajar, and I said so.

"Maybe she just forgot. That must be it. I know she has been so upset since the wedding." She looked over her shoulder at me. "Not that any of that is your fault." She walked to the kitchen door, and before I could stop her, she stepped into the kitchen and turned on the light. A second later, she screamed.

I rushed into the kitchen, not knowing what I would find.

Darcy lay on her side next to the cooktop. Her cheek was squished up to the linoleum, and her long blond curls covered her face. I feared the worst.

Iris broke down in tears and had to grab hold of the counter to keep herself upright.

I removed my cell phone from my pocket. "Iris, go outside. Call for help."

"You want me to leave you alone with her?"

"Please."

She looked this way and that. "What if whoever did this is still here?"

"Whoever did this isn't here," I said, even though I had no way to know that for sure. There weren't many places to hide in the café, but there was a walk-in fridge and a number of closets. Darcy's assailant could have been in any one of those spots, but Iris wasn't someone I wanted standing by me in case of an attack. She looked as if she might be sick any second. It would be best for her to leave the café.

"Here, take my phone and call for help. The dispatcher will tell you what to do." I held the phone out to her.

She looked down at the cell phone. "I don't know how to dial one of these."

I held it to my ear until the ringing sound came on, and then I put it into her hand. "Here. Now, go outside. Please."

She took one more look at Darcy on the floor and ran from the room.

I knelt next to Darcy and noticed that her chest was going up and down. I let out a sigh of relief. She was alive, and from what I could tell, she wasn't struggling for breath.

I lightly touched her arm, and she groaned.

"Darcy, are you okay?" I asked.

I saw her eyes move behind her eyelids, but they remained closed.

"I have the worst headache," she whispered.

I could see why. There was a knot the size of an egg on her right temple. She was going to have a bruise that even her grandmother's makeup wouldn't be able to hide.

"What happened?" I asked.

"Who's here?" She tried to sit up, but I gently pushed her back down with my hand.

"It's Bailey," I said. "I don't think you should move just yet. We don't know if you have a concussion."

She cracked her eyes open and blinked at me. "Bailey? Two Baileys?"

If she was having double vision, that wasn't a good sign.

She blinked again. "One Bailey." She said this with a sigh, as if it calmed her somehow to see just one of me. It made me feel a lot better.

"Just lie there until the paramedics come. Iris is calling for help."

She jerked as if she was trying to sit up. "Oh, no. Not Iris. She's coming in to bake this morning. She must be worried sick. What time is it?"

"It's almost six thirty. Iris is fine. She did the right thing and came to the candy shop for help. We are going to take care of you. Now, just relax."

She lay back down. "I can't relax. What if he comes back?" Her eyes were now open all the way, and they darted this way and that, as if she was afraid her assailant would jump out from behind the large stand-up freezer.

"You know someone hit you?" I asked.

"I think that's what happened. It makes the most sense. I was just getting the kitchen ready for the day. Then I saw a shadow behind me. I thought maybe it was Iris. I'd already unlocked the front door for her. And then I saw in the reflection of the stainless-steel freezer someone holding something over my head. I turned around and was hit."

"Did you see the person?"

"No, they were dressed all in black. My best look at them was in the reflection, and it was far across the kitchen and the image was warped. I couldn't even tell you if it was a man or a woman."

She touched the lump on her forehead and winced.

"It's hard to remember anything at all. I feel like there are blank spots in my brain I can't reach."

That didn't sound good.

"You probably have a concussion. What time did you come downstairs?" I asked. I wanted to gauge how long she had been passed out on the floor.

"Maybe just before four?" she guessed. "I like to come down early and get everything set up for Iris, so she can get straight to the baking. This morning I had trouble getting out of bed, which isn't like me, but then, I have a lot on my mind."

She certainly did.

"Bailey!" Aiden's voice rang out in the café.

"In the kitchen," I called back.

Chapter Twenty-one

I wasn't the least bit surprised that Aiden was the first officer on the scene. Our house was just a few blocks away, and I knew the dispatcher had called him the moment she heard that I was involved.

Aiden ran into the kitchen. He wore old jeans, a wrinkled T-shirt, and sneakers with no socks. He had his badge on his belt and his gun in his shoulder harness.

He took in the scene in a matter of seconds. "What happened?"

"We are just piecing that together. It seemed that someone broke into the café, and when Darcy interrupted them, they hit her on the head."

Darcy pushed herself up to a seated position.

"I don't know if you should move yet," I warned.

"I can't lie there on the floor like a dead fish while you all discuss this." She held her head, taking care not to touch the lump.

"That's swelling fast," Aiden said. "The EMTs will be here soon, but we should put some ice on it."

"There are ice packs in the freezer. Grams tends to be a little accident-prone in the kitchen, so we have a lot of them," she said. "Oh, Grams is going to be so upset that she wasn't here. She really would have wanted to use one of the weapons in her purse to whack the guy."

I jumped to my feet and went to the freezer to retrieve the ice pack.

"I'm going to ignore what I just heard," Aiden said. "I don't want to know what is in Lois's purse."

"No one does," Darcy reassured him.

I handed her the ice pack just as the two EMTs came into the kitchen. I moved out of the way, and they started to work on Darcy.

"Can you see my fingers?" one of the EMTs asked.

"Yes, but they are a little blurry."

"Probably a concussion," he said and glanced at Aiden. "Her pulse is elevated, too. We need to take her in."

"Let's get a stretcher," the other EMT said.

"I can walk," Darcy said. "If you will just help me up."

The EMTs shared a look.

"Please . . . I don't want to be taken out of my café on a stretcher."

"All right," the first EMT finally agreed, and Aiden and the two EMTs helped her to her feet.

She wavered for a moment when she was standing, but then she found her legs.

Aiden nodded. "Why do you think this happened?"

"I have no idea why anyone would want to break in here. I don't have any money. What little cash I have, I put in the safe in my apartment every night. None of my equipment is high end. Most of it I got secondhand."

"This had to have happened because of Jason's murder. It's the only explanation," I said.

Aiden frowned at me.

"But why? I don't know who killed him," Darcy said.

"Maybe they think you do."

Aiden gave me another *please stop talking* look, and I clamped my mouth shut.

"We really have to go," the first EMT said.

Aiden nodded and stepped aside.

Darcy touched her forehead, then winced. "I just remembered—I can't go to the hospital right now. This is one of the busiest days at the café, and Double Stitch is having their meeting here. I can't expect Iris to handle that. She's in the quilting club. I don't want to take her time with her friends away from her."

"They can reschedule the meeting," I said. "Or they can just meet at Millie's house like usual."

"Still . . ."

As the EMTs guided her to the door, she shuffled across the floor like she couldn't completely pick up her feet. I tried not to read too much into that. It was possible she was just being careful because she was dizzy. I would feel much better when I heard that she was okay. Concussions could be very serious.

"Can you call Grams?" Darcy touched the lump on her temple again, as if she had to keep checking that it was still there. "She will be so mad that she missed all the excitement this morning."

I knew Lois would be upset for many more reasons than that. Darcy meant the world to her. She would be furious that someone had hurt her granddaughter. When the culprit was found, I hoped Lois wasn't nearby, because there was no telling what she would do.

"I'll call her right now."

"She may not answer. It's Tuesday."

I nodded in understanding. Tuesday was Lois's flea market day. No one loved the large flea markets that dotted Holmes County as much as Lois did. She spent hours at each one looking for "treasures." Most of the things she bought were stored in her house near the square, and that was the end of their story. She always claimed that she planned to refinish them or fix them in some way, but the second step never seemed to happen.

The phone rang and rang, but Lois didn't answer. I didn't want to leave a voicemail about what had happened, so I just told her to call me back immediately and that it was an emergency.

The EMTs helped Darcy into the ambulance, and Aiden jumped into the bay after them. "Deputy Little will be here soon to process the scene."

"What about the café?" I asked. "Should Iris open it? Enoch will be here soon, I assume, to help her."

Aiden bit his lip. He knew how keeping a small business closed during the height of tourist season could be financially detrimental. There was always the risk the tourists would get fed up and not come back. "She can open, but just serve coffee, tea, and pastries that she can access from the front of the café. The kitchen has to be off-limits for a little while yet."

"I'll make some signs for Iris to hang up." I knew that Darcy would do the same for me if I was in the same situation.

Aiden nodded.

The EMT closed the bay doors, and the ambulance drove away. Deputy Little and another deputy arrived soon after that. I had Iris show them the kitchen while I ran over to Swissmen Sweets to type up some signs for Sunbeam Café on my computer.

By the time I got back with the signs, there was already a line waiting outside of the café for breakfast.

Iris stood at the doorway. She was flushed. "We have beverages, coffee, tea, pop, and pastries. The kitchen is closed this morning because Darcy had a family emergency."

Some of the guests were disappointed and turned to leave, but a good number still went into the café. Darcy's coffee was known to be the best in the county. The food wasn't the most necessary part of the morning for them.

I taped the signs to the front door, on the main counter, and on one wall, letting everyone know what was happening.

Enoch walked into the café with a backpack over his shoulder. "What is happening here?"

Iris hurried over to him and told him about Darcy.

"Is she going to be all right?" Enoch asked.

"Yes," I said. "She probably has a concussion, but she will be all right."

"Poor Darcy," Enoch said. "I wish I had been here. I would have put a stop to it."

"I know you would have, Enoch! You care so much

about Darcy and the café," Iris said. "It was a terrible shock. I'm still shaking over it, to be honest."

I rubbed her arm. "She will be all right."

Iris swallowed hard and nodded. "She will." She said this as if she was speaking more to reassure herself than anyone else.

"Does Lois know?" Enoch asked.

"Not yet," I said. "I left her a message to call me."

"Oh, it's Tuesday," he said.

I nodded. "Flea market day." The flea market opened promptly at six, but Lois always started her campout in the parking lot on flea market days at five, so she could be the first one to see all the new antiques for sale. There wasn't an antique that Lois wouldn't buy, as far as I knew. She was also so focused during that time that she usually turned off her phone. She didn't want any distractions.

I turned back to Enoch.

"You're in the kitchen here all day," I said. "What do you think the person was after?"

He shook his head. "I don't know. There is nothing of value in the kitchen. All the pots and pans are old and overused. The most valuable thing is the convection oven, but I can't see one man running away with that. It would be difficult for three men to take."

I shook my head. "It just doesn't make any sense, unless it is related to Jason Hackney's death."

"Do you really think it is?" Iris asked.

"It has to be," I said.

Iris covered her mouth as she considered the possibilities, but Enoch appeared to be far less convinced.

Iris hugged me before I left the shop. "*Danki*, Bailey. I couldn't have gotten the place open today without you."

"I'm happy to help. I just hope Darcy is okay."

"Me, too, but we will keep the café going until she gets back. I know that it's her pride and joy."

I hugged her. "I wish I could stay, but I need to get back to Swissmen Sweets until Emily can relieve me this afternoon."

"I understand."

And I knew she did.

"I just have one more request," Iris said.

I waited.

"Can you find Lois? We really need Lois here—and Darcy needs her even more."

It was an assignment I'd already planned to carry out.

"I'll find her," I said. "Even if I have to search every flea market in the county."

I hurried back to Swissmen Sweets. It felt like I had been gone for days, but it had only been a couple of hours, and the candy shop didn't open until ten. I still had much to do to prep for the day, though. I was tempted to call Emily and ask her to come in earlier, but I stopped myself.

It wasn't until I was back at Swissmen Sweets that I remembered my encounter with Abel Esh early that morning. Could Abel have been the one behind Darcy's attack? He had been threatening in the past and certainly untruthful, but I had never known him to be violent. Then again, I had never known him to be drunk, either. That could have skewed his normal behavior.

I considered calling Aiden, but then decided to wait. He would be at the hospital making sure Darcy was all right. He needed to concentrate to interview her while her memories were fresh.

Nutmeg, Jethro, and Puff were all in lined up in front of the counter when I walked into the shop. They stared at me with wide eyes. I didn't doubt for a second that they had been watching everything that was happening at the café across the square from the window the whole time.

I patted each one on the head in turn. "Darcy will be okay. Don't worry."

I went into the kitchen. The caramel that I had forgotten on the stove when Iris had knocked on the door was just beginning to smoke from being left on the hot burner for too long. I grabbed a towel to pick up the pan by the handle, then threw it into the sink. I doused the whole thing with cold water. That could have been very bad, indeed. I was lucky it hadn't caught on fire. Not to mention, the pot was a goner. I hoped this wasn't a bad omen for the rest of the day.

Chapter Twenty-two

Emily arrived at Swissmen Sweets at eight with both of her girls in tow. "I hope it is all right that I brought the girls again."

"The girls are always welcome here." I waved at Hannah, and she waved back. "I do appreciate you coming in. I hope it's not causing issues between you and your husband."

Emily removed her diaper bag backpack and set it on one of the dinette tables at the front of the shop. "Not at all. We are so grateful to you for what you have done for us over the years. There is no question that we want to help."

Emily removed Olive from the stroller and set her on the floor. The little girl wavered for a moment, as if she was considering walking around the shop. Then she had a change of heart and went to all fours.

"I was planning on staying here with you for a few hours, but I need to try to find Lois." I went on to tell her about everything that had happened that morning.

Emily gasped. "Is Darcy all right?"

"I think she will be. I haven't heard otherwise, but I know she would feel better with Lois at her side."

"It's Tuesday," Emily said.

I nodded. "She's got to be at one of the flea markets. I just don't know which one. There are several in the county."

"I would start with Harvest Flea Market on Route Sixty-Nine. I think that's a particular favorite of hers."

"Right. I know Aiden was going to try to send a deputy to track her down, but staffing is tight right now. He just doesn't have enough people to look for her."

"You go," Emily said. "The girls and I will be fine here."

"I have everything already made for you."

"I never doubted it, Bailey."

"Jethro is here, too. I called Juliet and asked her to come pick him up. She should be here soon."

Both girls were on the floor surrounding the animals and petting them with their small hands.

"There's no rush," Emily said with a smile. "They will distract the girls while I work."

"Jethro is very good at that," I agreed.

I hurried out the door and jogged back to my house, two blocks away. By the time I got there, I was out of breath.

My car was in the garage. I opened the garage door.

"Bailey!"

I jumped and looked over my shoulder. My elderly neighbor, Penny, stood on her back stoop in a bathrobe and curlers in her hair.

"Bailey, what is going on? You are always rushing about."

I grimaced toward the garage, but then turned back to Penny with the friendliest smile I could muster. "Good morning, Penny. I'm in a bit of a hurry right now."

She folded her arms across her chest. "I know. You are always in a hurry. I don't know what the issue is with young people today that makes them run this way and that."

"We can talk about it another time," I said.

She sniffed. "I heard your wedding was beautiful, except a man died at it." She paused. "You seem to attract death."

That wasn't something I wanted to be known for.

"I would have been there had I been invited." She narrowed her eyes.

"Everyone in Harvest was invited," I said.

"I'm not going to a wedding as part of a cattle call. If I am to be included, I expect to receive a proper invitation in the mail, which I did not."

"I'm sorry, Penny, but I really must go."

She glared at me.

Rather than stand there and take another one of her long-winded lectures, I got into my car and drove away. That would come back to haunt me, I was sure.

The Harvest Flea Market was about twenty minutes from the Harvest Square. The drive took even longer because I got stuck behind two Amish buggies. It was a common occurrence in Holmes County, and usually I was patient about it. However, today I anxiously tapped my fingers on my steering wheel, wishing they would go a little bit faster.

It was close to nine by the time I arrived, and the parking lot was full. I paid the two dollars to the Amish attendant at the gate so that I could park. To my relief, I saw Lois's ancient boat of a car parked as close as she could get to the entrance without using a handicapped spot.

I gave a sigh of relief. At least I wouldn't have to go to every flea market in the county to find her. That being said, this particular flea market was huge, sprawling through several buildings and across a few acres of land. Finding Lois could still take some time.

When I entered the flea market, the first thing that hit me was the noise. A cacophony of sounds hit my ears as vendors shouted out orders and shoppers—both Amish and English—spoke at the top of their voices to be heard. The second aspect to hit me was the smell, which was a mix of candle wax, fresh baked bread, garden soil, and coffee.

In front of me was Pearl's Coffee Cart, a vendor I wanted to see. Pearl and a young Amish woman were behind the counter serving the long line of customers as quickly as they could.

This would be a perfect opportunity to speak to Pearl, but I had to find Lois first.

I walked down the aisles of booths, making my way to the furniture section. Lois had a penchant for antique furniture that could not be understated.

I heard her before I saw her.

"You have got to be kidding me," Lois said to the large Amish man in front of her. "Two hundred is just too much." She pointed at a bright purple rocking chair. "Do you see how many layers of paint are on this thing? It will take me weeks and weeks to scrape it off. You're not going to find another customer who is willing to do that."

"All right. One fifty." The Amish man looped his thumbs into his belt.

"Are you joking? I'll give you seventy-five and not a penny more."

The vendor glared at her, and she glared back.

He looked away. "Fine."

"You're a smart man."

Jean Pierre stood a few feet away, watching Lois in awe as she made her negotiations with the vendor. I could have been wrong, but I believed he fell in love with her spunk right then and there.

Lois handed the vendor the cash.

He counted the money and stuck it into his money box. "It's yours."

Lois grinned.

The Amish vendor went to help another customer who was looking at a dresser.

Jean Pierre was immediately at her side and picked up the rocker. "This is heavier than I thought."

"It's solid black ash. That's hard to come by. When I refurbish it, I will be able to sell it for nine hundred, maybe a thousand dollars. People just don't take the time to research what they are selling, and savvy shoppers like me make out." She spotted me standing a few feet away. "Bailey! What are you doing here?" Her face fell. "What's wrong?" She hurried over to me and gave me a hug.

What I had to tell her must have been written all over my face.

"It's Darcy," I said. "We tried to call you."

The color drained from Lois's face. "Is she all right?"

After I told Lois about what had happened that morning, she was in a tizzy. "I have to get to the hospital right now."

"I'll go with you," Jean Pierre said.

"No. You would be stuck there all day with me."

"I don't mind." He set the heavy rocking chair back on the concrete floor.

"Bailey needs you to meet with the winemakers." Lois pulled at the reddish-purple tufts of hair jutting out from the top of her head.

I had never seen her so out of sorts before. "Jean Pierre can go with you. Darcy is more important," I said.

"No," Lois retorted. "Jean Pierre, you need to go with Bailey. Both of you go find out who killed Jason, because that person tried to kill my granddaughter, too." Her voice caught.

"What about the chair?" Jean Pierre asked.

"Can you take it home for me?"

"*Oui, ma chérie*. Whatever you need," Jean Pierre said.

"Okay, all right," Lois said. "I have to go." She rushed out of the flea market, leaving Jean Pierre and me standing in the middle of the aisle with the purple rocking chair.

Jean Pierre looked as if he might burst into tears.

I rubbed his shoulder. "She will be all right. She just needs to get to Darcy. When she sees her, she will feel so much better."

He sighed. "I wish she would have let me go with her."

"I know, but we can help by doing what she asked."

He blinked at me. "What is that?"

"Finding Jason's killer," I said.

Chapter Twenty-three

Jean Pierre carried the chair out to my car in the parking lot. I offered to help him, but he insisted that he could do it himself. I knew that he wanted to prove to himself that he could be useful to Lois, even if she wasn't there.

I opened the back hatch of the SUV. "Let me put the middle seat down."

"I got it, I got it," Jean Pierre said.

I squinted and cringed, half-convinced that he was going to send one of the chair arms through the back window. I couldn't watch. "There's someone I need to speak to in the flea market real quick. I will be right back."

I didn't know if he'd even heard me as he fought to get the chair into the car. I hoped when I returned that everything—the rocking chair, my car, and Jean Pierre—was all in one piece.

I was happy to see that the line to the coffee cart was much shorter than when I'd first arrived. I stepped in line behind two people, and when I got to the cart itself, Pearl asked, "What can we make for you?" Then she blinked. "Oh, Bailey, what are you doing here?"

"I wondered if we could talk."

She frowned. "It's very busy this morning."

"Please," I said.

There must have been something in my face that told her how desperate I was to speak to her. She turned to her barista. "Will you be all right if I step away for a few minutes?"

"*Ya*," the young woman said.

Pearl removed her apron and hung it on a peg behind her. "Just a few minutes," she said to me. "I can't be away for long."

"I understand. I have a shop, too. I know what it can be like when business is buzzing."

She nodded. "Let's talk over in the food court."

I followed her through the aisles of vendors to the very middle of the flea market, where there was open seating and a snack bar.

She sat at one of the high-top tables, and I sat across from her.

"This is about Jason, isn't it?" she asked.

I nodded. "It's now more important than ever to find out who killed him." I went on to tell her about what had happened to Darcy that morning.

She shook her head. "Poor Darcy."

"You don't seem to have any hard feelings toward her, even though she was dating Jason after your divorce."

"Why would I? Jason and I had been long over at that point. By the time we broke up, I knew what he was really like, and I wanted nothing more to do with him."

"Why's that?" I folded my hands on the tabletop.

"He was just so temperamental, and he thought that everyone owed him something. I don't think he thought he should have to work for anything. He wanted things handed to him. When his grandfather died and he inherited the vineyard, I think he thought life would suddenly be easy for him. I don't think he thought keeping the vineyard going would be so much work. He thought it could just run itself."

"But he'd already owned a vineyard in New York that went under," I said. "Wouldn't that have taught him how much work it really took?"

"I would think so, but he blamed that failure on the market and a whole slew of other things."

She stood up. "I need to get back. Sofia can't hold down the coffee cart too long without me. One thing that I will tell you about Jason . . . he was always looking for shortcuts. He would do anything for fast money."

"Anything?"

She nodded. "Anything."

After Pearl left, I walked outside to find the hatch opened to my little SUV and half of the rocking chair sticking out of the back.

A web of rope and yellow flags held it into place.

Jean Pierre waved at me from the passenger seat. "It took some work, but the rocking chair is secure."

I grimaced. It didn't look that secure to me. I checked my watch. There wasn't enough time left to take the chair all the way back to Swissmen Sweets before I was set to meet with Dakota at Swiss Valley Vineyard.

I walked behind the car and wiggled the rocker. It didn't budge. However, I did see there was a lot of rope involved. I mean a *lot*.

"It's not going anywhere," Jean Pierre called back to me.

I sighed. I would just have to take his word for it and drive slowly.

I got into the driver's seat. "We have to go straight to Swiss Valley Vineyard. I can't be late for my meeting."

He rubbed his wrinkled hands together. "Agreed. I'm ready to catch a killer and give him a piece of my mind."

That wasn't a terrifying thought or anything—not at all.

Chapter Twenty-Four

"I must say that in the time I've been here, I have really seen the charm of the place. The air is so clean and fresh." Jean Pierre stuck his head out the open car window and inhaled deeply.

I didn't tell him that the scent he was experiencing at the moment was cow manure, which the Amish farmers spread on their fields to enrich the soil.

I nervously glanced in my rearview mirror. So far, the purple rocking chair was still in place. Jean Pierre had packed it into the back of my car so tightly, now I was worried we would need the Jaws of Life to get it out.

"I'm happy that you appreciate it, Jean Pierre. I know it was difficult for you when I left New York."

"Difficult? It almost broke my heart in two. I had planned for so long for you to take over the chocolate shop. Now, though, seeing you here, I can understand why you defected. I myself am tempted to stay, if all goes well with lovely Lois."

I glanced at him as we turned onto the winery's road. "You're that serious?"

"Oh, yes. I have never met a woman quite like her before."

That, I believed.

"Please, be careful. I care about both of you. I don't want you to move so fast that one or both of you gets hurt."

"You have to understand, *ma chérie*, at our ages, there isn't that much time left. If I don't take the leap, I might be six feet under when the next one comes around."

On that cheerful note, I turned my car down the long driveway that led to Swiss Valley Winery and Vineyard. On either side of the wide driveway were rows and rows of grapevines, tethered into place with wooden stakes and wire.

When Jean Pierre had asked me which winery we were going to visit first, I told him, without question, we were heading to Swiss Valley—the winery that had belonged to Jason. I had to learn what Dakota knew about her boss's death, along with what she had been reluctant to share at the meeting with Margot and the other vintners on the square.

I was certain she knew more than she was leading us to believe.

The parking lot was empty when we turned into the winery. There wasn't so much as an Amish scooter to be seen.

Jean Pierre peered through the windshield. "Are you sure this is the right place?"

"I'm sure. Look at the sign," I said.

"Well, it doesn't seem like anyone is here."

"It doesn't." I parked the car. "But let's take a look around before we leave to go to the next stop."

He raised his bushy eyebrows. "Will we be snooping? Is that what you call it?"

"That's what Lois calls it. I call it just looking around."

He opened his door. "My dear, that's the same thing."

I couldn't argue with him on that.

Swiss Valley Vineyard was pristine. The concrete parking lot didn't have so much as a scuff on it. It looked brand-new, and the flowers in the flower beds along the front of the modern farmhouse–designed building were at peak bloom. Nothing was out of place—except for the CLOSED sign on the front door.

I went up to the front window, shuffled behind the hydrangea bush there, and cupped my hands next to my eyes up against the glass.

The interior lobby was beautiful. Wine shelves running the length of the wall were fully stocked, and the counter where the tastings were set to be held was made of polished marble. Jason, or maybe it had been his grandfather, had spared no expense when it came to the business.

And now the business was shuttered. I couldn't say I was that surprised. Dakota had wanted to keep the winery open in honor of her boss, but she was only an employee. She really didn't have any authority to do that.

"See anything?" Jean Pierre asked.

I shook my head. "No."

"Well, there has to be more to this." Jean Pierre

marched around the side of the building, and I had no choice but to follow.

The back of Swiss Valley was even lovelier than the front. Acres and acres of grapevine rows stretched down the hillside to the west, where there was a pergola and an outdoor café area. I could just imagine all the parties and wedding receptions that would happen here in the summer. It was little wonder that Jason hadn't been overly impressed with the setting of my wedding.

"Wow," I said.

Jean Pierre nodded. "You know, I have always wanted a vineyard."

I stared at him. "What? You never told me that."

"Hmmm, I suppose that it was something I kept to myself. Who is to have a vineyard in New York City? I thought that someday I would retire to upstate New York and have one there. You know I could never completely stop working. Maybe I should revisit that dream in a new location?"

I raised my eyebrows, but tried not to read too much into it. Jean Pierre was a big idea man. He had always been that way. Once he'd told me that he planned to make a full-sized replica of the Statue of Liberty out of chocolate. That had never happened, but I knew that if he set his mind to it, he could do it.

My shoulders drooped. I would have to find another way to talk to Dakota. I hoped she still planned to come to the Summer Soiree, but if I were her, I would stay as far away from it as I could possibly get. "Let's go on to the next winery. I don't want Emily to be stuck at Swissmen Sweets for too long."

We circled back around to the front of the building

to find that my car was no longer the only one in the parking lot. A small sports car, not well-suited for rural Ohio, was parked as close to the front door as possible. A tall, thin woman was at the door taping a sign to it. She wore a flower dress that cinched in on her narrow waist. Her hair was curled and fell to the middle of her back.

"Carly?" I asked.

She jumped and dropped a roll of masking tape on the ground. It rolled into a neighboring garden bed.

"You scared me close to death," she accused. "What are you doing here?"

"I was supposed to meet Dakota to discuss her wine-candy pairing for the Summer Soiree."

"It's not *her* wine pairing," she said hotly. "She has zero claim to the wines from Swiss Valley Vineyards. I have told Margot as much, but she still insisted on letting Dakota showcase the wines. It's an insult to both my grandfather and myself, if you ask me."

"Who has a claim to the vineyard?" I asked.

"Obviously, it's me. It should have been me from the start. It would have been if my selfish cousin hadn't come back to Ohio."

"No one else has a claim to it?" I asked.

She scowled at me. "It did belong to my family, and I am the last one standing—other than my own children, of course, but they are little still. It should all go to me so I can pass it down to them. I knew in his heart of hearts that's what my grandfather would have wanted. Jason came back to Holmes County, confused my grandfather—who was already slipping mentally—and got his way."

Jean Pierre retrieved her masking tape from the garden. She thanked him and took it from his hand. "I don't believe we've met before."

"This is Jean Pierre," I said. "From JP Chocolates in New York. He's visiting me this week, and he offered to help with the wine and candy pairings."

She placed a hand on her cheek. "JP Chocolates? I always go there when I am in the city. It is such an honor to meet you." She held out her hand for a handshake.

Jean Pierre bent over her hand and kissed the back of it. "The pleasure is all mine."

"Oh," she said with a blush.

If Jean Pierre wasn't careful, she was going to faint right then and there.

I peeked around Carly, who was still swooning over Jean Pierre, to look at the sign she had taped to the door.

It read, *Swiss Valley Vineyard closed. Visit Hackney Family Winery for the best vintage*. The address and phone number for the Hackney Family Winery were listed below that.

"Did you close Swiss Valley?"

She sniffed. "What kind of question is that? I had nothing to do with any official closing, but I did hear that it was closed today."

"So you thought it was a good idea to put a sign on someone else's business to come and patronize your own?" I asked.

Her face flushed. "How dare you? I am only trying to tell any customers who might drive all the way out here that there is another option close by. We aren't on the beaten path. Would you rather they completely waste their time?"

She was trying to steal her cousin's business.

"Did you ask Dakota if you could do that?" I asked.

"Why would I ask that girl anything at all? She has no claim to the business. How many times do I have to say that?"

I raised my brow.

She adjusted the tennis bracelet on her wrist. "Now, if you would like to meet at my winery, where you will be able to do a candy pairing, let's go. As you can see, there is no one for you to meet with here."

"How far is your winery from here?" I asked.

She lifted her chin. "It's just a half mile down the road."

That was awfully close.

Chapter Twenty-five

Carly's winery and vineyard was just as lovely as Swiss Valley, but it was clear the property wasn't as well-established. There weren't as many rows of grapevines, the main building was under construction, and the bushes and flower beds around the grounds were small, as if they hadn't been there for more than a season.

However, there were still customers about. A bus of elderly tourists was just walking into the tasting building as we pulled up. I wondered if they were there because they had intended to come to Hackney Family Winery in the first place or because Swiss Valley was closed.

Jean Pierre and I walked to the main door, and he leaned over. "Let me do the talking," he whispered.

I raised one eyebrow at him.

"It's clear she has a bit of a chip on her shoulder over how you criticized her sign." Jean Pierre made a *tsk*ing sound.

"I didn't criticize her sign, but you have to admit that it was in poor taste." I pressed my lips together.

"It was, but now she doesn't care for you. She loves me, as most people do. Let me do the talking. You get more bees with honey, as you Americans say."

"How are you going to know what to ask?"

"Not to worry." He shook his index finger at me. "Lois gave me tips. She gave me a whole lesson on the art of investigation while we drove out to the flea market this morning. She is a fascinating woman—and so knowledgeable on the subject, too."

I wrinkled my nose, afraid of what those tips might be. At least he wasn't carrying a giant purse that could be used as a weapon.

We went inside, and the laughter and chatter in the front room was almost deafening. The ceilings had to be twenty feet up, but the space was relatively narrow, causing an echo-chamber effect.

It seemed to me I was the only one who wanted to plug their ears, however. The tourists from the bus were having a grand time, as the three vintners at the front counter poured them flights of wine in mini-wineglasses and told them what each one was.

Carly wasn't in the room.

A young woman came up to us. "Welcome to Hackney Family Winery. Would you like a sample?"

I shook my head. "We have a meeting with Carly about the Summer Soiree, to be held on Harvest Square this week."

She smiled. "Oh, yes, you must be Bailey. I should

have recognized you the moment I saw you. I love your show." She looked around the room. "Is Jethro with you?"

I shook my head. "Not today."

Her brows knit together. "Will he be at the Summer Soiree?"

"I doubt he would miss it," I said and wondered what Juliet had dreamed up to make Jethro the focal point of the Summer Soiree.

"I'm so glad. I have to get a picture with him. I'm Anna Grace, and I will be helping Carly at the soiree. I asked specifically if I could go so I could meet Jethro. If he wasn't there, I would be just heartbroken. Let me go find Carly for you." She walked away.

"I think the pig is more popular than you are," Jean Pierre said.

"This is a fact I accepted years ago."

Anna Grace returned a moment later with Carly at her side.

Carly smiled at Jean Pierre and me. "I can't thank you enough for coming to the winery for the meeting. I know the other wineries are bringing their wines to you at the factory, but we have a big event tonight."

"What's the event?" Jean Pierre asked.

A strange look crossed over her face. "It's a private corporate party."

I wrinkled my forehead. I didn't know many corporations that held their parties in Holmes County.

"I, for one, am glad we could come here to visit the winery," Jean Pierre said. "It's so inspiring to me. I was just telling Bailey on the drive that I've always wanted a vineyard. I never thought of Ohio as a place for wine."

"There are so many wonderful wines coming out of this state. For the most part, the prosperous vineyards are in Holmes and Geauga counties, close to Amish communities."

"Doesn't that strike you as odd?" Jean Pierre asked.

Carly shook her head. "No, the land is fertile and great for growing grapes in those two areas, and the tourists are already coming here to see the Amish culture. It's just another way to bring tourism into the area."

"Margot would agree with you on that," I said. "That's why she wanted to do this Summer Soiree. I just wish I'd had more warning about the candy pairings."

"You being involved wasn't Margot's idea. It was Jason's."

"I had heard that," I said. "I have to say, I'm a little surprised. Usually Margot isn't that open to other people's ideas. She always thinks hers are best."

She gave a slight smile. "I have been learning that as I spend more time getting ready for the soiree. She's a bit of a control freak."

I didn't correct her on that point, because she was right.

She wrinkled her nose. "Jason thought it might be a good way to get the Amish to buy in to the soiree, since you and your candy shop have so many ties to the Amish."

"I don't think it's helping, to be honest," I said.

"That was nice of him wanting to be inclusive, though," Jean Pierre said.

"Jason could be inclusive if he thought he would get something out of it," Carly said. She then cleared her throat. "I have three wines for you to taste, and I hope one of these can be paired with a candy."

She walked over to a table by the window. It was already set up for the tasting.

We sat down, and Anna Grace, the young waitress, was immediately at Carly's side.

"In front of you, we have a rosé, an ice wine, and a pinot noir. The ice wine is by far the sweetest, so I decided to include it since candy was involved."

Jean Pierre shook his head. "I can already tell you the ice wine would be a bad pairing. Too much sweet on sweet."

"That is a good point," Carly agreed.

I had the feeling that if I'd given her that same advice, she would have dismissed it, but since it came from Jean Pierre, it made perfect sense.

"Let us start with the rosé, then," Carly said.

She poured a small glass for each of us.

I took the tiniest of sips and was about to make a suggestion when Jean Pierre spoke up. "It's not this one, either."

Carly's eyes went wide with concern. She had only one wine left for us to try. She had to be worried that Jean Pierre wouldn't believe this next one was a good fit, either.

She poured the third and final wine into the waiting glasses. It was a deep red, almost black. I sipped the wine, and it was very good.

Jean Pierre also tasted it, but said nothing at first.

Carly watched him nervously as he sat at the table, staring into the glass as if deep in thought.

Carly might have been surprised by Jean Pierre's quiet reaction, but I wasn't. I recognized this as one of those moments when he was getting one of his very best ideas.

Carly looked as if she was about to open her mouth to say something to him, and I gave her a quick shake of my head. To my surprise, she heeded my wordless advice and said nothing.

Another several minutes passed. And then Jean Pierre held up his glass and said, "I have it! Peanut butter."

"Peanut butter?" Carly asked.

"Yes, elevated peanut butter truffles with sea salt. It will be the perfect pairing with this. The acidity and deep fruit flavor of the wine will be just the things to complement the saltiness of the candy."

I took a tiny sip of the wine. "Jean Pierre, I think you are right on this, and we don't sell peanut butter truffles at the shop. It would make it a special treat."

He smiled. "Maybe I will be a sommelier in my final act of life."

I set my wineglass down. "It's not your final act. You have many more acts in front of you."

"From your lips to God's ears."

"I do agree that will be the right candy," Carly said, sounding happier than I had ever heard her. "It will almost have a peanut butter and jelly taste to it, but far more sophisticated."

"Yes," Jean Pierre agreed, before taking another

long sip from his glass. "And I think we should do different-flavored truffles for each winery. They are relatively easy to make. There are no molds involved. A mold can be finicky, as you know, Bailey, and we do not have the time to fight with a candy mold. Time is of the essence."

"That's the perfect idea, Jean Pierre," I said.

He gave a half bow in his seat. "Sometimes inspiration will strike." He took another long sip of the wine. "This is truly delicious."

Carly beamed at his compliment.

I was very glad that I was driving, as this was only our first wine tasting of the day. We had two, maybe three, in total, if I could find Dakota, and more at Swissmen Candyworks that night. At least tonight, Jean Pierre could walk to the inn from the Candyworks.

She stood up. "I will make sure that we have extra cases of this wine at the soiree. I have no doubt this will be the most popular pairing at the event." She got up and hurried over to where Anna Grace was moving around the room with a tray of water glasses for the guests.

I leaned over the table. "Good job, Jean Pierre, on the tasting, but we need to know more about Jason and the murder."

He waved his cloth napkin at me. "Do not worry. I have it all under control. Step one in questioning a suspect is to make them like you."

I raised my brow. "Lois taught you that?"

He nodded.

Carly returned to our table with a bottle of wine.

"Please take this back to the factory with you, so you can taste it with the truffle while you're trying to perfect the recipe."

"Lovely." Jean Pierre stood up and accepted the bottle. "And if it is not too much to ask, could I have a tour of your winery and vineyard? Being here has reignited my dream of having a vineyard someday, and you have everything so well ordered. I can't think of a better place to get a full understanding of what it takes."

Carly blushed. "I doubt you need any type of advice from me. My business will never be on the level of JP Chocolates."

"Don't sell yourself so short," Jean Pierre said. "I don't grow the cocoa that goes into my creations. You do everything here from beginning to end. That is what I need to learn. I admire the fact that you can say you have a hand in every part of the creation of your wines. It's inspiring!"

Carly glowed under his praise, and then glanced at me as if she'd just remembered that I was there. "Bailey, would you like to come on the tour, too?"

I was about to open my mouth and say that I would, when Jean Pierre spoke up. "No, Bailey is just going to wait here for me. She's feeling a little under the weather. I told her it was because she hadn't rested in weeks due to the wedding preparations and all the excitement since her big day. Isn't that right, Bailey?"

I nodded and knew he'd gotten the advice from Lois to fib.

Carly looked at me as if waiting for a confirmation.

I placed my fingertips to the side of my head. "He's

right. I guess all the buildup to the wedding is catching up to me."

Jean Pierre patted my hand. "Rest and drink some water."

Carly appeared to be relieved that I wouldn't be accompanying them.

As he walked away, Jean Pierre looked over his shoulder at me and mouthed the word, *"Snoop."*

He didn't have to tell me twice.

Chapter Twenty-six

I didn't know how I felt about Lois teaching Jean Pierre about the art of investigation. Amateur detective work was one of her favorite pastimes. It made me believe their flirtation might be more than a passing amusement. I didn't remember Lois sharing those tips with any other past boyfriends—and there had been many.

I sipped from my water glass and looked around the room. The guests from the bus tour were having a great time tasting all the wines. A burly man with a cane held up his glass. "This one. It's the best one. Gladys, we are going home with a case."

"Bert, we will never be able to drink all of it," was his wife's rebuttal.

"Speak for yourself."

She shook her head. "I just wish that Swiss Valley was open. We came on this trip specifically to visit them."

"Didn't you hear?" a woman with a silver bob standing next to her said, "The owner was murdered."

"No!"

"Yes! And everyone is saying his ex-girlfriend was behind it."

"Who is the ex-girlfriend?"

"Darcy Woodin. She owns Sunbeam Café in Harvest."

"No! I love that place. They have the very best coffee." She shook her head. "I would hate to have to boycott it because the owner is a killer. It would be just a horrible shame."

"I know, but I'm not going there ever again. I'm not taking the risk of being poisoned."

"Poisoned!"

"Yes, he died from poisoning. Apparently, whatever he ate that day killed him, and what's more, Darcy was catering a wedding that day, and she made all the food."

"She could have easily put poison in it, then."

"Exactly," the second woman said. "It all sounds very cut and dried to me. I wouldn't be surprised if Darcy is arrested very soon."

"How soon?" The first woman wrapped her arms around her chest as if she felt a sudden chill.

"Maybe even today," the second woman said excitedly.

I shifted uncomfortably in my seat. It took all my willpower to stop myself from jumping into the conversation to defend Darcy.

Even if it was proven that she was innocent—which

I knew was the truth—her business, and her reputation, were all at risk. If people stopped coming to her café for fear of being poisoned . . . that was a terrifying possibility. The sooner we found out who was behind Jason's death, the better.

I stood up and walked to the back of the showroom. There was a hallway that led back to the offices. All the doors were open, and from what I could tell, the offices were all empty.

Anna Grace carried a box into the hallway. "Can I help you?"

I shook my head. "I'm just waiting for Jean Pierre. Carly is giving him a tour."

"Oh, yes. Carly was so excited that he asked. I think she was as excited to meet Jean Pierre as I will be to see Jethro at the soiree."

I had to make sure Jethro would be at the Summer Soiree because Anna Grace really wanted to meet him.

"Carly has a lot to be proud of when it comes to her vineyard," I said.

"She does! This vineyard was in terrible shape when she took it over. She even planted most of the new vines herself. She's an inspiration."

"I thought she and Jason grew up at the Swiss Valley Vineyard."

"They did, but when her grandfather died, Jason took it all." Anna Grace shook her head. "It was awful. No one saw it coming. We knew Mr. Hackney's time was short, which was sad in and of itself. He was such a cheerful, kind man. He would give you the shirt off his back if you asked him. I actually saw him do that once. No joke. A man had spilled his cabernet, and

Mr. Hackney just whipped his button-down shirt right off so the other gentleman wouldn't ride home wet and stained."

"How was Jason able to take everything?" I asked, wanting to see if Carly's version of events added up the same as Anna Grace's.

She sighed. "From what Carly said, he had his grandfather write a new will. The old will had said that the vineyard would be divided between his two grandchildren. Jason took his half years before and sank it into a failing winery in New York State. When it went bankrupt and he came back to Holmes County with his tail tucked between his legs, he somehow convinced Mr. Hackney that Carly would never keep the winery after he died, that she would sell it off. He played on his grandfather's worst fear—that the winery and vineyard would be parceled up and sold. That's how he got him to change the will. I heard all of this from Carly, of course, so take that how you will."

"And Carly didn't know what was going on?" I asked. "Wouldn't she have been told if the will had changed?"

She shook her head. "You don't have to get permission from the people in your will to change it."

That was a very glaring motive for murder, but their grandfather had died years ago. If Carly had wanted to remove her cousin, it would have made more sense for her to have done it back then. Unless, I thought, she'd just bided her time until she thought no one would suspect her anymore. If that was the case, though, I didn't think she'd given it enough time at all. When I'd seen her and Jason together at the wedding, it was clear they weren't getting along. At the time, I hadn't known they were cousins.

"When was the will changed?" I asked.

She wrinkled her brow. "A few years before their grandfather died."

"When did he pass?"

She thought about it. "About two years ago. Carly was furious. She loves winemaking, and she had essentially run Swiss Valley for those last ten years her grandfather was alive because of his health."

"How did she end up with a new winery so close by?" I asked.

"This was a small mom-and-pop hobby winery, so there were already some vines here that were mature enough to produce some grapes. The three wines she let you sample are the only ones from this vineyard. Carly got it all for a steal because the land was in foreclosure, but even as cheaply as she got it, she's still in some serious debt. The property taxes are out of this world. We are barely making ends meet. I don't know how much longer she can hold on." She wrinkled her nose. "I've said too much. It's just, for everyone who works here, what will happen to the winery is top of mind. Carly won't be the only person out of a job, and we came here for her. We invested our lives into this, too."

I raised my brow. I didn't know much about wine tasting, but I thought a winery only sold its own vintages. However, I could see why she might sell others. If the winery didn't have enough ready to sell to customers, it would make sense for them to sell other labels.

"She's doing what she can to make ends meet. She will figure it out. I have faith in her. She even bought some wine from Jason to sell here, to make a little extra cash. I think the Summer Soiree will really put Hackney Family Winery on the map, too."

"She bought Jason's wine?" I asked.

"She's proud of what her grandfather accomplished, so she bought wine wholesale from her cousin to sell here. If he was willing to sell it to her, I don't see anything wrong in that."

I supposed that was true, but it still seemed odd to me.

"How do you know about that?" I asked.

"Oh, I worked for Jason for years. I conducted the wholesale transaction for her the first time she made the request. Before her grandfather died, I was at Swiss Valley, too. When she asked me to come work for her after he passed, I jumped at the chance. I was excited to join a winery when it was just starting out. When I'd joined Swiss Valley, it was a well-run machine. But after a while, I was looking for a way out. Jason wasn't the world's best boss."

"How was he a bad boss?" I asked.

"He was just so critical. He was the most critical man I had ever met—and my dad was in the marines and could really get on my siblings and me for any little thing. I loved working for Swiss Valley because being a sommelier from there was such a respected position. By the time Carly left and then offered me another job, I had the experience I needed from Swiss Valley to be respected in the industry, and I could more easily leave." She peered over her shoulder. "I should get back to the counter and help the others. They're all new to this business, and another bus of thirsty senior citizens just pulled into the parking lot."

"One more question."

She waited.

"Has the winery always been this busy? It's clear you are off the tour route, and Carly mentioned there was to be a corporate party here tonight. I was kind of surprised to hear that."

"It's been a lot busier since Swiss Valley closed, and this is our first party like this. They were in a pinch and needed a new vineyard where they could hold their event."

"And let me guess. Swiss Valley was the original host."

She nodded.

Chapter Twenty-seven

Jean Pierre buckled his seat belt on the passenger side of my car as I told the GPS on my phone to take us back to Harvest Square.

"Does that work here?" he asked.

"Yes, GPS works in Holmes County." I paused. "Most of the time."

"I'm terrible with directions myself. I always trust what my phone tells me to do," Jean Pierre said. "It's only steered me wrong a few times. Once it advised me to walk right into the Hudson River. I will have you know that I ignored that instruction."

"Thank goodness for that." I drove out of the parking lot and was a mile down the county road when I saw a sign that read, BILLINGS FARM SUPPLIES, RIGHT TWO MILES AHEAD.

When we reached the intersection where the sign for Billings Farm Supplies had said to turn right, my phone instructed me to turn left to return to the village center.

I turned right instead.

Jean Pierre sat up straight in his seat. "The phone said to go left."

"I know that." I closed the phone's map application. "We need to go this way first. It's important."

He leaned back into his seat. "Whatever you say, *ma chérie.* I trust you as much as I trust my phone's navigation."

I didn't know whether that was really a compliment.

Billings Farm Supplies was a huge complex. The many signs on the grounds advertised that it sold everything from manure to chicken feed to tractors. It was the tractors that I had the most interest in.

"You need chicken feed?" Jean Pierre asked as I put the car into PARK.

"I don't have chickens."

"I'm just trying to figure out why we are here."

"Remember what Raellen said at the quilting circle? Her cousin, Carson Lee Gleib works here. Carson Lee is Pearl's brother, and Pearl is Jason Hackney's ex-wife."

"Oh!" he said as if it was all beginning to dawn on him. "Yes, yes, an angry brother is just the type of suspect that we need."

I shushed him when he said "suspect."

A stocky, muscular Amish man walked over to us. He had a light blond beard that was going white, and he wore glasses on the very tip of his nose. It was a marvel that the glasses didn't fall off altogether. His name badge read, CARSON LEE.

Perfect. Just the man I was looking for.

"May I help you folks?" Carson Lee asked.

"I hope so," I said. "I'm Bailey King, and this is my friend Jean Pierre."

Carson Lee frowned as if he was wondering why I was telling him this.

I took a breath and continued. "I know your cousin, Raellen Graber."

Knowing came into his expression. "What does Raellen need now? She only calls on me when she needs a favor."

I shook my head. "It's nothing like that. You see, we're trying to find out what happened to Jason Hackney, and Raellen said you might know something since he used to be your brother-in-law."

He looked from Jean Pierre to me and back again. "You two are trying to find out what happened to Jason, and you came to me? I don't know anything about it. I barely knew that man."

"But your sister, Pearl, still knew him?"

"Barely," he muttered. Carson Lee walked away from us. "If you're not going to buy anything, then get out of the warehouse."

Jean Pierre grabbed the smallest-possible bag of chicken feed from a nearby shelf. "We are buying this . . ."

"Jean Pierre," I said.

"You never know. You *might* get chickens," he whispered. "And really, what we are doing now is paying for information, is that not right?"

I guessed this was another tool of sleuthing he had learned from Lois.

Jean Pierre proudly took his small bag of chicken feed to the cash register, where Carson Lee waited.

"You have chickens?" Carson Lee asked.

Jean Pierre shook his head. "But I am really giving it a lot of thought."

"Most people get the chickens before they buy the feed."

"I'm not most people," Jean Pierre said proudly.

"I can see that," Carson Lee said as he rang up the sale.

Jean Pierre didn't take any offense.

"Pearl is your sister, is she not?" I asked.

He scowled at me. "Yes, Pearl is my sister. I still care about her, even if she decided to leave the church to be *Englisch*. The family wasn't so much upset that she left the church to be *Englisch*, but that she left the church to marry that man. Anyone with eyes knew he was trouble from the start."

"Why do you say that?" I asked.

He scowled and glanced at the sliding-glass doors as if he were willing another customer to come in, so he would have an excuse not to talk to us. I didn't think Jean Pierre's purchase of the chicken feed was going to go a long way in convincing Carson Lee to continue answering our questions.

"He takes shortcuts. Always has. I never trusted him, and my sister never should have, either."

"Is Pearl still upset over the divorce?"

"It was over twenty years ago."

"But she never remarried."

He frowned at me. "That's a strange comment coming from an independent *Englisch* woman. Maybe she didn't want to remarry. She loves her work."

"I know that. Her flowers are gorgeous."

"Her coffee tastes even better than her flowers look. You should try it."

I promised him I would. "If you don't mind me asking, where were you and Pearl on Saturday during my wedding reception?"

He stared at me for a long moment, and I thought for sure he wasn't going to answer. But then he spoke. "I was at a barn raising in Wayne County all day Saturday, from before dawn until dusk. There were hundreds of Amish there. If you need to know where I was, ask any one of them."

I noted that he gave an alibi for himself, but he didn't have one to give for his sister. Maybe he didn't know where she was that Saturday, or maybe he was just covering for her by not telling us. As an Amish man, he wouldn't want to lie, but there was nothing to stop him from withholding the truth.

The automatic doors opened, and three Amish men in dirt-covered overalls walked inside.

Carson Lee jumped up from his post at the register. "I have to help them. Please take your chicken feed and leave."

Jean Pierre picked up the bag of feed. "We will put it to good use."

Carson Lee simply shook his head before he went over to the men and began to speak to them in Pennsylvania Dutch.

After we left Billings Farm Supplies, on the drive back to town, I told Jean Pierre all that I had learned from Anna Grace.

He sighed. "I really like Carly. She's ambitious and

determined to make her vineyard as great as her grandfather's was. I was inspired in listening to her talk about how much pride she takes in making wine. It was like listening to myself talk about chocolate when I was first starting out. I hate thinking she's a killer."

"We don't know that she killed anyone." I turned the car onto the square and planned to park by the Candyworks so we could start preparing for our meeting with the other wineries.

"I guess you're right, since Darcy is being arrested." He rolled down his window and stuck his head out for a better look.

"What?" I looked in the direction of the Sunbeam Café, and I recognized Aiden's department SUV out front.

Deputy Little walked Darcy out of the café.

Lois had a tea towel in her hand that she was waving in the air. "Unhand her! Darcy did nothing wrong. Sheriff Aiden Brody, I have known you since you were a child. You cannot do this to my family. I would have expected better from you!"

"Oh, no," I said.

I parked the car in the first semi-legal spot by the square that I could find, and then jumped out. Jean Pierre was right behind me.

"What's going on?" I asked.

Lois spun around and faced me. "Bailey! Your husband is arresting my granddaughter! What are you going to do about it?"

I licked my lips and glanced at Aiden, who had a pained expression on his face. "There must be some kind of explanation," I said hesitantly.

Darcy opened her mouth to speak.

Lois held up her hand. "Don't say a word. They will hold it against you. I learned that when my third husband was arrested on more than one occasion. He always said too much."

Darcy closed her mouth and looked down. I could tell by the way she shifted back and forth on her feet that she was dying to speak. But she said nothing.

"I don't understand," I said. "The last I knew, you were going to the hospital, Lois, to be with Darcy."

Lois nodded. "Yes, they were releasing her just as I arrived. Thank heavens she only has a mild concussion, but they told her to take it easy the rest of the day and watch for signs of blurred vision and headaches. I had it set in my mind that I would take care of her. We would watch old movies and make popcorn. Iris and Enoch could watch over the café while we took it easy, but then your husband showed up and is carting her off to jail."

I looked to Aiden when she said this. "Aiden?"

"Darcy is under arrest for the murder of Jason Hackney."

Lois adjusted her purse strap on her arm, as if she wanted to remind the people around her that it and its myriad of contents were there. "Outrageous!"

Aiden's face was tight. "Deputy Little, please escort Miss Woodin to the station."

Darcy looked around as if she didn't even know what was happening. I wondered how much of that was from shock and how much was still from the lingering concussion. I knew both Aiden and Deputy Little would be kind to her after her injury, but I wondered why all of this couldn't wait until she was feeling better.

"Don't worry, Darcy. I will get on the horn with an attorney right away," Lois said. "I will take care of this!"

Darcy didn't say a word as Deputy Little helped her into the back of the cruiser.

Jean Pierre raced to Lois's side. "My dear, let's call my attorney. He will know what to do. I will call him right now." Jean Pierre pulled his cell phone from the pocket of his jacket.

Lois watched the deputy's car drive away with a look of horror on her face. As I glanced back toward the café, I saw the same expression on the faces of all the guests inside. Abject horror.

Jean Pierre ushered Lois into the café, and Aiden turned to walk back to his car.

Chapter Twenty-eight

"You're just going to walk away from me?" I asked.

He turned to face me. "Bailey, I can't talk to you about this."

I walked over to him and lowered my voice, so the people gawking at us from around the square couldn't hear. "You arrested Darcy? Why?"

"Bailey, I can't talk to you about an open case."

"You can't arrest her now. She just got out of the hospital."

Aiden frowned. "Time is of the essence when we are in the middle of a homicide investigation. We will take very good care of her while she is at the station."

"But what if she starts feeling worse as the night progresses?"

"I will have a deputy with her at all times. Please, Bailey, I can't answer any more questions about this."

Even though he'd asked me not to ask any more

questions, I couldn't stop myself. "How can you think that Darcy could be responsible for what happened to Jason when she was attacked herself just this morning?"

"Bailey . . ." He sighed.

"Aiden, you know she would never have done this."

He removed his department ball cap and ran his hand through his hair before setting the hat back in place. "It's the evidence that we have. I don't have any other choice. The toxicology report came back. Jason was poisoned with wild mushrooms. The death cap mushrooms that were found in her knife case? They were baked into the tart he ate. The tart that she handed to him."

In my mind, a scene from *Snow White* played out, but instead of it being the old woman handing Snow White a poisoned apple, it was Darcy handing Jason Hackney a poisoned mushroom tart.

My mind immediately flashed back to the day before the wedding, when Juliet, Aiden's *mother*, had come into Swissmen Candyworks with Jethro and insisted that Darcy use those very mushrooms in the hors d'oeuvres because Jethro had foraged them. Darcy said that she would because she knew the mushrooms were safe. Had she been wrong? Would this make Juliet and Jethro accomplices in the crime, as well?

"That doesn't prove anything about Darcy. That only means that someone tampered with the food. It doesn't mean she did it herself."

"No, but the witness saw her give the tart to Jason. She said she wanted him to taste-test it for her."

"Who's the witness?"

"You know I can't tell you that."

"Maybe you can't, but I can certainly find out on my own." I spun on my heel and walked away.

"I have to get back to the station," he said.

I turned back and placed a hand on his arm. "Just please remember who Darcy is."

His face softened. "I will, Bailey, but I can't promise that will change anything. I don't want it to be her as much as you don't, but I have to follow where the evidence leads, and right now it is pointing directly at Darcy Woodin," Aiden said, then walked to his SUV.

I watched him drive away with a pit growing in my stomach. Darcy was my friend. I knew she hadn't done this. However, a tiny voice in the back of my head said, *You didn't even know she was dating anyone. How well do you really know her?*

I turned and went inside Sunbeam Café. All the customers who'd had their eyes glued to the windows watching Darcy being taken away by Deputy Little soon had their eyes back to their own tables after I'd stared them all down.

Iris hurried over to me. "Oh, Bailey, this has been the most terrible day. I don't know what to do. Should I close the café? I asked Enoch if that was what we should do, but he thinks we should keep it open."

I bit my lip. The last thing Darcy needed was a loss of business in the middle of the summer. She likely would need bail money now, too, but it wasn't my call to make.

"Where's Lois?" I asked.

"She and your friend, the Frenchman—I'm sorry, I forgot his name—went upstairs to Darcy's apartment."

She bit her lip. "She said something about a council of war. Do you know that that means?"

When it came to Lois, it could mean a number of things, but what I knew for sure was that she wouldn't rest until Darcy was safely back home at the café.

"Okay, you keep the café running for now. I think Enoch is right. Darcy is going to need the money now more than ever."

"*Ya*, you are right. We will stay open for Darcy's sake." There was a determined set to her jaw as she came to her decision.

It was common assumption among the English that Amish women were submissive pushovers, but in my time in Ohio, I had learned that couldn't be further from the truth. They were some of the toughest people I knew, and I counted my grandmother, and now Iris Young, in that number of sturdy Amish women.

I walked into the kitchen. Enoch was leaning against the cold stove with a faraway look in his eyes.

He blinked at me. "Oh, Bailey, I thought you would be here at some point. It's been an eventful day. How is Darcy?"

"She's on the way to the sheriff's department."

He nodded. "I thought as much."

"I'm sorry." I apologized even though I hadn't been the cause of any of the troubles for the staff at Sunbeam Café.

He shook his head. "I know you're married to the sheriff, but he is making a big mistake blaming Darcy for this. The wrong people are always the ones who suffer the most." He picked up a dish towel from the counter and threw it on the floor before stomping out the back door of the kitchen.

I wondered whether I should go after him. It was jarring to see Enoch Unger, who was usually known for being so upbeat, angry. But then again, I didn't think he'd ever been in a situation like this before.

There was a set of stairs behind the kitchen that led up to Darcy's apartment. I had only been up there once before. I walked up the open wooden stairs that squeaked and creaked as I went. The building was old, and the stairs appeared to be original. I hoped I wouldn't be the person whom they finally gave out on.

The door to the apartment was painted bright purple, with a floral wreath hanging on it that looked like it had been there for a good decade. I knocked on the door.

"Who is it?" Lois yelled.

"Bailey," I said.

"Come in."

I opened the door and stepped into Darcy's sparsely furnished, one-room apartment. The kitchenette was in one corner. She didn't have a closet; her clothes hung on a rolling clothing rack pushed up against the wall by the one window in the room. There was no bed, and I could only assume the ancient-looking couch was a pullout or she just slept on it as it was. Her end tables were plastic milk crates, and there was one closed door in the room. I could only guess that led to her bathroom.

I recognized the signs of a young woman who was putting every cent she made back into her business.

I had lived in many apartments like this while in New York, and at the time, it had been with two or three roommates. It was clear to me that Darcy spent most of her time downstairs in the café. The apartment was the place where she slept, and that was all. I could see why she didn't put as much effort into making it homey, but the surroundings made me depressed. I promised myself that when she was released—and I knew she would be—I would convince her to redecorate. Her grandmother was an expert on the flea market circuit. I was surprised Lois hadn't already redone the whole apartment herself. It wasn't like Lois to have so much restraint.

"Bailey, I'm so glad you're here. Jean Pierre has been on the phone with his attorney. He has a friend he went to law school with who's a practicing defense attorney in Canton. She's driving to the sheriff's office right now. I hope Darcy has enough good sense not to say anything until she gets there."

"I think she will," I said. "Tell me what happened."

Lois sat on the prehistoric couch, and it swallowed half of her body. So much so that her feet came off the bare wooden floor. She yelped. "Now I remember why I never sit down when I'm up here. I have to convince Darcy to let me furnish this place. I have enough furniture in my house to take care of her. This is no way to live."

I agreed with her on that point, but I was more interested in hearing what had happened before Jean Pierre and I arrived.

Jean Pierre sat on the couch next to her, and he sank at least a foot into the seat, as well. He reached out and took Lois's hand. He was a far cry from his penthouse in Manhattan, and oddly, he didn't seem to mind it.

"Jean Pierre and I are leaving soon to go to the sheriff's office to meet with the attorney."

"Bailey," Jean Pierre said, "I won't be able to meet the winemakers with you. I am sorry."

"There is no reason to apologize," I said. "I'm wondering if I should cancel it. It seems silly to be making candies to pair with wines when Darcy is in so much trouble."

"You have to keep your appointment with the winemakers," Lois said. "It might be the only chance we have to find out who is really behind Jason's death. Don't you remember that they were all there when Juliet flounced into the Candyworks with Jethro's mushrooms?"

They *had* all been there. Jason had been, as well.

"You think one of them saw the mushrooms and hatched a plan?" I asked.

"That's what I would do if I really wanted someone dead. I would look for the perfect person to frame. In this case, there is no one better than my granddaughter."

I shivered and tried not to consider how much Lois had thought about this.

"And when you figure it out, because I know you will, I want you to tell me who did it." Lois hugged her giant patchwork purse close to her chest.

Chapter Twenty-nine

I didn't think that if I revealed who the real killer was to Lois, she would do something rash. I mean, I didn't know that would happen for sure. In any case, I planned to tell Aiden before anyone else, and that was still assuming I would be able to find out who it was.

Before I went to the factory, I stopped in at Swissmen Sweets to check on Emily and her girls. I still felt awful that they had been at the shop for so long. I knew Emily would never complain about it, but I didn't know how she ran the shop and kept an eye on the children. I could barely run the shop and keep an eye on Jethro—but then again, Jethro had always been a special case.

The bell over the shop door rang when I went inside, but I was surprised to find it wasn't Emily behind the counter but her sister, Esther.

"I didn't expect to see you here," I said.

"*Nee*, I wouldn't think that you would. Emily had to go home. The little one started to fuss and was running a fever. She's teething."

"I'm sorry to hear that. Emily could have closed the shop if it came to it."

"She asked me to help. I was almost out of pretzels for the day with no plans to make more, so I could help. I brought the last of my pretzels that I made for the day over here, so I could sell them to customers who might stop by."

"That's a great idea." I still couldn't get over the fact that Esther was in my candy shop helping me.

As if she could read my mind, she said, "I'm not doing this for you. I'm doing it for Emily. The baby was getting fussy and needed to go home—and I am doing it for Clara, too."

I didn't mind that I wasn't on her motivation-for-helping list. I would have been shocked had I been.

"Thank you for helping. I know my grandmother would appreciate it. I will let Emily know that she doesn't have to come in tomorrow. I will ask two of the ladies from the factory to come and help in the shop."

She nodded. "*Gut.* I know Emily would come in tomorrow if you ask her, but she should really stay home with her little girls."

I nodded.

"Are you here now? Can I leave?" Esther asked.

"I have a meeting at Swissmen Candyworks with the wineries that will be at the Summer Soiree. That being said, you can leave. You have already done so much for us. I will just close the shop a little early and put a sign up to go to the Candyworks for candy."

She sniffed. "Maybe that should have been your solution to the problem this morning."

I didn't say anything. Over the years, I had learned it

was just best to let Esther feel self-righteous. It was the emotion that made her the most comfortable.

"I really can't thank you enough for your help," I said.

She started to pack up the few soft pretzels she had left. "It was the Christian thing to do."

I glanced at Nutmeg and Puff, who were sleeping together in Nutmeg's cat bed by the window. Jethro was there, too. "Juliet didn't come and pick up Jethro," I said.

Esther pursed her lips. "Does it look like she did? She stopped by not long after Emily left and said she had a meeting at the church. Since Jethro was sleeping so peacefully with his friends, she said he might as well stay here. She said you wouldn't mind."

Of course that's what she said, I thought.

"I hope the animals didn't give you any trouble," I said.

"They kept their distance, which was fine with me."

She closed her pretzel box, removed her apron, and hung it up. "Well, if that is all you need, I will be on my way."

I thanked her again.

At the door, she paused. "I'm sorry your friend killed that man."

I blinked at her. "Darcy? She didn't kill anyone, and the truth will come out."

"Oh? I don't know about that. My *bruder* told me that the two of them had the most terrible arguments and the man had threatened her more than once." She paused. "Perhaps she wanted to get to him first. Some women are like that."

"When did Abel hear this?" I asked.

"It is not my place to say. I know my *bruder* wants nothing to do with it. He doesn't want to be involved."

"If he's already said something to you, he's now involved."

She scowled. "I shouldn't have said anything. I was only trying to tell you that I was sorry."

"If Abel knows something, he needs to tell my husband. I know he and Aiden have their past, but if he knows something about Jason's death, the right thing would be to tell the sheriff."

She sniffed. "Abel doesn't need to do anything. I don't know why you are always harping on my *bruder*."

"I don't want anything to do with Abel, if I'm completely honest, but he's the one who's been creeping around the square all hours of the night. And the last time I saw him, he was clearly intoxicated. Despite everything he has done, I'm worried about him."

She glared at me. "He's none of your concern. He is just trying to live a quiet Amish life."

I almost laughed when she said that.

"Leave Abel out of whatever mess you are putting yourself in again. When will you learn to leave well enough alone?"

The answer to that question was, *most likely never*.

Chapter Thirty

After Esther left Swissmen Sweets, I quickly closed up the candy shop and rushed over to the factory. I was running late, but I had already told Charlotte to start without me if I wasn't there on time.

I stepped into the factory to find the shop buzzing. A large family with matching T-shirts that said O'Connell Family Reunion were milling about, waiting for their factory tour, while Charlotte stood in one corner of the lobby with the winemakers, Jon Michael and Angel, and much to my surprise, Dakota.

One of my staffers came into the room and rounded up the guests for the tour. They trooped through the glass doors that led into the factory. When the doors closed after them, the noise level dropped considerably.

Angel touched her right ear. "I thought they were never going to leave. It makes me grateful that I don't have a big family. I couldn't stand all the noise."

Charlotte waved at me. "Bailey, you just made it!

We haven't started yet. I was waiting for the tour to leave the room. It was a little too loud in here to speak. I have everything ready."

Charlotte had set up a folding table in one corner of the room and covered it with a pink linen tablecloth. There were enough chairs around it for each of us to fit. I sat on one side of the table next to Charlotte, and the winemakers were on the other side with their bottles of wine lined up in front of them. I could always depend on Charlotte to have my back.

"Thank you, Charlotte. This is perfect," I said.

She beamed under my praise.

I smiled at Dakota. "I'm surprised you're here. Jean Pierre and I went to Swiss Valley this morning and found it closed."

She blushed. "I know. I was the one who closed it. It was just too much for me to keep it open. None of the staff was willing to come back after they heard about Jason. Not that I blame them, but I can't care for the place all on my own." She looked down at her hands. "I feel like I've let Jason down."

"You haven't," Jon Michael said. "I wish I had an employee who was so loyal to me that they would want to keep my business going after I was gone. I can't say I have that."

Angel sniffed. "You act like Jason would appreciate it. He wouldn't care. The only person he cared about was himself. Now that he is dead, what use is the Swiss Valley to him?"

I arched my brow at her reaction and wondered what Angel's relationship with Jason had been.

Dakota sat up a little straighter in her chair. "Jason

appreciated what I did for Swiss Valley. He told me more than once that I was his most trusted employee."

"Compared to who? Anna Grace?"

Dakota's face flushed red at the mention of Anna Grace's name.

"Anna Grace is the only one who stuck around for any length of time, but as soon as she could, she left to work for Carly. I can't say I blame her. If anything, I can't believe you didn't leave with her. I thought the two of you were friends," Angel said.

Dakota stared down at her hands.

"Don't be so hard on her, Angel," Jon Michael said. "What's done is done. It is not Dakota's fault."

Angel pursed her lips but didn't say anything more.

"Should we get on with the tasting?" I asked. "Dakota, let's start with you. It seems that you still want Swiss Valley to participate."

She glanced at Angel, then took a breath. "Yes. The soiree was so important to Jason. I might not be able to keep the winery itself open, but there is plenty of wine that can be used for the Summer Soiree. I believe Jason would have liked that."

"I think so, too," Jon Michael said. "This was really his brainchild."

"And Darcy's," Angel added. "They went to Margot together to propose it. I personally thought it was a lot for Darcy to take on. Your huge wedding, and then an event on the square just days later that would bring nearly a thousand people to Harvest? At least that was the number Margot was projecting."

"When Darcy saw him here at the factory the day

before the wedding, it was clear they'd had some sort of falling-out," I said.

"They sure did," Angel said. "He fired her from being part of the soiree and broke up with her, all in the same breath."

"How do you know that?" Jon Michael wanted to know.

While we were talking, Dakota sat at her corner of the table, still staring at her hands. She didn't move. If I didn't know better, I would have wondered if she was even breathing, she was so still.

"I saw him do it with my own eyes. He ousted her right in the middle of the square just a few days before the wedding. It did not please Margot because they didn't have much time to find someone else to supply the food, but he told Margot that if she kept Darcy on, he was out."

This was news to me, and by the look on Jon Michael's face, he hadn't known this, either. But apparently, Dakota wasn't the least bit surprised that Angel knew, and I had a feeling that was an important detail to remember.

"Why did he break up with her?" I asked.

Angel shrugged. "I guess you will have to ask Darcy that herself if she gets out of jail."

I grimaced.

By the end of the meeting, we had decided on the three truffle flavors for the wineries. Jon Michael would get vanilla bean; Angel, salted caramel; and Dakota, raspberry.

"How many of each flavor will you need?" Charlotte asked.

"At least five hundred," Angel said. "That way each guest can taste two truffles if there are really a thousand people there as predicted."

"Five hundred?" Charlotte gasped. "You're saying we need to make two thousand truffles in less than two days!"

Angel arched her brow. "Is that a problem? I thought you were a world-class candy factory."

"We are, but that's a lot of truffles." Charlotte glanced at me.

I felt ill. To make that many truffles and keep up with our normal production at the factory would be a challenge. No, it would be more than a challenge. It would be close to impossible, but I couldn't ignore how much it would help our business.

"We can do it," I said.

Charlotte's green eyes bugged out of her head.

"Good. Margot said you were the best, and that's what we are expecting. The best." Angel stood up. "I need to get back to my vineyard to prepare."

Dakota and Jon Michael stood, too.

Before Dakota could leave, I asked her if I could speak to her for a moment.

She looked this way and that, as if she was trying to find a way out of the situation. When Jon Michael and Angel walked out of the Candyworks, her shoulders sagged as if she was trapped. She forced a smile. "I think the raspberry truffle will be a perfect pairing with Jason's wine. I know if he were here, he would be pleased with it, too. Is that what you wanted to talk about?"

"Why are you doing this?" I asked.

She blinked at me. "Doing what?"

"Trying to promote Swiss Valley Vineyard. You're not getting paid right now, are you?"

She shook her head. "No."

"I know you care about the business, but you're putting a lot of work into this. I don't see what you're getting out of it."

She pursed her lips together. "I know that not too many people have a lot of nice things to say about Jason, but he was kind to me and gave me a chance when I needed work. It's the least I can do since the soiree was so important to him. And after working there for so many years, I guess the grapes and vines have become as important to me as they were to him. I know I can't do much more for the vineyard after this, but if it helps people recognize what Swiss Valley has to offer, I want to do that."

I nodded. "I can understand that. I feel the same way about Jean Pierre. He gave me my start in New York. I'm not sure I would have made it in the city if he hadn't taken me under his wing."

She nodded. "Jason had a good side. It's just that sometimes his bitterness snuffed it out."

"And where was the bitterness from?" I asked.

She shook her head. "I have to go. I promised an Amish friend I would give him a ride home." She hurried from the factory, leaving me to wonder who her Amish friend was.

Chapter Thirty-one

After the candy shop and the factory had closed for the evening, I climbed into my car and drove to Millie and Uriah's farm.

As I pulled into the driveway, Uriah was out in the yard trying to talk some sense into Phillip and Peter, the goats. He waved his arms at them. "It's time for the two of you to get into the barn for the night. Don't make me go inside and get your *maam* to shoo you in."

Phillip didn't seem too nervous about the threat as he hopped this way and that, doing all he could to stay out of Uriah's grasp.

I got out of the car. "Do you need some help?"

Uriah shook his head. "*Nee,* it's clear to me that the two of them need to burn off some more steam. They are too worked up to go to the barn for the night yet. There are times when they won't go in for me until well after dark, but then Millie comes out and whistles at them, and they fall into line." He sighed. "I wish I had that kind of power over the goats, but it is a skill that only my wife has."

I laughed.

Uriah waved at the goats. "Fine with that, both of you. You can stay out here a little while longer while Bailey visits with Clara."

The goats hopped all around me with glee. It was as if they knew I had given them a reprieve from going into the barn for the night earlier than they wanted to.

"Ornery rascals." Uriah removed his felt hat and shook his head. "That's what Millie always calls them, and they have sure earned the title." He started to walk toward the farmhouse, and the goats fell into step beside him.

I laughed and then my tone turned somber. "How's *Maami* today?"

"She's been in some pain—not that she would admit it to us, but you can see it on her face. The doctor said this would be the worst day for the pain. We are praying to the Lord that that is true."

"I wish she was staying with Aiden and me. Don't get me wrong, I know you and Millie are giving her the very best care, but she is my grandmother and my responsibility."

"I know you wish she was at your house, and that makes you an exceptional granddaughter, but you have to remember that Clara is where she needs to be right now."

I nodded. "I know that, but it doesn't make it any easier."

"I would imagine not."

Uriah held the door for me while I went into the house. Peaches was sleeping in a cardboard box under the quilt frame, but Millie wasn't in the front room.

"She's upstairs with Clara. She likes to sit with Clara to keep her company, even if the two of them are just there in silence."

I smiled and knew that *Maami* was in the right place to recover. I would never be able to sit by her bedside all day, especially this week, between the soiree . . . and the murder.

"You can go on up," Uriah said as he walked into the kitchen. He turned on the tap to wash his hands.

As quietly as I could, I walked up the stairs. I found the door to the guest room open, and I peeked inside. Millie was reading a book in a rocking chair, and *Maami* was asleep on the bed.

Millie stood with her book. "I'll give you two some time alone."

Before I could tell her she didn't have to do that, she was out the door.

Maami looked so small on the queen-sized bed in the Schrocks' guest room. Her hands were folded over her chest like she might have been lying in a coffin.

I shook the comparison away in my head. She wasn't going to die anytime soon—and certainly not from the stent in her heart.

She opened her eyes and smiled at me. "Bailey." She reached out her hand. "Have you been here long?"

I gave her a small smile.

"You should have awakened me. I have been looking forward to seeing you all day."

I pursed my lips, and guilt clutched at my heart. "I'm

sorry I didn't come sooner. There has been so much going on with the factory and the soiree." I looked down at my hands. "I know that's a terrible excuse. You have to come first."

She arched her brow just a little. "And the murder investigation?"

I scrunched up my nose. I didn't want to worry *Maami* about the murder.

"You don't need to hide anything from me. I've already heard much of it from Lois when she's been here to see Millie. You know what a talker Lois is, especially when she's worked up about something. I would imagine having her granddaughter accused of murder would get her riled."

"I would imagine," I agreed and touched her hand. "But let's not talk about it. I don't want to say or make you think of anything that would give you bad dreams."

"Don't be silly. I need other things to think about besides the fact that I'm stuck in this bed while I recoup. Murder just might be the ticket as Lois would say."

I wrinkled my nose. "Are you sure?"

She patted the side of the bed, encouraging me to move closer to her. "Tell me all about your murder investigation." She smiled. "Because if I know my sweet girl, she is sticking her nose into other people's business."

I moved closer to the head of the bed, where she wanted me to sit. "I don't think anyone knows me as well as you do."

She smiled and closed her eyes as I told her everything I had learned about Jason Hackney's murder so far.

* * *

The next morning, I was at Swissmen Sweets by five. Puff and Nutmeg were curled up in bed together again. It was too early for them. They could barely eat their breakfast before they went back to sleep. There were times when I thought my animals had the right idea when it came to living life. I would love to sleep in until ten in the morning someday, but that wasn't the nature of a candy maker. Even on Sunday, I was up early, perfecting new recipes and working.

After eight, Lida and Neva, both young Amish candy sellers at the Candyworks, came into the store. They would be running the shop for me today, so Charlotte and I could make the bazillion truffles we needed to make. Maybe that was an exaggeration, but it would feel that way.

I was walking around the shop showing my staff what needed to be done. They had brought plenty of candy from Swissmen Candyworks, so there would be no shortage in what was to be sold.

"How is Clara?" Lida asked.

"She's improving. I went and saw her last evening, and she was up and alert. I believe she loves Millie, but I could tell she was ready to come home. I would feel better if she stays with Millie a couple more days, just to be sure that everything is working properly." I knew she wouldn't want me to sleep in her apartment above the candy shop with her, but if she insisted on leaving Millie's too early, that was exactly what was going to happen.

The door opened, and Enoch Unger walked inside. His smile was as radiant as ever. His grizzled Amish beard was neatly combed, and his collar was perfectly straight. He had a carrier of coffees in his hand. "I thought you all would need this today."

We gratefully accepted the coffee.

"Any word on Darcy?" I asked.

He nodded. "I have some *gut* news. Lois and your friend Jean Pierre stopped by this morning. They were on the way to the station to bail her out."

"That has to be expensive," Lida said. I knew she must have been thinking of the number of times her late brother had been arrested.

"It's more money than I have sitting around," he replied. "Lois said that Jean Pierre offered to pay it."

"Wow," Neva said. "That is awfully generous."

It didn't surprise me at all. Jean Pierre could be generous to a fault, but in this case, I thought he was putting his money to good use. It would be far more difficult for me to find out what had really happened between Darcy and Jason if I couldn't speak to her.

Aiden likely shared more with me than he really should about his cases, but I knew he would never let me into the jail cell to question Darcy.

"When is she getting out?" I asked.

"Around ten, from what Lois said, but she warned me it might be longer. It's hard to know how long these things will take." He shook his head. "I just can't believe that anyone could think that Darcy would or could do such a horrible thing. She doesn't have a mean bone in her body."

"What she does have is poor judgment in men," Neva said. "It seems to me she always picks the wrong one."

I had to agree with Neva on that point. I just wished Darcy could meet a nice man who wasn't corrupt in one way or another. So far, that hadn't been the case for her.

"I know when Darcy gets back, she will want to jump right back into work," Enoch said.

"Sometimes work is the best distraction," Lida said.

He nodded. "I know it has been that way in my own life. It can be a flaw, too. It can make you avoid the things that are really bothering you."

I nodded. "How is the café? Has business been impacted by Darcy's arrest?"

"The café is doing well. I believe some folks are actually coming in because they want to hear all about Darcy's arrest." His face fell. "It's just awful what happened. I wish I had done more to stop it."

"There was nothing you could have done," I said. "And if you'd gotten involved, you could have been arrested, too. Darcy wouldn't want that. You are doing the best thing for her. You and Iris are keeping the business running. I know she appreciates it."

The front door to Swissmen Sweets flew open, and Juliet came inside. She was wearing her overalls again, and they were streaked with mud. "Oh, Bailey, I'm so glad you're here. I'm in desperate need of your help. Jethro is lost in Harvest Woods, and it's all my fault." She burst into tears.

"What happened?" I asked.

"I felt just awful about that man dying, so I called my mushroom club, and we went out into the woods this morning. We headed back to the spot where we'd collected the chanterelle mushrooms. We wanted to make sure that's what was really growing there. If there are death caps nearby, then maybe I did grab one by mistake and give it to Darcy!"

"You have a mushroom club?" Enoch asked.

Juliet wiped at her eyes and lifted her chin. "Yes, it's called the Fungals."

Enoch's eyes went wide, and it looked like he was holding back a laugh. I might have laughed, too, if I hadn't been so worried about Jethro and the fact that Juliet might be unintentionally complicit in the murder.

"How did Jethro go missing?" I asked.

Juliet took a deep breath. "We were back on the trail of the mushrooms, and I removed his leash. That's what I always do when we are mushroom hunting. He needs the leeway to work."

I grimaced. Removing the leash was Juliet's second mistake. The first was thinking Jethro's calling in life was to be a mushroom hunter, but I kept my mouth shut on both of these thoughts.

"He was on the scent of the mushrooms. He had his snout down in the mud. I knew we were close—and then, out of nowhere, a giant barred owl came down and swooped over his head. It gave us all a fright, but no one more than Jethro. He squealed and took off. By the time we'd all realized what had happened, Jethro was gone." She placed a hand to her chest. "I'm terrified that the owl flew off with him." She was on the edge of tears again.

"I think Jethro is a little too big for a barred owl to carry him off," I said, even though I didn't know this for sure. The alternative was too gruesome to consider.

"The Fungals are still out there looking for him, but I came here because I knew if anyone could find him, it would be you. He trusts you. Please come. He must be scared. I will never forgive myself if something happens to him."

"Let's go." It wasn't even a question.

As I was about to walk out the door, Enoch handed me my coffee. "I think you are going to need this."

He couldn't have been more right.

Chapter Thirty-Two

Harvest Woods was a large acreage of trees just outside of Harvest proper. I had been there before—in fact, this wasn't the first time I had traipsed through the woods looking for a pig. Jethro really needed to stop making a habit of running off. One of these days, I might not be around to find him.

With a heavy foot on the accelerator, Juliet drove us back to the spot where she'd left the Fungals. I understood she wanted to get back to the woods to find her pig as soon as possible, but she wasn't cut out for the Indy 500, that was for sure.

At the edge of the woods, a group of five women were waiting by the side of the road. Their clothes were as mud-streaked as Juliet's. I had the feeling I would look much the same very soon.

I got out of the car weak-kneed.

"Ladies," Juliet said to the women when we were out of the car. "Bailey is here, and she will find Jethro.

They are kindred spirits. He will come out of his hiding place for her."

The Fungals all clapped, and I hoped I could live up to Juliet's promises. To be honest, I was worried about Jethro, too. The woods were dense, and there were bobcats, coyotes, and a myriad of other wild animals that could hurt the little pig, or he could hurt himself by tripping over a fallen log or branch. He wasn't the most agile bacon bundle on earth.

"Where did you lose him?" I asked.

"It was about eight hundred feet down the path," one of the women said. "He just took off. Who knew a pig could run that fast?"

I did. I had seen it more times than I could count.

"Okay, why don't all of you just stay here for a moment, and I will go look alone first. I think all the commotion might be scaring him even more. If I don't find him in ten or fifteen minutes by myself, I will come back, and we will regroup."

Juliet grabbed my hand. "Thank you, Bailey." She blinked away tears. "You have to find him. I don't know what I would do without him."

"I'll find him." I had to stop making promises that I didn't know whether I could keep.

I went into the woods, and even with the shade of the trees, I was sweating within seconds. A small creek ran to my left, and the humidity under the canopy of leaves had to be twice what it was by the road.

I lifted my hair off my neck and pulled a hair tie from my pocket. I always kept one there for when I was making candy. I wrapped my hair up in a bun on the top of my head. That was just a bit better. At least the back of my neck wasn't burning up.

"Jethro!" I called in a calm voice. "Jethro, it's Bailey. Where are you, boy?"

There was no response. Not that I had expected one. He was a pig, after all. Was I expecting him to *oink* back at me?

"Jethro? If you come out now, you can have some pumpkin pie from the café."

Pumpkin pie was his favorite, and he especially liked Darcy's. I hoped there actually was some at the café—it wasn't exactly the season for pumpkin.

"Jethro?" I called again.

I felt a tightening my chest. All around me were trees, fallen logs, brambles, and bushes. He could be in or under any one of them, and I would never know it. How was I going to find him? The only way was if he decided to reveal himself to me.

I had been walking for close to ten minutes when I thought about turning back. If I didn't return to the road soon, Juliet and the Fungals might come after me. Any one of them could get lost in the woods themselves, and then we would have a much bigger problem.

I stopped in the middle of the path. I was reluctant to venture out into the brush by myself. If I did, I just might be the one who was lost.

"Jethro," I called again, and then, with all my concentration, I listened.

Overhead, birds twittered away, and to my right, there was a scuttling of leaves from a chipmunk or maybe a squirrel. It was too small to be that of Jethro.

I hung my head. I had to go back.

I had just started to turn around when, out of the corner of my eye, I saw a mushroom. It was large, a golden-yellow color, and growing at the base of a large beech tree.

I took a picture of it with my phone and searched the internet browser with the picture. It soon informed me that it was a chanterelle mushroom. It did look exactly like the ones that Juliet had brought to the Candyworks the day before my wedding.

I didn't pick it, though. I wasn't taking any chances.

I stepped off the path but told myself I wasn't going to go too deep into the forest. I would always keep the path in my line of sight. I couldn't trust the Fungals to come into the trees after me. They meant well, but they were a group of older ladies. If they were to fall and get hurt, they wouldn't be much help.

Would Jethro have gone back on the trail of the mushrooms after the near owl attack? It was the only lead I had.

The next large tree had a bunch of five mushrooms at its base, and the third had even more than that. At the fourth tree, I found Jethro curled up like a cat. His head was facing the tree and pressed into the dirt.

He was covered with so much mud it was hard to know which were his black spots and which were splotches of dirt.

I crept toward him, trying not to make a sound. I was afraid he might run off again if I startled him.

Within two feet of the pig, I lunged forward and scooped him up with both hands. He kicked his legs in panic, squealing like I was the owl who had returned to take him to its tree hollow. The piercing sound broke my heart.

"Jethro, Jethro, it's me." I held him out from me so he couldn't kick me with his sharp little hooves.

When he finally realized it was just me, he went limp in my arms, as if he couldn't believe he was safe.

I cradled the little pig to my chest and kissed the top of his muddy head. He shoved his snout into my neck and snuffled. If I hadn't known better, I would have said he was crying with relief.

Of all the scrapes that Jethro had gotten into in his short little life, it seemed to me that this one he found the most terrifying.

"Don't worry. It won't happen again. I won't let Juliet take you out mushroom hunting anymore."

As if he understood what I had said, he sighed.

"Bailey! Bailey!" I heard voices calling my name in the woods. I had overstayed my fifteen-minute allotted time in the trees.

"Over here!" I called. "I found Jethro!"

I kept shouting until I saw the Fungals break through the trees. When Juliet saw Jethro, she burst into tears. "My angel! I'm so sorry. Are you okay?"

When she reached me, she took the pig and hugged him hard. Jethro's eyes bugged out of his head as he gasped for air.

I touched Juliet's hand. "You might be squeezing him a little too tight. He's been through a lot today."

"Oh, you're right," she cried, and to my relief, she loosened her embrace and hugged the little pig much more gently.

"Jethro found a stash!" one of the women cried.

"What is it, Megs?" Juliet asked between her tears.

"Those are chanterelles, to be sure. He's gifted! He's found another stash."

Juliet hugged her pig close to her chest. "You really are good at everything that you try, Jethro."

Except staying with his person, I thought. He wasn't great at that.

"This is a gold mine," Megs said. "Ladies, let's gather these up. I don't know if we will ever find so many in one place again."

The women started to gather up the mushrooms with gusto. It was as if the terror of losing Jethro was all but forgotten as they chattered together while collecting as many mushrooms as possible. Juliet simply watched as she cradled her pig. I was just about to suggest that Juliet, Jethro, and I head back to town when I noticed to the east that the trees started to thin out.

Unable to withhold my curiosity, I walked to the edge of the tree line.

There, I spotted a small clearing, with a pond and a field of wildflowers. Wild bee balm and daisies filled the field, and bees and butterflies fluttered from blossom to blossom. There was an impression between the wildflowers and the pond—with a ring of white. As I stepped closer, I saw it was a ring of mushrooms growing in the damp earth. My mother would have called it a fairy ring, but I knew it was much more sinister than that.

Chapter Thirty-Three

Megs came into the field. "You were such a big help to us today, Bailey. Do you want some of these chanterelles to take home? They are excellent in soup, or even on the grill."

"I'll pass," I said. It might be a long time before I ever ate a mushroom again.

She shrugged as if it made no difference to her. "This is one of the best hunts I have ever been on. Did you find more mushrooms?"

"Yes, but I don't think you want to pick these." I pointed at the fairy ring just five feet from the edge of the pond.

Megs whistled through her teeth. "*Amanita phalloides*. More commonly called death cap mushrooms. You're right. You don't want to pick those. Don't even touch them. You could get a rash or worse if you somehow get the oils from it in your mouth. You'd get sick or even die if that happened."

"This is what killed Jason Hackney," I said.

"Really?" Megs arched her brow. "He ate them?"

I nodded.

She shook her head. "Dumb move, but a few people do every year. They look like friendly mushrooms, but I can assure you they are not."

"I don't believe he ate them on purpose."

"Someone gave them to him to eat? Sinister. It's a death sentence."

"The sheriff's department," I said, knowing very well that I was talking about my own husband, "believes one was put in the mushrooms that Darcy used to make the tarts. Those mushrooms were given to her by Juliet."

"I don't believe that. Juliet would not have put those mushrooms in her basket to give to Darcy. We would never pick those. Juliet has never gone mushroom hunting without me, and I know my stuff. There is no way I would have let her pick one of those up." She shook her head. "And Darcy would know better. She used to be a member of the Fungals when we started. When her business picked up, she no longer had the time. But if anyone knows how to cook with wild mushrooms, it's her."

I raised my brow. This was new information to me. Darcy had said the day before the wedding that she knew about wild mushrooms, but she hadn't mentioned the Fungals. I don't know if that meant anything at all. She had no reason to say she was part of the group, and she had been clearly uncomfortable with Jason in the room.

I looked up from the fairy ring. "What's on the other side of the trees, at the other end of the clearing?"

"I thought you would know that, since you have been there before. It's Carly Crestwood's winery." She wrinkled her nose. "I can't remember the name of it. It's new."

"Hackney Family Winery," I said.

She nodded. "That sounds right. I'm not much of a wine drinker, but I drive by it every few days or so on the way to forage. I've seen the sign many times, and that name rings a bell."

I felt a shiver run down my spine. "And how far is it from here to the winery?"

"No more than a quarter of a mile, I would guess." She rubbed the back of her neck. "It's been a good day for foraging. But I do think we should ask Lois to leave Jethro at home after this. We can't take the risk." She turned to head back to the path. "Are you coming?"

"I'll be right there," I said. "I just want to take a look on the other side of the clearing."

"Ahh, you have foraging in your blood now. I'll warn you. It can be addictive." She walked back into the trees.

But it wasn't mushrooms I was looking for.

I removed my phone from my pocket and quickly snapped several photos of the fairy ring. I even knelt down and took some close-up shots. I knew I needed the proof that they were there and so easily accessible.

My knees cracked when I stood up, and I jogged around the small pond and through the line of trees. From there, I had a clear view of the land beyond. In the distance, I saw Carly's vineyard, and beyond that, Jason's vineyard as well.

* * *

When Juliet, Jethro, and I returned to Harvest, we were all covered with streaks of mud. Juliet dropped me off in front of the Swissmen Sweets, and she and Jethro headed home to get cleaned up.

As she drove away, I could hear Juliet chattering away to her little pig. She really did love him. I hoped she loved him enough to take mushroom hunter off his list of attributes. He already did more than most pigs; he could sit this one out.

Lida and Neva were at the candy shop, and with their help, I knew I didn't have to worry about the shop today. I was thinking of walking home to get myself cleaned up before I went to the factory to help Charlotte make the hundreds of truffles, when a car pulled up in front of the Sunbeam Café across the square.

Darcy got out of the passenger seat.

She was just the person I needed to talk to, because I had questions—more than I'd had when I'd gotten up that morning.

The bell on the café's door rang when I went inside. It was close to lunchtime, and the place was starting to fill up. Iris greeted me at the door. "Are you here for some lunch?"

I shook my head. "I saw that Darcy was home, and I wanted to check on her."

Iris nodded. "She's in the kitchen."

Lois came out of the dining room with a stack of menus and pulled up short. "What happened to you?"

"Jethro got lost in Harvest Woods."

She held up her hand. "Say no more. We've all fallen

on our faces once or twice chasing that pig. Heaven knows I have."

I looked down at myself. "Is it really that bad?"

"It looks like you mud-wrestled that spoiled pig. You'd better go home and clean yourself up before Margot sees you. You know she expects all the businesses on the square to have a certain level of decorum."

"I was planning to, but I wanted to check on Darcy first," I said.

Darcy came out from the kitchen. Her face was drawn, and her eyes were sunken in. It was clear to me that the one night she had spent in jail had taken a toll. I don't know how she stood it. I would have lost my mind being there for just an hour.

"I'm right here," she said in a quiet voice. "I was expecting you would be over soon wanting to talk."

Everyone in the café seemed to be on the edge of their seats, trying their best to hear the conversation.

"Why don't we go for a walk," I suggested.

Darcy wrinkled her brow. "I don't know. I have already been away from the café for a whole day. I should stay and give everyone who has been covering for me a break."

Lois shook her head. "You go. Iris and I have got this, and Enoch is in the kitchen. There's nothing we can't handle."

Darcy nodded, removed her apron, and handed it to her grandmother. "We won't be gone too long."

Darcy and I walked out of the café and onto the square. There was a bench near the gazebo. It was amazing to see the square was already in the process of being transformed. Uriah had outdone himself for the Summer Soiree. It was a shame he wouldn't be there to see the results of his good work, but he and Millie would not attend because of the alcohol. I wondered how many other members of the Amish community would stay away.

Darcy glanced at me. "You really are a mess. What happened?"

"Jethro."

"Oh." She nodded and asked for no further explanation.

"How are you feeling?" I dusted a patch of dirt from my knee.

"Are you asking how my head is feeling or how I'm doing emotionally?" she asked.

"Both, I guess."

She touched the bump on her head and winced. "It's still tender, but the headache is gone. I will say that it was very quiet and dimly lit in the jail cell. I was the only one there. That helped calm my headache."

I grimaced.

"I mean that, Bailey. It wasn't horrible. I'm not saying it was fun, but I knew Grams would get me out. Also, Aiden was kind to me. He gave me lots of extra pillows and blankets, and he made sure the deputies did all they could to make sure I was safe and comfortable." She paused. "Don't get me wrong. I never want to be in that situation again. I'm praying that the real killer is found, so my innocence will be proven."

"I'm doing my best."

She nodded, then winced, as if it still pained her to move her head up and down. "I know you are." She sighed. "To tell you the truth, it was worse being arrested than being in jail. I was humiliated in front of the entire café. I never thought something like that would ever happen to me—and definitely not for murder." She turned on the bench to face me. "Bailey, I promise you I didn't do this. I would never hurt anyone, let alone someone I cared about as much as Jason." She looked down at her hands. "I know now how misguided my feelings were for him. We didn't work out. That was it. I didn't care enough to kill him."

"Did you love him?"

"We weren't in love. We hadn't been together long enough for that, but I really liked him. He was so sophisticated and different from the other men I'd met in Holmes County. I think that was why I was so attracted to him. I hadn't had much luck with the usual type you meet around here, so I was happy that someone different had taken an interest in me."

"What's the 'usual type'?" I asked.

"You know, a country guy. Jason lived in New York for a while. He was so different from the guys who grew up here and never left." She kicked at a tuft of grass at her feet.

I raised my brow. "Why did he move back?"

She nodded. "His grandfather's vineyard brought him back. He'd had a vineyard in New York and said he closed it down. He always planned to come back to Holmes County and take over his grandfather's business. At least that's what he told me."

I remembered something that Cass had said. "Did he tell you he had to close his vineyard in New York because of financial trouble?"

She shook her head.

"When did he move back here?"

"Maybe three years ago. Not long after that, his grandfather passed."

"And how long were the two of you dating?"

"Officially, nine months, if that."

I gave up trying to pick all the dirt off my clothes. It was a lost cause. "Did you know about Jason convincing his grandfather to change the will before his grandfather died?"

She shook her head. "I knew nothing about it until Carly told me."

"When did she tell you this?"

"Maybe a month ago. She said she'd heard that Jason and I were dating, and she wanted to warn me about him."

"Did you tell Jason about that conversation?"

"No, but it is why he broke up with me. He thought I'd betrayed him by talking to her." She paused. "Carly came to my café and told me the whole story while she was there to eat lunch. What was I supposed to do, kick her out of the café? That wouldn't look good to the other customers in the room."

"Was Lois there?"

She shook her head. "No, but if she had been, she would have pumped Carly for information about Jason. She didn't like him. I don't know if that's fair. Grams wasn't so great at picking men, either."

That was true.

"How did he find out you spoke to Carly?"

"He must have heard it through the grapevine. You know how people in this village talk. Nothing is ever done in secret. There were at least seven tables full there when Carly came in. Any one of them could have gossiped to the wrong person about it, and one way or another, it got back to Jason."

I nodded. It was very difficult to keep any kind of secrets in Harvest, and that was especially true at the café, where the whole village went to mingle and talk.

"You asked Margot to add her to the Summer Soiree," I said.

She kicked at the grass again. "I did. I felt bad for her, and I was already starting to question how I felt about Jason. I couldn't really be with someone who would do such a terrible act, not only to his cousin, but to his grandfather. I would do anything for Grams. I would never take advantage of her or let someone else do it. Hearing what Carly had to say made me feel uneasy."

"He broke up with you after that."

She nodded. "I was at a meeting about the Summer Soiree with Margot and all the winemakers when Carly showed up. He wanted to know what she was doing there, and Margot said I had invited her. He was furious. Jason said he was done with me, and if Margot didn't fire me from the soiree, he was out." She looked at the gazebo. "I don't blame Margot for cutting me out of it. Swiss Valley was the most well-known winery participating. Losing Jason would have been a real loss, much more so than losing me. And like I said before, it was sort of a blessing in disguise that the event was so close to your wedding, I didn't know how I could do both well."

"Carly was there when this happened?"

She nodded.

"Wasn't he as mad at her as he was at you?"

"I guess so. I was in such a state of shock over what was happening, I can't say that I noticed much else."

I frowned. "I'm surprised he didn't say she had to be out of the soiree as well."

Darcy dug the toe of her sneaker into the grass under the bench until it made a small dent into the earth. "I never thought about that, but you're right."

"There has to be a reason that he let her stay and made you leave."

She shrugged. "Whatever it was, I don't know. I didn't even see Jason again after that, until the day before your wedding at the factory. I was shocked that Margot brought him there. Margot knew what had happened—she was there."

"I don't think that means all that much. You know Margot. She is always thinking of her events on the square above everything else. It probably didn't occur to her that you would be there, or if you were, that you would be uncomfortable."

She nodded. "In a way, it came as a relief. I realized that I'd taken on too much with catering the wedding, keeping the café open, and catering the soiree. Losing the money hurts, of course, but if I want this catering business to be strong, I need to grow it more slowly. Your wedding was the perfect start. At least it was until . . ." she trailed off.

She didn't have the finish the sentence. I knew what she was going to say: "*until Jason died.*"

"Let's go back to the day of the wedding. What was Jason doing in the factory?"

She looked down at her hands. "He said he wanted to apologize for the way he had treated me. He wanted to talk in person that day. I said I couldn't because of the wedding, and then he just showed up."

"Did he apologize?" I asked.

"He never got a chance. I was running around doing all the final touches for the reception. He said he would wait in the kitchen until I had some free time to talk to him. The next time I saw him"—she closed her eyes—"he was dead on the floor."

"How long were you there before I walked into the kitchen?"

"I don't know. Ten minutes, one minute? I had never seen a dead body before. I was in shock."

I nodded. I remembered the first time I ever saw a murder victim. It still lived in my memory and haunted my nightmares.

"What's odd to me is that you said he was waiting for you in the kitchen. There was so much staff working that day, didn't anyone see anything? People had to be going in and out of the kitchen all the time."

"They were," she said. "And I was in and out, too. I didn't see Jason after I first told him I couldn't talk. I assumed that he'd left. To be honest, I was relieved. I wanted to put that relationship behind me. I realized soon after he broke it off that it wasn't good for me. I never felt like I was enough for him. I got the sense he was just interested in me because of my connections to Harvest. Once he was in with Margot, he didn't need me any longer."

"I heard the Summer Soiree was your and Jason's idea."

She nodded. "Yes, we came up with it together and presented it to Margot. She loved it. I knew she would.

Anything that promised to bring a crowd to Harvest was welcome."

"And you weren't nervous about the Amish reaction?"

"I was, but I knew they just wouldn't come. I thought there would be enough Englishers from out of town to make up the difference. I even talked to Millie about it, and she said that for the most part, the Amish would ignore it. Although she did promise me that Ruth Yoder would have an opinion, and she did."

"What about the Amish who work for you?" I asked.

"Enoch and Iris?"

I nodded.

"I didn't want them to be uncomfortable, so I told them they didn't have to take part in anything related to the soiree. Iris, I know, was relieved. Her husband wouldn't have liked it. Enoch said he would help because he didn't have any family to get upset with him. He was going to help me cook beforehand, but I don't believe he was going to be at the soiree itself. We really didn't get to hammer out the details because by the time I really needed to be planning for it, I'd been ousted. Like I said, I think that was a blessing in the long run."

"Did Enoch help you cook for my wedding, too?"

She nodded.

"Who made the mushroom tart?"

"Are you asking me whether Enoch or I put death cap mushrooms in the tarts?"

I nodded.

"We didn't. I didn't, and Enoch never touched the tarts. Those were all on me."

"But they got death cap mushrooms in them somehow."

"It was just in the one."

"The one that Jason ate?"

She nodded.

"You know your mushrooms, you said. Was that because you were a member of the Fungals?" I asked.

She blinked at me. "How did you know about that? I haven't gone foraging with them in years."

"It's the group that Juliet and Jethro joined. Megs told me."

She nodded. "Juliet joined long after I was gone. We were never in the group together. I enjoyed it, but I had to quit because the café was so busy. Foraging is time-consuming."

Especially when a pig runs off into the woods, I thought.

"But you're right. I know my mushrooms. I did use the ones Juliet gave me for the tarts, but I swear they were all chanterelles. I washed and prepared them all myself. No one else touched them."

I frowned. Darcy wasn't making herself look any better by saying that. "Someone told me there was a witness who saw you give a tart to Jason."

She bit her lip. "I did. When I first saw him, when he was trying to talk to me, he said he was hungry. I had a tray of tarts, and so I gave him one. He said something about liking them, which was odd to hear because I had never made them before."

"And that was the one with the death cap mushrooms in it."

"I don't know. I guess so. I don't know how it would

have gotten there. The tray was cooling on the kitchen island while the waitstaff was running in and out of the kitchen. I suppose anyone could have gone in there and tampered with one of the tarts. The rest I took to the wedding guests, and no one else got sick.

"But how would they have known which tart I'd hand to him? Or that I even intended to take one to my ex?"

"Was he already sick when you first saw him?"

"He looked sweaty, but it was a hot day and he was clearly upset about something. I thought it was about us. Maybe it wasn't."

"Did you know that Jason's assistant, Dakota, will be bringing some of his wines to the soiree?"

She frowned. "I didn't know that, but I'm not surprised. Dakota was loyal to him to a fault, even though I can vouch that he wasn't always nice to her."

"How was he unkind to her?"

"He promised to help her pay for wine school. The closest one was in New York State, so she would have had to leave the Swiss Valley to do that. Later, when Carly opened her winery and stole all his employees, he said she had to stay. He couldn't lose another person. I think he still promised to pay for school, but it was indefinite at that point. I suppose it won't happen at all now."

"Why didn't she just leave?" I asked.

"That's a question you will have to ask her."

And I would.

Chapter Thirty-four

After my chat with Darcy, I went to the Candyworks and spent the rest of the day making truffles. So. Many. Truffles.

Charlotte and three Amish women who worked for me were already hard at work. Charlotte gave a sigh of relief when I came in. "Bailey, now that you're here, I know we will pick up speed. The most tedious task has been rolling the truffles. We have all been on that, and it seems like we're going slower, not faster." She sighed.

Three of the completed truffle flavors were dipped in chocolate and dusted with cocoa. The peanut butter truffles were being made in another room so there was no cross-contamination for anyone who might have a peanut allergy, but the process was much the same.

In the prep room, the truffles sat on parchment paper–lined steel trays to be moved to the walk-in refrigerator. They would be packed for the soiree just before it began the next evening. With the heat, we couldn't risk taking them to the square too soon for fear they might melt.

I grabbed an apron off the wall, rolled up my sleeves, washed my hands, and donned gloves. "I'm ready to work. I can roll truffles and give you all a break."

Charlotte sighed. "Thank you. My fingers were going numb. We have about four hundred truffles done and a lot more to go."

While Charlotte went over to the stove to mix up the next truffle recipe, I sat on a metal stool by the rolling table. I took a teaspoon's worth of the raspberry truffle mix and rolled it in my hands. I set the truffle on the table and went to roll the next one. I did this over and over. And over. I knew Charlotte and the other ladies had tired of rolling truffles, but I found something therapeutic in the task, and it gave me time to think.

My thoughts went to the murder. I tried to put the timeline straight in my head, and I believed it all started when the Summer Soiree became a Harvest event. Jason and Darcy approached Margot and suggested the idea of a soiree on the square—an elevated event that included a wine tasting. A select number of wineries would participate. Hackney Family Winery, which was owned by Jason's cousin, Carly, was one of the wineries that was invited—at Darcy's suggestion. This already sounded odd to me. Why was Carly asked to participate if she and Jason didn't get along? Was it just because Hackney Family Winery needed the recognition? That's what Anna Grace, who worked for Carly, had seemed to imply.

A few weeks before the event, Carly found out Jason and Darcy were together, and Carly went to the café to bad-mouth Jason. Instead of being upset with Carly, he dumped Darcy and got her fired from the soiree. I shook my head. It just didn't make any sense.

To me, it could only mean that Jason had a reason he couldn't touch Carly. Did she know something about him? Was she blackmailing him? But if that was the case, why wouldn't she just blackmail him to get the rights back to their grandfather's vineyard?

Did she kill him for the vineyard? Whom would it go to now? That was the biggest question—other than who'd killed Jason Hackney.

I finished another tray of truffles and took off my gloves and apron.

Charlotte looked up from across the room where she was pouring melted chocolate over the truffle balls. "Where are you going?"

"I need to ask someone a question," I said.

"But what about the truffles?" she squeaked.

"I'll be back tonight to finish. You all do as many as you can until five and then go home. You don't have to stay. I'll finish up. I just have to go right now."

"You are going to solve Jason's murder." Her forehead creased in concern.

"I hope so," I said before I ran out of the door.

On the drive to Carly's vineyard, I played over in my mind how the conversation should go. I would ask Carly what she had on Jason, and she would tell me. Simple.

I knew it wasn't going to go that easily. If Carly didn't see the benefit in telling me what she knew before, she wasn't going to tell me just because I asked now.

I drove by Harvest Woods a second time that day.

Death cap mushrooms were common in the damp ground of Ohio, both in the forests and in the fields this time of year. The mushroom that killed Jason didn't have to have come from the fairy ring that I'd found by that little pond in the clearing, but the proximity could not be ignored.

I parked outside of the winery. It was close to closing time. A group of tourists came out of the tasting room carrying wine bags and cases of wine. It looked like Carly had just made a great sale—maybe she would be in the mood to talk to me.

I went into the tasting room and was surprised to see Enoch standing at the counter.

I walked over to him. "Enoch, I didn't expect to see you here."

He gave me his customary wide smile. "I didn't expect to be here. Uriah was busy, and Margot asked me to stop by Carly's winery to pick up more posters for the soiree to post around the county. I'm taking them to some shops in Berlin and Charm."

"That's kind of you, especially given how the district feels about the event," I said.

"No one in the district feels anything about the event expect Ruth Yoder, and I don't know if you could even count on one hand the things that she likes. The Amish have been ignoring the *Englisch* ways of amusement for years. This is no different, and by hanging up the posters, I'm helping Uriah out. He and Millie have always been *gut* to me. If I can do this so he doesn't have to, I will."

The back door to the room opened, and Carly walked

in. "Here are those posters Margot wanted. This is the last batch I'm going to print. The soiree is tomorrow evening. If people don't know about it by now, they aren't coming." She blinked when she saw me standing there with Enoch. "What are you doing here?"

"I just wanted to fill you in on the meeting at Swissmen Candyworks about all the candy pairings for the soiree."

She frowned. "I really don't care what the pairings are, as long as I get the one I want."

"You still have peanut butter," I said.

"She came all this way," Enoch said. "You should hear her out."

Carly frowned at him. "Fine."

Before she could change her mind, I quickly told her about the other wines and truffles.

She nodded. "It sounds to me like mine will be the most popular. Jean Pierre was the one who suggested it, so it makes sense that it would be the best."

"They all sound delicious," Enoch said with a smile. "Bailey, if you could save me one of each truffle, I would be grateful. I won't be partaking of any of the wine."

Carly frowned at him. "Don't you have signs to hang up? You should head out if you want to visit all those shops in the county before they close."

He looked at the clock on the wall. "You're right." He waved goodbye to us both. "I'll see you back in town, Bailey."

After Enoch left, Carly shook her head. "I wish I was as happy as he is. He can smile at any situation. I just don't have that gift. My husband complains that I have a permanent scowl on my face, and it's just gotten worse." She scowled as if to prove her point.

"Because you didn't get Swiss Valley Vineyard?" I asked.

She frowned at me. "That is part of it. Jason stole it from my family and me. I worked with our grandfather for years at the vineyard. My husband and children were part of the business, too, and Jason just swooped in one day and took it all out from under us. I have every right to be angry about it."

"You do," I agreed.

She frowned as if she were suspicious by my answer.

"I was surprised to see you so comfortable with Enoch," I said.

"Why's that? I have known him since he was a teenager."

"Oh, did your family have ties to the Amish community?"

"Not really, but he worked for my grandfather when he was on *Rumspringa*. My grandfather was the best of men. His son worked for my grandfather, too."

"Enoch has a son?"

"Had. The boy passed away rather young."

"How awful," I said.

She nodded. "It was terrible."

"And did Jason know Enoch, too."

"I wouldn't know how. Jason was in New York sowing his wild oats at that time. We never thought he would come back, and I wish he never had. He knew Joseph, of course. That was the son who died. Joseph worked at the vineyard for Jason even after my grandfather passed."

"Enoch never mentioned that he worked at Swiss Valley."

"Why would he? It was twenty-five years ago, if not more. He was just a kid then."

"Was he thinking about being *Englisch*?" I asked.

"I don't think so. He had an Amish sweetheart. I think he was married at eighteen and was a father by nineteen."

This was interesting. Enoch had never mentioned having children to me. He did say that his wife had died young from cancer. I just thought it was before they were able to have children. He never remarried, which was unusual for a young Amish widower, but he seemed happy. Who was I to question it? When he came to Sunbeam Café to work for Darcy, he'd said he'd taught himself to cook from living alone for so long and enjoyed it. That was unusual for an Amish man, as well.

Darcy had been elated to find a cook who was able and willing to work the long hours that she needed at the café. It freed her up to do other things, like start her catering business.

"What did he do at the winery?" I asked. "Did he make the wine?"

She laughed. "No, he harvested the grapes and cared for the grounds. Joseph did the same work when he worked for Jason years later, but from what I heard, he wasn't as big of an asset as his father had been. Joseph just wasn't as well-versed in plants. My granddad said if you wanted to know anything about the flora and fauna of Holmes County, you should just ask Enoch. He knew it all. He told me once he'd learned it from his father, who was an herbalist of some sort. His father knew every last herb and plant that could heal a person."

An unwelcome thought tickled the back of my brain. "And would he know the poisonous ones, too?"

"He would have to, wouldn't he?" she asked.

CHAPTER THIRTY-FIVE

My alarm went off way too early the next morning. I had been at Swissmen Candyworks long after midnight finishing the truffles. Charlotte had still been there when I returned to the factory after my quick trip to Hackney Vineyard. I made her go home early at four. She had been working on the truffles much longer than I had, and she deserved a break. After that, I rolled up my sleeves and finished the last of the truffles alone. And considering how many we'd had to make, finishing in the wee hours of the morning didn't seem at all that late. I hoped that the Summer Soiree was as much of a success as Margot predicted because otherwise I didn't know who would eat all two thousand truffles we had made. It certainly wouldn't be me.

Aiden rolled over in the bed, wrapped his arms around my waist, and pulled me close. "Do you have to leave already?"

I buried my face into the pillow. "Yes, it's the day of the soiree. Margot can't be there for the setup."

He pulled back from me. "And let me guess. You agreed to do it for her."

"It wasn't so much as agreed on as it was conceded."

He chuckled, but then his tone turned serious. "I'm sorry about this week. I will make it up to you. We will go on our honeymoon, I promise."

I rolled over to face him. "I know we will. And I know what I signed up for when I married a cop."

Aiden leaned in for a kiss when Puff bounced in between us.

Aiden pulled back as the rabbit wedged herself in the middle of the bed. She was nearly thirty pounds. Puff did what Puff wanted to do.

"I don't know how I feel about Puff sleeping in our bed," Aiden said.

"Are you going to kick her out of the room?" I asked. "She's your daughter, too, now."

"You should do it. You know her better."

I glanced down at Puff's snow-white face. She twitched her little pink nose at me. "I'm not doing it. Look at how sweet she is."

Aiden shook his head and laughed.

Before I headed into town and started working on the soiree, I needed to check on my grandmother. I hadn't been able to go to Millie's house last night to visit her like I'd planned, and the guilt of not checking on her ate away at me.

Phillip and Peter, the goats, greeted me when I arrived at Millie's farm. They leapt three feet in the air.

Uriah stood at the screen door. "Calm down, you two nuts! Bailey isn't here to see you."

I held my hand out, and both goats ran over for a

head scratch. Then they skipped behind me as I walked toward the house.

"I wish I had that kind of energy in the morning. On the drive over here, I just drank the biggest coffee I could make at home, and I still feel like I could sleep for a year."

Uriah laughed. "No one has the energy that Phillip and Peter do. They aren't even kids any longer—they are firmly in middle age for goats. You'd think that would slow them down, but I think it just makes them more determined to be excitable." He held the screen door open for me.

Maami was sitting in a recliner by the cold, potbellied stove in the middle of the room. "Bailey, my girl."

I hurried over to her. "I didn't expect to see you out of bed this early."

"We couldn't make her stay put," Millie said from the kitchen. She placed a steaming loaf of banana bread on the counter. It was fresh from the oven and smelled heavenly. "As soon as I told her that you'd called the shed phone and were coming over this morning, she insisted on being up and out of bed."

"I'm so happy to see you, *Maami.*" I squeezed her hand. It felt cold and small in mine.

"Would you like some banana bread?" Millie asked.

"Just a small piece. Unfortunately, I can't stay too long. Margot put me in charge of the setup of the Summer Soiree since she had to take her husband for some medical tests."

Maami smiled. "Margot always seems to be able to convince you to do things you don't want to do."

"You would think after all these years, I would have

learned to say no to her. It's clear I haven't. Not only am I in charge of the setup, but I was at the Candy-works after midnight last night making truffles to pair with the wines. Margot owes me big-time for this one."

"I wish I could help you more," Uriah said. "But all the tables, chairs, and everything you need are set up. I know it will be a great event. I just hope Margot doesn't get it into her head to have more alcohol-related events on the square. Harvest is a family-oriented community, and I believe it should stay that way. It's asking for trouble, if you ask me."

"Trouble how?"

He shook his head as if he didn't want to answer the question.

"Alcoholism is a major issue in the Amish world, just as it is in the *Englisch* world," Millie said. "Our community just doesn't talk about it as much."

"They treat it like a dirty little secret," Uriah said. "I think that is a mistake, too. Children have to know the dangers. If they aren't told the dangers, they will learn about them one way or another—and it might be the worst way possible."

I thought of Abel Esh stumbling around the square in the early morning hours. I didn't know whether or not he was an alcoholic, but I did know he'd gone to jail for selling moonshine to other Amish people. The Amish who did drink alcohol kept it very quiet. Abel was the exception to that. Maybe it was because he didn't care anymore. He had already gone to prison once. He didn't have any reputation left to save. He certainly didn't seem to care how his behavior impacted his sisters, Esther and Emily.

But the Amish hiding their vices didn't just apply to drinking. It was also true for gambling, drugs, and other habits the church preached against.

I knelt by my grandmother's recliner. "How are you feeling?"

She placed a wrinkled hand on my cheek. "Much stronger. I am hoping I can go home today."

I glanced over my shoulder at Millie, and she gave a slight shake of her head. I turned back to *Maami*. "I think it would be best if you stayed with Millie for a little while longer, especially today. The village is all abuzz over the Summer Soiree. It would be better for you to wait until things calm down."

Maami sighed. "How is Nutmeg?" she asked. "I didn't know I would ever feel this way, but I miss that little cat—and Puff and Jethro, too. Peaches, Millie's cat, doesn't care for me much."

"He doesn't like me, either," Uriah piped up. "He is a one-woman cat."

Millie shook her head. "He may come around for you yet, Uriah."

Uriah shook his head as if he didn't believe that.

"All the animals are fine and causing their typical amounts of mischief."

Maami smiled when I said this.

"Jethro had a big scare yesterday," I added.

"What did that little pig get into now?" Millie asked.

I told them about Jethro getting lost in Harvest Woods. "The strangest part was finding so many death cap mushrooms nearby. Both Jason's and Carly's wineries are just a short walk away from the clearing where I saw them."

Millie handed *Maami* a cup of tea. "It's herbal. No caffeine for your heart right now. Keeping calm are the doctor's orders."

Maami accepted the cup. "*Danki*. It is difficult to keep calm when you know so much is happening in the village without you."

Millie sank into the rocking chair on the other side of the potbellied stove. "You will be back home, right in the thick of the village happenings, soon enough." She picked up her own teacup from the side table. "Would you like anything to drink, Bailey?"

I shook my head.

"Please let me know if you change your mind." She sipped her tea. "You think it's noteworthy that the mushrooms were so close to the vineyard."

"It could be. Carly's vineyard is on the same county road, less than a quarter mile away."

"If you want to ask someone about mushrooms," Uriah said, "you should speak to Enoch. He's very knowledgeable."

"Enoch Unger? Carly said he worked for her grandfather during his *Rumspringa* and knows everything one can know about nature."

He nodded. "*Ya*, his father was an herbalist, and he picked up all he knew about plants from him. Many times, for church, he would prepare the most wonderful salad made with ingredients he harvested from Harvest Woods—microgreens, wild berries, dandelion greens, and so many delicious herbs. If there were any death cap mushrooms in the woods, he would know. That's his favorite place around here. When he sold his farm, he moved to a little cottage at the edge of the woods so he could walk in the forest every day."

"Isn't it unusual for an Amish man to sell his land? I thought most wanted to pass their property down to the next generation."

"He didn't have anyone to pass it down to," Millie said. "He and his wife only had one child, a son."

"Carly told me that Enoch's son worked at the winery and passed away at a young age. I don't know much more than that."

Millie nodded. "It was so tragic. The boy would have been eight or nine at the time his mother died. He passed away himself a few years later."

"What happened?" I asked.

"The poor boy died in a tractor accident. He was young at the time. Do you remember how old he was, Uriah?"

"Just turned sixteen," Uriah said.

"It was so awful," Millie added.

"Did the tractor flip over?" I leaned forward.

"Don't know exactly how," Uriah said. "But it was in the middle of the night. He and some other boys stole a tractor from a local shop and went joyriding."

"Were the other boys hurt?"

"*Nee*. I don't know if the sheriff deputies even knew who they all were. None of them ever came forward."

"Then how did anyone know his son wasn't alone?" I asked.

"They stole the tractor from an *Englisch* shop. The shop had cameras. There were clearly three young men on the cameras, but their faces were covered. The sheriff at the time was only able to identify Enoch's son because his body was found with the stolen tractor."

Uriah swallowed. "Jason always denied it, but there was a rumor. I hate to say it."

"What?" I asked.

"There was a rumor that Jason had some part in underhanded dealings in the county. He got into some trouble for having stolen goods not long after he moved back. He claimed he didn't know how the stolen items got in his garage. His grandfather had a lot of influence in the county and made it all go away."

"Why hasn't Aiden said anything about it?" I asked.

"I think this was when Aiden was working for BCI," Uriah said.

I nodded. Aiden had moved away from Holmes County for over a year because he and the old sheriff hadn't seen eye to eye. At that time, he'd worked for the state's Bureau of Criminal Investigation. It had been the hardest time in our relationship, and for a while, I didn't think we would make it.

"Just based on Jason's history, a lot of folks believed he'd put the boys up to stealing the tractor."

"And Joseph died in the process." I shook my head. "Poor Enoch. You would never know that something like that had happened to him. He's always so positive."

Uriah nodded. "He's a *gut* man. He's had so much loss, but he's still been able to find the joy in life. I don't think too many other men would have been able to do that."

"No, they wouldn't," I agreed.

Chapter Thirty-six

Uriah was a man of his word. He'd said that everything was set up for the soiree, and he'd meant it. When I reached the square later that morning, I found the tables and chairs out and the gazebo decorated in lavender-and-white bunting. White twinkle lights that had been there for my wedding were still in the trees, with the addition of crystal ornaments that spun and sparkled in the sunlight. They would look even more dazzling after dark.

Charlotte walked from the direction of the Candyworks, pulling a wagon that had all our display pieces for the truffles onto the square. It was far too early bring out the truffles, though. It wasn't even ten in the morning, and the temperature hovered at eighty degrees, with enough humidity to make my dark straight hair frizz. I would be wearing my hair up in a bun for the duration of the soiree.

Charlotte must have been thinking the same thing as her hair was also up, and she'd traded her typical long skirt for one that fell just below her knees. I knew it was hot when my modest cousin was willing to show her ankles.

"It's so pretty, isn't it?" Charlotte said.

"It is."

"I think Margot was right that we do need that cooling station at the Candyworks. By the time the soiree begins late this afternoon, this place will be boiling."

Charlotte shielded her eyes from the sun. "I'm already on it. If we have to cool people off, we should just keep the lobby and the shop open. I have three of our non-Amish employees in the shop working until the soiree ends. We will have cold water and iced tea ready for visitors, and of course, we will be willing to sell them all the chocolate they want." She grinned.

I smiled. "I don't think I even have to come up with any ideas any more. You are always on top of everything."

She wrinkled her nose. "The staff who are staying will all go over their usual hours, so we will have to pay them overtime."

I waved away her concern. "That's fine. If Margot is right and a thousand people come through the square tonight for the wine tasting, we will more than make up for their wages." I looked around the square. "We can tuck the truffle displays under the tables until the actual truffles come out. I'm not sure what else we can do until the vendors arrive."

Charlotte reached into the wagon and pulled out Margot's clipboard. "Well, she left you a list."

I took the clipboard from her hand. "I would have been surprised if she hadn't."

Looking over the clipboard, I saw that the soiree was to begin at three. The wineries and vineyards would be arriving between one and two o'clock, depending on how much time they needed for setup.

At the very top of Margot's list, she'd written, *Make a cooling station at the candy factory!! It will be close to ninety when the soiree starts!!*

I grimaced. "Was it really necessary for her to use that many exclamation marks?"

Charlotte chuckled.

"I'm relieved that you've already handled that one," I said.

"I was relieved that you finished the truffles. I was dreading coming into the Candyworks today to make more. My wrists still hurt from moving them this way and that to make the truffle balls. How late did you stay at the factory last night?"

"I left after midnight," I said, then looked over Margot's list again.

The second item on her list was *Meet the florist!* There was that exclamation mark again.

It said she would arrive at ten thirty.

I checked my phone and realized she would be there any minute.

"Isn't it a little early for the florist to show up? The flowers will be out in the heat for four hours before the event," I said.

Charlotte shrugged. "She is Jason's ex-wife, though. It will give you another chance to talk to a main suspect."

I tapped my pen on the side of the list. "There is that."

Charlotte cleared her throat. "Is Aiden even still investigating the case? He must have felt pretty confident to arrest Darcy."

I sighed. "He did, but I still can't believe she did it, even when the overwhelming amount of evidence pointed at her."

"Neither can I." She paused. "I'm glad Darcy is back home."

"She's just out on bail," I said. "She's not cleared of the murder."

Charlotte bit her lower lip. "I hope this isn't causing problems between you and Aiden. You didn't have much time to settle into married life before everything happened."

"We had no time at all," I admitted. "Of course this doesn't make things any easier, but we have had disagreements in these types of situations before, and we always made it through. I don't see this case being any different—especially when I find the real killer, because I *know* it's not Darcy. It can't be."

Charlotte shook her head. "Who do you think did it?"

I had an inkling, but I was afraid to say it out loud. Thankfully, I was saved from answering as Pearl Gleib arrived at that moment in her white florist van.

Pearl climbed out of the driver's seat, and her brother, Carson Lee, jumped out of the passenger side. When Carson Lee saw me standing at the edge of the square holding Margot's clipboard, he scowled. I guessed I was the second-to-last person he wanted to see. The very last person would have been his sister's ex-husband, Jason Hackney, and he was dead.

Pearl walked over to Charlotte and me and gave us a nervous smile. "I'm looking for Margot. Is she here?"

"Margot's husband had a medical appointment today. She will be here just as the soiree begins. I'm in charge until then," I said.

"Oh," she said. She clearly wasn't thrilled about that. "She asked me to bring the flowers this morning."

"Isn't it a bit early? Won't they wilt?" I asked.

"I was worried about the same thing, so I thought it would be best to put them in the shade until the wineries arrive. Then I can decorate their booths with them. All the flowers are lavender, purple, or white at Margot's request."

"There are a couple of shady spots we can put them in, under some of the larger trees and in the gazebo," Charlotte said.

Pearl nodded. "That would be fine."

"We can help," I said.

"Oh, that won't be necessary. I have my brother here with me. He will help me." She glanced back at Carson Lee, who had opened the back of the van and was unfolding a collapsible dolly. "I know that you spoke to my brother at his work."

"I did," I admitted. "I had heard about him from—"

"From my cousin Raellen. I know. She told me. She can't even keep her own confidence, let alone that of others."

"Raellen didn't mean any harm."

"She never does," Pearl said. "Leave my brother out of this. He wasn't even in the county the day of the wedding. He was helping with a barn-raising that day in Wayne County. Hundreds of Amish women and men from all over saw him."

"I know that," I said quietly. "I wasn't accusing him of anything."

Carson Lee stomped over to us. "Pearl, where do you want me to put these flowers? I am only here on my lunch hour, and I have to get back to work soon."

Pearl's face flushed. "I know. I'm sorry, brother. We are going to put them in the shade of the trees for now. I will come back later to decorate."

He scowled at me. "And what is she doing here?"

Rather than let Pearl answer for me, I spoke up. "Margot can't be here until later. I am just helping out until then."

He tugged on his beard. "It seems you are always around to *help*." He turned to start walking back to the van.

I called after him. "Carson Lee, what do you know about the night when Joseph Unger stole that tractor?"

Charlotte stared at me. That wasn't the question she'd been expecting.

Carson Lee turned around and glared at me. "What did you ask me?"

I took a few steps closer to him so I could lower my voice. I didn't want to shout my questions at him. The Sunbeam Café was just across the square, and I knew Enoch was inside working. "Can you tell me what happened the night when Joseph Unger stole the tractor from Billings?"

Carson Lee narrowed his eyes. "Why are you bringing up painful memories from so many years ago? Joseph was misguided."

"Why? Because Jason Hackney put him up to it?" I asked.

He narrowed his eyes. "Of course Jason put them up to it. He would do anything for money. He wasn't satisfied with anything in his life—he just wanted more and more. The best thing that ever happened to my sister was when he divorced her and moved to New York. I only wish he had never come back. Our lives would be much more peaceful, and Joseph would still be alive."

I shivered. "How are you so sure that Jason put Joseph and the other boys up to stealing that tractor?"

He scowled at me for a long moment. "I do not want to answer your questions, but from what I know of you, you will give my sister and me no peace until I do. This will be the last time I speak on the matter. After this, I will never speak on it again. I spoke to the other boys who were there that night."

"Who are the other boys?" I asked. "There were three on the video footage, and we already know one of them was Joseph Unger."

"I'm never telling anyone that," he said. "They lost their friend and afterward turned their lives the right direction. They learned their lesson from that night and will have to live the rest of their days knowing what happened to Joseph. That is punishment enough for them. I gave them my word that I would never share their secret, and to this day, I have not."

"Did you ever speak to Jason about what happened to Joseph?" I asked.

"Why would I? He wasn't going to change his ways. He was a greedy, spiteful man. I knew he chose the tractor to be stolen from Billings because I worked there. He surely enjoyed that little detail." He rubbed the back of his neck. "I am sorry that he is dead because he ran out of time. He can't make amends for what he did to others during his life, and he will have to answer for that. But I am not sorry that he is gone. I can breathe a little bit easier now that he's no longer on this earth." With that, Carson Lee walked back to the van and started to unlock the containers of fresh flowers.

Without looking at me, Pearl ran to her brother and started to help.

Charlotte walked over and stood next to me. "Should we help them put the flowers in the shade?"

I shook my head. "No, they don't want our help."

Chapter Thirty-seven

By two thirty that afternoon, all the wineries had arrived, and Charlotte and I were running this way and that, helping them set up. Staff from the Candy-works brought the truffles out onto the square in large coolers to keep them fresh throughout the evening. Some of the truffles were artfully displayed on the tables while the rest remained in the coolers until they were needed.

Pearl had done a beautiful job arranging the flowers around all the booths. The purple and white blossoms were the perfect touch of elegance that I knew Margot had wanted for the soiree. After my conversation with her brother, Pearl avoided me for the rest of the day. Any time I was within five feet of her, she would scurry away like she'd suddenly remembered another task she had to do that was as far away from me as possible.

I couldn't say that I blamed her, and I truly didn't believe that she or Carson Lee had anything to do with Jason Hackney's murder. Carson Lee had an airtight alibi, and Pearl, in my opinion, was too naturally avoidant to kill anyone. Besides, she and Jason had divorced nearly twenty years ago. She had two successful businesses, between her coffee cart at the flea market and her growing flower enterprise. When would she have time to worry about Jason?

I still wasn't ready to admit, even to myself, who I really thought was behind the murder, but I knew I would have to face that suspicion soon.

I went from station to station, asking the wineries if there was anything they needed. "We are ready to go," Carly said when I got to her table. She was much more cheerful than I had ever seen her to be.

"You seem excited about the event," I said.

"Why wouldn't I be?" she said with a smile. "I learned today that I will be getting back my grandfather's winery."

I frowned. "You're inheriting Swiss Valley?"

"I am." She didn't even try to hide her glee. "My cousin doesn't have any heirs, so I am the next of kin."

"Did you know this was a possibility? That you would inherit?"

"No. I would have thought someone as business savvy as Jason would have created a will. If he had, there was no way he would have listed me in it. It was no secret how we felt about each other." She smoothed the edge of the cloth on her table. "It's fitting that it would come back to me, though. And with Hackney Family Winery so close to Swiss Valley, we can combine the two and make it even better than when my grandfather was alive. If my grandfather had been in his right mind when he died, this is what he would have wanted. I was the one who stayed in Holmes County and worked with him all those years, while Jason was sowing his wild oats in New York."

To me, it sounded like a twisted version of the Parable of the Prodigal Son.

She opened one of the bottles of wine on the table in front of her and let it breathe. "Things have been set back to the way they were meant to be."

"Because Jason died," I said bluntly.

She scowled. "That's not how I would have wished for it to happen. And it is not my fault he died. Are you saying I shouldn't accept the vineyard because of how I received it?"

I shook my head. "No. But it must be upsetting how you got it."

"It's not ideal," she agreed. "But it also spares me from working with my cousin, and I would be lying if I said I wasn't happy about that."

I arched my brow. Carly might as well have come out and said she was happy that Jason was dead.

Dakota was in the next booth, and I saw that she was watching us with a peculiar look on her face. It was as if she felt a mix of judgment and sympathy for Carly. As far as I knew, Dakota was the only person who was truly sorry that Jason had died. She felt so bad about it that she'd even tried to keep his winery going by continuing to host a booth at the Summer Soiree.

I turned back to Carly. "Are you in charge of the Swiss Valley booth tonight, too?"

"Technically, yes," Carly said as she carefully set wineglasses out on the table in front of her.

"Are you keeping Dakota on?" I asked.

She looked up from the wineglasses. "To be honest,

I haven't made that decision yet. She was loyal to my cousin, and that rubbed me the wrong way. She's a talented sommelier, but I want to work with people who are on my side."

"I think you should give her a chance," I said.

"We'll see." Her tone was noncommittal, and if I were Dakota, I would start looking for a new job immediately.

It wasn't quite three o'clock, and the tourists and wine aficionados were already milling around the square. Jon Michael walked up to me with a wide smile. "Margot came through with her promise. The place is already filling up, and we haven't even officially opened yet."

I shook out the skirt of the lavender dress that I'd put on for the occasion. I hoped Margot noticed that I'd stuck to her purple palette for the soiree. "Margot always comes through," I said. "It's just that the methods she uses to get there could use a little more finesse."

He laughed. "I wanted to tell you that you and your team did a bang-up job on the truffles. I tasted one of the vanilla bean ones, and it was out of this world. It was the perfect pairing with my wine."

"I'm glad."

He glanced over his shoulder as if to check whether his staff at his booth were doing all right. It appeared they had everything in hand. "I heard that Darcy Woodin was arrested for Jason's murder."

I raised my brow. This wasn't the direction I'd expected the conversation to go.

"I just have to say—and no offense to your husband—but the sheriff has it all wrong. Darcy didn't do it. If I was really looking for the killer, I would have my eyes on Enoch."

"Why do you think that?" I asked.

"Because he hated the guy. I mean, *hated* him." He paused. "I guess he had good reason. If Jason had never come back to Ohio, his son, Joseph, might very well still be alive."

I swallowed. Jon Michael had just verbalized the very thoughts I had been trying to avoid for the last few days. I tried to wrap my head around the possibility that cheerful Enoch Unger could have killed Jason. The facts were that he had the means and opportunity just as much as Darcy did, but he also had something she did not: a much, much stronger motive, to avenge his son's death.

"Bailey, Bailey, Bailey!" Margot called as she fast-walked across the square toward me.

I looked back to where Jon Michael had stood, and he was gone. He'd fled back to his booth. I couldn't say that I blamed him.

"Everything looks perfect. From the booths to the flowers to those delectable truffles that you made. I knew you could do it. Maybe I should leave you in charge more often."

Please, no, I thought.

For the soiree, Margot had swapped out her HARVEST VILLAGE T-shirt for a plain purple T-shirt and her denim capris for khaki. That was as fancy as she was going to get. Margot wasn't one to dress up, and I appreciated her unwavering commitment to her personal uniform.

"How is your husband?"

"Oh, he's fine. The poor man has an ulcer. I told him it was from all the junk he eats on the road while driving his rig. He's going to have to change his diet." She made a *tsk*ing sound. "It's not going to be easy. You try to convince a sixty-something man to stop eating gas-station hot dogs."

I grimaced.

Margot held her prized clipboard in her hand. "The truffles are phenomenal, Bailey. I knew you could do it. It just proves to me that you don't need much time at all to pull off such a task."

"If you want me to do something like that again, I will need way more warning, or I'm not doing it."

She laughed. "You always say that, but in the end, you always pull through. I'm going to see how many vouchers we have sold so far. There must be four hundred people milling around the village right now. This is wonderful! One of my best ideas yet."

"I thought it was Jason and Darcy's idea."

She waved her clipboard at me. "It might have been, but no one can put together an event like I can." She walked away.

I shook my head.

After my conversation with Jon Michael, I couldn't put off my suspicion any longer that Enoch might be involved in Jason's murder. I knew I had to call Aiden. He had planned to come to the soiree at the end of his shift, but there was no time to waste.

I pulled my phone from my pocket and started texting him. Before I could hit SEND, something smacked into the back of my bare leg, and the phone went flying from my hands.

Chapter Thirty-eight

"Oomph!" I said as the impact on the back of my legs rocked me forward. Thankfully, I was able to keep my balance and didn't topple over. I looked behind me to find a purple blob on the ground with a white, curly pig's tail sticking out the back end of it. "Jethro?"

The little bacon bundle tried to look up at me, but he couldn't see around his costume, which, I believed, was supposed to resemble grapes. His little body was covered with purple pom-pom balls, and a patch of leaves was taped to the top of his head. He did look like a bunch of grapes . . . if you squinted hard enough.

"Oh, Bailey, you have found Jethro again," Juliet said, hurrying over to us in a white-and-lavender polka-dot sundress. Her hair was up in a twist, and even though the soiree was being held on the grass, she wore heels. I wouldn't have expected anything else from my mother-in-law. "He always seeks you out. It's clear to me that he feels safest with you."

That could be because I would never make him wear a grape costume, and he knew it.

I fished my phone out of the grass. "Are you sure he's okay in that thing? It's very hot out."

"Oh, I know. I am only making him wear it for a short while for pictures with his fans. I don't think I bought the right size for him. It's so hard to determine sizes when you buy pig clothing online."

I had always found that to be true, too.

"He can't see very well in his costume, but isn't he the cutest bunch of grapes you've ever seen?" Juliet wanted to know.

"It's a statement," I said.

She beamed like I had given her a compliment.

"I think you should get your pictures and then get him out of the costume. It's just too hot for Jethro to wear it much longer."

She nodded. "You're right." She looked around. "I was wondering, since you will be on the square all evening anyway, would you look after him for me? Reverend Brook and I never have any alone time with Jethro around, and we would like to go out to dinner in Canton."

I sighed. "Sure."

What else could I say? I was their designated pig sitter.

Juliet gave me a hug. "Thank you, Bailey. You are truly the best daughter-in-law any mother could wish for."

At least I had that going for me.

Juliet shuffled away on her heels toward the church as if she was afraid I would change my mind.

I looked down at Jethro. "Sorry, buddy."

Anna Grace ran over to me. "Ohmigawd! Is that Jethro? I want a picture with him." She wrinkled her small nose. "But can you take off whatever he's wearing? No one will know it's him if I take a picture with him in that."

"Gladly," I said and squatted in the grass to remove the grape costume.

When he was free of the puff-ball grapes, Jethro licked my cheek in thanks.

"Sometimes your mom can take a theme too far," I told him.

He licked my cheek again in agreement.

I stood up, and Anna Grace handed me her phone. I took at least a dozen photos of her and Jethro while she posed with the pig. Jethro seemed to enjoy it. He did have a little bit of a diva complex.

When I handed her back the phone, she excitedly scanned through the pictures.

"Did they come out okay?" I asked.

She nodded. "I've already posted two." She grinned. "I'm so glad he's here. My friends are going to die when they see it. We're all big fans."

"Juliet will be glad to hear it." I picked up Jethro.

"I should get back to the booth. Carly will be annoyed if I'm gone for too long, but I thought of something."

"About Jethro?" I asked.

"No. About Dakota."

I blinked. "What was it?"

Across the square, I could see Dakota was pouring wine for guests and handing out truffles. She appeared to be happy. It was clear to me that she really loved her job as a sommelier.

"You asked me why I thought Dakota had stayed at Swiss Valley."

"I did."

"It was for Joseph," she said.

"Joseph?" I asked.

"Joseph Unger. He was Amish. He and Dakota were really close. She wouldn't leave Swiss Valley as long as he was still there. Everyone thought she was in love with him. Nothing would have come of it. It wasn't like she was going to become Amish, you know?"

I nodded. "He was killed in an accident."

"Yeah, it was a couple of years ago. Dakota was a mess after that." She shrugged. "I don't know if it will help you, but I wanted to tell you that."

I thanked her and watched as she ran back to Carly's booth.

I looked down at my phone. The text I had started to write to Aiden was still on the screen. I thought about what Anna Grace had just told me, then closed the messaging app. I needed to think over this more before getting Aiden involved.

He would be there soon. Maybe it would be better to tell him in person, so we could sort it out together before confronting Enoch.

I set my suspicions of Enoch aside for the moment and looked around the square. The oddest thing about the soiree was the lack of Amish folks. They were still in Harvest. I could see Amish young women walking around the square, pushing baby strollers, or men on the way home from their work in the shops, but none of them set foot on the square itself. There was a clear division. I didn't know that I liked it. The best part of Harvest was when the Amish and English communities got together.

I tossed Jethro's grape costume behind a bush and promised myself I would retrieve it later. I didn't want to carry the hot piece of purple fabric and puff balls around all night. With the offensive costume safely stowed, I snapped on Jethro's leash.

He pressed his snout into the grass and inhaled deeply.

If anyone thought it was odd that I had a polka-dotted, potbellied pig on a leash, they didn't show it. Jethro was just part of the charm of Harvest.

I debated my next move. I thought it would be best for me to go to Swissmen Candyworks and see how my staff there were doing with hosting the cooling station. I pulled on the collar of my dress. With this heat, I knew the Candyworks would be a very popular spot.

Before I could head that way, though, I saw Enoch across the square. He was locking up Sunbeam Café for the night. I waved at him and started his way, and he waited for me on the sidewalk.

I hoped I wasn't making a huge mistake.

"Hello, Bailey," he said with a smile, and then he looked down at Jethro. "Weren't you wearing grapes earlier?" he asked the pig.

"Yeah, we eighty-sixed those as soon as we could."

Enoch laughed. "Can I do anything for you, Bailey?"

"Is Darcy here?" I asked. "I wanted to check on her. She's had a rough few days."

"That's an understatement." He shook his head. "She's not home. Lois and Jean Pierre took her to New

Philadelphia for dinner. They wanted to get her away from the soiree in case it reminded her too much of Jason."

"I can understand that." I paused. "Uriah told me you know a lot about plants and nature."

"I know my fair share. My father was an Amish herbalist, so I learned a lot when I was young."

"You didn't follow in his footsteps?" I asked.

He shook his head. "I wanted my own farm. I was eventually able to acquire one, but it took time. Most farms are passed down from generation to generation, but my father didn't have any land."

"But then you sold your farm." I wrapped Jethro's leash more tightly around my hand.

He raised his bushy auburn eyebrows. "You seem to know a great deal about me."

"I'm sorry. I wasn't prying. You just came up in conversation because when I was looking for Jethro yesterday, I found death cap mushrooms in Harvest Woods. I mentioned it to Uriah when visiting my *maami* this morning. He said you would be the person to ask if I wanted a positive identification of them."

He nodded. "I know most of the plants, flowers, and fungi in the county. I can tell you the ones that are native and the ones that are invasive. My *daed* was particularly committed to native plants, and this was before so many others were talking about it. Did you take a picture of the mushrooms?"

"I did." I glanced over my shoulder to make sure I wasn't needed at the soiree, but with the truffles made and Margot back, I wasn't really needed anymore. I was happy to see that the guests appeared to be enjoying the truffles as much as they did the wine.

I pulled the picture of the fairy ring up on my phone and handed it to him to see.

He nodded. "*Ya*, those are death caps to be sure. Very dangerous. You shouldn't even touch them. You would become very ill then."

"It's what killed Jason."

Jethro looked up at me as if he was hearing this news for the first time. I would never admit it to Juliet, but there were times when I thought Jethro knew more about what was going on in the village than we gave him credit for.

Enoch handed the phone back to me. "I didn't know that. It's a very uncomfortable way to die. Whoever gave it to him wanted him to suffer." He stuck his hands in his trouser pockets and rocked back on his heels. "It's just terrible," he said, but with very little emotion.

I shivered at how coldly he said that.

"Uriah happened to mention that you have a cottage near Harvest Woods."

"*Ya*, I moved there two years ago, after I sold my farm. I was the only one living on the farm, and it was too much for one person. It was a difficult choice to make, but in the end, all is well, as Darcy gave me a job. I do love cooking at the café. I know it's not a normal job for a man."

"Maybe not for an Amish man, but there are many English male cooks and chefs."

He nodded. "I had to teach myself to cook after my

wife died, and I found that I like it very much. It gave me solace. It brings me joy to feed people and make them happy."

"And you are so good at it. Darcy is so grateful for your help," I said, hoping the compliment would put him back in a better mood.

"She is kind. I enjoy working for her." He smiled.

"What did you think when she was dating Jason Hackney? I haven't heard that many people say nice things about him."

"Why would they?" he asked. "He came back to Ohio and tricked his senile grandfather into giving him the winery. No one can respect a man who would treat an elderly man so poorly, especially someone like Mr. Hackney, who really cared about his employees and customers. As far as I knew, Jason Hackney only cared about himself."

"Did you know Jason?" I asked.

He nodded. "I knew him."

"Did you know him well from when you were younger? I heard that you worked for him when you were young."

He removed his hands from his pockets and looped his fingers around his black suspenders. "I did not work for him. I worked in the vineyard for his grandfather. It paid well and allowed me to save enough to buy a farm when I was ready to marry. I was no longer working there when Jason came back to Ohio. I barely knew the man."

"But your son knew Jason and went to work for him when he was in *Rumspringa*."

His face clouded over. “Did Uriah tell you that, too?”

“Carly did,” I said

“Carly likes to talk,” Enoch said. “I wish she wouldn’t speak on such things.”

“She’s here with her booth tonight.”

He eyed me. “I know.”

“And Dakota is here tonight, too, hosting a booth from Swiss Valley Vineyards. She must have worked with your son.”

He scowled. “Dakota’s a fool to be doing anything for Swiss Valley now. What has she even gotten from Jason? She doesn’t owe him anything.”

Before I could make a comment on that, he asked, “Why are you speaking to so many people about me, Bailey? If you have questions about me, come to me.”

I swallowed. “You’re right. I just didn’t know about your son or his connection to the winery. I was surprised to hear it.”

“It is not something that I simply talk about. It is not the Amish way to dwell on the past. I still grieve my son—and my wife, for that matter—but they are mine to grieve privately.” He dropped his hands to his sides. “It is not for the whole county to know.”

My face flushed red. “You’re right. I’m so sorry if I upset you.”

His face cleared, and his usual cheer was firmly back in place. “I know of your inquisitive nature, Bailey. Do not worry. I don’t take offense.” He put his hands back into his pockets and seemed at ease.

But a cloud of unease had fallen over me. “I’m glad.”

"Now," he said, "I should get home before Ruth Yoder sees me at the soiree. I do not want any issues with the bishop's wife or, in turn, the bishop."

I nodded.

With his hands still in his pockets, Enoch whistled to himself as he walked away.

I bit the inside of my lip, then turned back to the square, where I saw Dakota watching Enoch leave with tears in her eyes.

Chapter Thirty-nine

I returned to the soiree to find Ruth Yoder in the middle of the square holding up a sign. DRY HARVEST! NO ALCOHOL IN HARVEST! She held her sign without speaking and while standing perfectly still. Tourists walked by her with raised eyebrows.

"Bailey!" Margot shouted at me. "Where have you been?"

"I just went to see if Darcy was around," I said.

She waved her hands in the air. "Fine. That doesn't matter. We have a situation here. You have to do something about this!"

"You want *me* to do something about Ruth?" I asked.

"Yes, about Ruth." Margot pulled at the curls on the top of her head. When she let them go, they sprang back into place. "And do it now, before it becomes worse. This is going to be the only thing people talk about at the soiree. An Amish protest! They will forget about the elegance, the fabulous wines, and your delicious truffles. Your truffles will even be lost in the gossip. I can't have that. Bailey! Do something!"

I picked Jethro up and tucked him under my arm like he was a football and I was ready to run fifty yards. In truth, I would much rather run fifty yards away from Ruth Yoder than confront her. By the set of her jaw as she held her sign, she meant business.

"What do you want me to do?" I asked helplessly.

Margot pushed me toward Ruth. "I don't know. Just get rid of her. She's your friend."

I wouldn't call Ruth Yoder my friend in the least.

Margot gave me another shove, and I stumbled through the crowd to where Ruth stood. I cleared my throat. "Hi, Ruth, everything okay?"

She flipped the sign around. The handwriting read, *I am not speaking. This is a silent protest against the English who would destroy the village of Harvest, which does and always will rightfully belong to the Amish.*

"Oh, well, okay," I said and adjusted Jethro under my arm. "I understand you can't speak, but you need to take yourself and your sign off the square."

She flipped the sign back to its original message and glared at me. Her feet were firmly planted into the grass. She wasn't going anywhere, and she wanted me to know it.

I wasn't going to be the one to throw the elderly bishop's wife off the square. My *maami* had enough problems with the leadership of district because of me. I wasn't going to add to it, especially when my grandmother was so unwell.

I decided to blame it on Margot, who, if I was honest, was the one who was truly at fault. "Margot asked me to ask you to leave."

She glared at me.

"I know the two of you have your differences, but neither of you would want to do anything to make Harvest look bad. A protest is your right, and it will bring attention to the village. But not all of that attention will be good."

Still, she said nothing. She didn't even blink. Ruth had this vow of silence thing down pat.

Jethro pressed his wet snout into my arm as if he thought it would bring me comfort. He meant well.

"You have every right to protest. Free country and all, but can't you go across the street or something?" I asked. "You can still make your argument, but just a little out of the way. I'm sure everyone will still see you from there."

She glared at me again.

"I'll take that as a no." I bit my lower lip. "I think you've made your point, and I completely understand. Harvest has a long-standing tradition of being a dry village. I can see why you are upset."

Just when I thought there was no way I would ever get Ruth to move, Jethro held his nose up in the air as if he smelled something delectable. He kicked at my side.

I yelped and dropped the pig, and he raced across the square in the direction of a vendor selling gourmet popcorn. Jethro had a very soft spot for popcorn. Caramel popcorn was his favorite, even though it got stuck on his molars. I knew this because Juliet had asked me to brush his teeth once after a caramel popcorn binge. Juliet claimed that she asked me to do it because Jethro trusted me more, of course.

If Juliet was any judge to the fact, Jethro trusted me to do just about everything.

The popcorn vendor was just handing a young woman a bag of popcorn as Jethro jumped two feet in the air and grabbed the bag before running off.

I threw up my hands. "Jethro!"

"Loose pig! Runaway pig!" someone in the crowd cried.

In any other place in the world, this would have been a very shocking announcement, but here, it was just part of life in Harvest. Jethro would get loose, and pandemonium would ensue. It was just part of the fabric of the village. Unfortunately, it seemed to be my job to deal with the aftermath of Jethro's antics.

I knew from experience that the best way to catch Jethro wasn't to chase him, but to wait until he was tired and scoop him up. Unfortunately, it seemed the tourists at the soiree didn't know this, and at least a dozen people began to chase the little pig.

Jethro's eyes rolled back into his head as he bobbed and weaved around them. A man in a blue suit ran right at him causing Jethro to make a sharp turn and rip right through the sign Ruth had been holding at her side like a bullfighter holding a red cape. I was just on the other side of the sign, and I caught the little pig in my arms.

There was a cheer from the tourists.

I heard one of them say, "I didn't know that this

event had entertainment, too! I will definitely come back if they have the Summer Soiree again."

"There is always something going on with the pig when you come to Harvest," a man standing next to her said.

"That horrid little pig ruined my sign." Clearly dismayed, Ruth held up both pieces of her sign, which had been ripped into two.

I guessed that now that her protest sign was ruined, she didn't have to keep her vow of silence any longer.

She glared at Jethro. "You horrid, little pig. You're always making trouble."

I held Jethro close. "Ruth, that is no way to talk to a pig."

"Everyone else in this village talks to him like he is a person. Why can't I—espccially when he's done something wrong?" She narrowed her eyes at me. "And *you*, Bailey King. I will be speaking to Clara about you just as soon as she is feeling better. I won't burden her with your behavior when she is unwell, but you should have more respect for the Amish."

"I respect the Amish very much."

"Not as far as I have seen."

I rolled my eyes. I wasn't going to gauge my respect for the Amish on how Ruth felt about it.

"Do you need to make a new sign?" I asked. "We have poster board over at the Candyworks."

She scowled. "*Nee.* I have made my point. You just let Margot know that if she has another event like this in Harvest, she will have much more than a sign to contend with." She folded up the ruined sign and marched off the square.

I looked down at Jethro. "Nice work. You did what I could not—you got Ruth's protest off the square."

He wiggled his body.

"You're one heck of a pig. Now, let's get you some popcorn, and we are going to pay for it this time, like upstanding citizens."

He licked my nose in thanks.

Chapter Forty

Around eight thirty, the sun was making its downward slide into the west, and Jethro and I were walking back from the Candyworks, where we had gone to check on Charlotte and the other English candy sellers. I was happy to see that business was booming. Hosting the cooling station in the factory while keeping the shop open to sell candy had been an excellent idea.

The soiree was set to end at nine, and by the time Jethro and I stepped back onto the square, it was clear that things had begun to wind down. The long lines of guests waiting for samples had died down, and from what I could tell, most of the truffles were gone. That was good news for me. I was on a serious truffle break.

Lampposts began to flicker on around the square and up and down Main Street. The twinkle lights in the trees reflected off the petals of Pearl's flowers.

Margot walked up to me, clapping her hands. "Well done, Bailey King, well done. You did very well, and your truffles are all but gone. They might even have been more popular than the wine. Don't tell the wineries I said that."

"I won't," I said, then made sure Jethro's leash was secure before I set him down in the grass. I looked around the square for Juliet. I had expected her to come back at some point after her dinner with Reverend Brook to collect her pig, but there was no sign of her. It looked like Jethro was going home with me for another night.

Aiden would be thrilled to have another pet in our bed.

I checked my phone to see if there was any update from my new husband. He had planned to come over to the soiree at the end of his shift, but like so many other times, he hadn't made it, likely from being caught at work with another issue or emergency. It was something I'd become used to as his girlfriend and then fiancée. It was also something I would just have to accept as his wife. He wasn't always able to come home when he said he would.

I was happy to see he had texted me.

I know the soiree is ending. I'm heading that way now. I will meet you at the candy factory. So sorry, babe.

I sighed and stuck the phone back into my pocket. I wasn't sighing so much over Aiden missing the Summer Soiree—I had expected that—but I was sighing over the conversation I needed to have with him about Enoch. I didn't want to accuse an innocent man of murder. If I was wrong, it could cause more hardship for Enoch Unger, who had already been through so much.

At nine o'clock sharp, Margot climbed to the top of the gazebo stairs. "Thank you all for coming," she announced. "The Summer Soiree was a hit, but sadly it has now come to an end. I want to thank all our fabulous wineries and vendors for taking part in this event, and in particular, Bailey King and Swissmen Candyworks."

I smiled. I didn't need the public praise from Margot, but it was nice to hear. On second thought, I wondered if she was just buttering me up for the next favor she wanted to ask of me. I bet it was the latter. Margot was smart like that.

As the four wineries packed up their empty bottles and leftover wine, everyone looked to be in good spirits. The Summer Soiree had been a success despite the unexpected antics of Jethro the Grape and Ruth Yoder's inconvenient protest.

I looked down at Jethro, who was tucked under my arm like a football. He seemed to still be in shock over the soiree's events.

When Margot had finished her brief speech, she walked over to me. As if she could read my mind, she said, "I do plan to have a few words with Ruth. She almost ruined the whole event."

"Peaceful protests are allowed," I said, "even if it's only one Amish woman."

Jethro looked up at me with questioning eyes. It was going to take him a few days to get over this one.

"Since when do the Amish stage any protest, peaceful or otherwise? If Ruth won't take my complaint seriously, I will go to the bishop." She shook her clipboard at me. "Mark my words, Ruth Yoder doesn't want to go toe to toe with me..This means war." She stomped away.

Now that the Summer Soiree was over, it was apparent that Margot had moved on to her next big project: putting the bishop's wife, Ruth Yoder, in her place. I wished her luck with that. She was going to need it.

Charlotte rolled a wagon of coolers filled with candy over to me. "We're all packed up. It's mostly empty containers. I can count on one hand how many truffles were left. I just gave them away to anyone who would take them."

"Fine by me," I said. "Between the wedding and this, I need a truffle break."

She nodded toward her wagon. "I'll take this back to the factory and then go home."

"Don't be silly," I said. "I live much closer than you do. You're not going to get home until after eleven as it is, and you have been at work since five this morning. I'll take the wagon. Go on home. Besides, Aiden just texted me to say he was at the factory."

"He's already there," she said. "He was just walking in as I was leaving to collect the coolers. He looked exhausted."

"It's been a rough week."

Charlotte sighed. "I wish that wasn't something you had to say about the week after your wedding. You should be enjoying this time."

"We will get a chance to enjoy our marriage. The soiree is over now, and when *Maami* is recovered, we can start thinking again of going on a honeymoon. But I don't want to go anywhere until I know that she is all right."

Charlotte nodded. "I understand. We are all so worried about her. She is such a treasure to the community."

I blinked back tears and reminded myself of what the doctors had said. If *Maami* was willing to change her diet, she was sure to make a full recovery. I knew she wouldn't be happy to have to give up some of her favorite Amish foods, but I also knew she would do it for me. She loved me that much.

With my free hand that wasn't holding Jethro, I took the wagon handle from Charlotte. "I've got this. Go home and relax—and come in late tomorrow. I know the long hours you have been working leading up to the wedding and now with the Summer Soiree."

Charlotte laughed. "If you're sure."

"Charlotte, I'm sure."

"Okay. Luke is waiting for me in his car, parked in front of the candy shop." She gave me a hug. "Another great event, Bailey. You should be happy."

I waved at her as she climbed into the car with her husband, Deputy Little.

I turned and started to walk across the square, waving at Jon Michael and Angel as they got into their separate vans. Both seemed very happy with the soiree. It had been a success, but I still didn't know how I felt about having events on the square that were clearly so offensive to some of the Amish in Harvest.

Chapter Forty-one

Dakota was the last to finish packing up. She snapped the lid closed on the final rolling case of Swiss Valley wines that she'd brought to the soiree.

I rolled my wagon over to her. "You're all set?"

She jumped. "Oh, I'm sorry, Bailey." She rubbed her eyes. "I guess I'm tired. It's been a long day."

"I can understand that. I feel dead on my feet. Where are you parked?"

"I—I parked by the market," she said.

"Perfect. I'm going the same way." I nodded at the wagon. "I have to drop this off at the factory. I'll walk with you."

My arm was tired of carrying Jethro, so I moved around some empty containers in the wagon and made a little nest for him. When I set Jethro in the wagon, he looked around in confusion, but then he seemed pleased with his new hideout among the empty truffle containers. Perhaps he felt comforted by the scent of chocolate.

With the many hours he spent around it in Swissmen Sweets, he was certainly used to the smell. He quickly curled up into a ball and went to sleep. We were all tuckered out from the day.

Dakota scrunched up her face as if she was trying to think of a way to get out of walking with me. "All right."

We walked in silence for a few paces, and the factory wasn't far. I didn't have much time to ask all the questions swirling in my head.

"Carly told me she would be inheriting Swiss Valley," I said. "Are you going to stay on there?"

She glanced at me. "It's not really my decision, is it? I'm only glad that Carly let me sell Swiss Valley's wine tonight at the Summer Soiree. As soon as I heard she would be inheriting the winery, I thought she would put a stop to it."

"Carly is too smart of a businesswoman to do that," I said. "Now that Swiss Valley is hers, she wants it to succeed. The soiree was great publicity for the brand, and she knows it."

"I guess." She shrugged.

"Do you want to stay at Swiss Valley?"

"I—I don't know. There are a lot of other wineries in Holmes County I could look into. It might not work with me staying on at Swiss Valley. Carly is pretty set on the idea that I was just loyal to Jason, but that's not true. It's really her grandfather, Mr. Hackney, that I loved. I worked with him and Carly for a couple of years before Mr. Hackney passed away. He was a kind and thoughtful man, but Carly has never liked me. It only got worse when I didn't leave the winery after

Jason took over. I don't think she will want me there now. It doesn't matter how close I was to Mr. Hackney, does it?"

"How long were you at Swiss Valley?" I asked, trying to get the timeline right in my head.

Jason had returned to Ohio three years ago. In his first year back, he'd convinced his grandfather to let him take over the winery. His grandfather then wrote a new will, stating that Jason would be the sole heir. He died a year later. The same year he died, Joseph Unger also died in an accident after stealing a tractor from Billings Farm Supplies. According to everyone who might know, Jason had put Joseph and his two anonymous friends up to stealing the tractor so that he himself could sell it.

And then Jason had died by a poisoned tart—laced with a death cap mushroom—at my wedding reception. It was a tart that Enoch, Joseph's father, could have easily tampered with, because he was Darcy's cook and he had been in and out of the Candyworks kitchen throughout the day of the wedding.

I was more convinced than ever that Enoch was behind the murder, and Dakota might be able to confirm it because she'd cared so much about Joseph. Surely she would know Enoch, then, as well as what he might be capable of.

She bit her lower lip. "I've worked there for five years. I started right after high school. It was just a summer job at first."

"You could serve wine when you were underage?" I asked.

"No, but I could harvest grapes and work with the vines. My mom has a huge garden. I grew up with plants and always loved them. I moved from the vines and eventually into the tasting room. Jason needed help there, and he said I had a knack for pairing the wine with what people were looking for. I don't know where it came from. I grew up with a single mom, and she was against drinking almost as much as the bishop's wife. Although I don't think she would have staged a protest like Ruth Yoder did."

"Ruth is in a class by herself. Hopefully, Jethro will recover. I don't think that when Margot asked Juliet if Jethro wanted to take part in the soiree, this is what they thought would happen." I chuckled. "Do you still want to be a sommelier?"

She shook her head. "I don't know. I think I need to do something new—and as far away from here as I can get."

"I know it was hard when you lost Joseph."

She stopped at the edge of the parking lot. One side of her face was lit up by a lamppost, and the other was in the dark. "Joseph?"

"Anna Grace told me that you and he were close."

"He was my friend." Her voice was low.

"But maybe you wanted it to be more?"

"Who told you that?" she snapped.

"Anna Grace said you had feelings for him. She believes Joseph was the reason you stayed at Swiss Valley. It wasn't loyalty to Mr. Hackney, who had passed away."

Her face flushed. "Anna Grace has no right to be

gossiping about me. Besides, Joseph was Amish—I'm not. It never would have worked. I cared about him, but we were just friends. It doesn't matter if I wished it could be more. It wasn't reciprocated that way, but we were friends. Best friends."

I glanced back at Jethro and was pleased to see he was happily sleeping in the wagon. It had been quite a week for the little pig, too. I turned back to Dakota. "That must have been hard to have feelings for your best friend."

"It was," she said, thus admitting that was how she'd really felt about Joseph. "But I wasn't going to do anything to mess up our friendship. I wanted to stay friends with him even after he was baptized and joined the Amish church."

Now that Joseph was gone, there was no point in telling Dakota that likely wouldn't have worked. In the Amish world, having unmarried friends of the opposite sex, especially when you were married, was strongly discouraged. Add that to the fact that she was not Amish, and it was almost impossible.

"Can you tell me about the night of his accident?" I asked.

She stared at me. "What does that have to do with anything?"

"Was Joseph working for Jason?"

"Yes, you already know that. He worked in the vineyard." She quickened her pace across the parking lot.

I matched her stride for stride. "Was he stealing for Jason? Did he steal the tractor as part of his work for Jason?"

She stopped in the middle of the almost-empty

parking lot. There was one buggy with no horse by the market's door, and only a few cars spread about. I spotted Aiden's department SUV near the factory entrance. I had to find a way to get her to come into the factory with me, so we could talk all of this over with Aiden. I knew Dakota was the key to finding out who the killer was.

Instead, she increased her pace and made a beeline for an older-model sedan. It was just the kind of car a young person would drive around the county when they were just starting out.

I quickened my steps to catch up with her.

Jethro made a whimpering sound as the wagon bumped over the uneven spots in the pavement.

"There is a rumor that Jason had young men stealing farming equipment for him." I paused. "And Joseph was one of them. That's what he was doing that night, correct?"

Dakota hurried to her car, unlocked the trunk, and tried to throw the rolling case inside. But it was too heavy for her to move that quickly. It bounced off the bumper and landed on her foot. She squealed.

I ran over to her. "Are you okay?"

"Get away from me!" she shouted and shoved the case off her foot. She tried to stand up but couldn't. She crumpled back onto the ground. Her foot was bent at an odd angle.

"I can help you," I said.

"I don't want your help. Just leave me alone. I wish everyone would just leave me alone and stop telling me what to do!"

I stepped back. "Okay, but at least let me call an ambulance. Your foot looks broken."

She whimpered.

I knew she had to be in terrible pain.

"No." She fished a small plastic bag out of her pocket and opened it. She then held whatever was in the bag in front of her mouth like she was going to eat it.

It didn't look like gum or a mint to me.

"What's that?" I cried. "What do you have?"

"A death cap mushroom. I saved some for myself just in case. I'm glad I did. I should have known it would go this way. Nothing ever works out for me."

My stomach dropped. I let go of the wagon handle and took a step close to her. "Dakota, give that to me."

"Don't come any closer or I will eat it." She held the bit of mushroom in front of her mouth.

"Please don't," I whispered. I was afraid to move. I was even afraid to take my phone from my pocket and call for help. Any movement might push her over the edge and make her eat it.

I should have gone to Aiden first before talking to her, or at least have asked him to come to the parking lot. Now it was too late.

"I loved Joseph, and I didn't stop him when he left that night. I knew what they were planning to do, but I was so angry at him. I—I called an anonymous tip in to the sheriff's department that someone was going to steal a tractor at Billings Farm Supplies." Tears ran down her cheeks. "I thought I was teaching him a lesson. I didn't know that Jason had put him up to it until later. I always thought he and his friends just did it on their own."

"How did you find out Jason's involvement?" I asked.

"I told her," a deep voice said behind me.

I jumped and turned around to see Enoch Unger step out into the light.

"I'm sorry, Enoch." Dakota began to sob. "It's my fault that Joseph is dead. I was the one who called the sheriff."

"*Nee.* It was Jason's fault," Enoch said in a soothing voice. "It was always Jason's fault. The score is settled now. We have no more work left to do."

I looked from one to the other and back again. "You were in on Jason's murder together?"

He shook his head. "*Nee.*"

"But you told me to do it." She rubbed her foot. "You gave me the mushroom and told me which tart to put it in."

"*Nee.* I never said to do it. I just told you how *I* would do it if I made that choice. To consider it is one thing. To act on it is another. I didn't make the choice to kill him—you did."

She held the mushroom to her mouth again. "Then it's just me who needs to be punished."

With a great squeal, Jethro leapt out of the wagon, ran across the parking lot, and jumped on Dakota's broken foot.

She cried out in pain.

The bit of death cap mushroom flew out of her hand and landed just feet away from me. I stomped on it with my shoe like I was squashing a bug.

Enoch knelt next to Dakota and held her close. She cried into his chest. "I know you loved him," he said into her hair. "I am grateful someone cared for my son so much before he died."

"Bailey!" I heard Aiden shout from the direction of Swissmen Candyworks. "I heard a scream."

"Over here!" I called as I scooped up Jethro.

I guessed the little pig was a good mushroom hunter after all.

Epilogue

As Aiden and I settled into our seats on the airliner, destined for our honeymoon, I took his hand in mine. He smiled at me. "You nervous?"

I shook my head. "I fly all the time. I have no reason to be nervous."

He touched my wrinkled brow. "Then what are these little creases about?"

I gave him a half smile. "I was just thinking about Jason, Dakota, and Enoch. Even Joseph. It's all so sad."

Aiden nodded. "It is. So many times, when I close a case, I dwell on it for weeks, or even months, afterward."

"How do you get over it?" I whispered.

He squeezed my hand a little more tightly. "I think about the fact that I did the best I could to bring justice to the situation, and then I feel grateful for my own life." He paused. "For you."

I smiled at him. "I'm grateful for you, too." I looked

out the window. "But I can't help but feel sorry for Dakota."

"I can understand that, but she's young. She could very well get out on good behavior someday and rebuild her life."

I nodded and thought about the shy young woman. The night of the Summer Soiree, Dakota had broken her foot, and Aiden took her to the hospital after arresting her. On the way to the hospital, she'd confessed to it all. Hours before the wedding, she'd added a piece of the death cap mushroom to one of Darcy's tarts and had given it to Jason, telling him it was a peace offering from Darcy. Jason had wanted to make up with Darcy so badly that he ate it without question. The tart Darcy gave him herself during the reception was the second mushroom tart he'd eaten that day. Dakota had killed Jason Hackney to avenge Joseph's death.

I didn't know what Enoch was guilty of other than putting the idea in her head. He'd never told her to do it, so Aiden said there wasn't a strong case for an accessory charge. However, he did confess to being the one who had attacked Darcy in the early morning. He was in the café looking for the death cap mushroom that he believed Dakota had hidden there to frame him. As it turned out, she'd had it with her all the time.

Darcy had unwittingly walked in on Enoch when he was searching, and he panicked. He hit her on the head with a frying pan. Every time I thought about it, I shook my head. Enoch worked at the café. He could have just claimed he wanted to start work early that day.

Lois was fit to be tied over the attack and wanted

Darcy to press charges. She refused. In the end, she'd had compassion for Enoch for all he had been through, losing his wife and son. Still, she wasn't comfortable with him working at the café any longer, so she'd let him go. I prayed he would finally find peace over the loss of his family.

If I were Enoch, though, I would watch my back. Lois was still walking around Holmes County with a brick in her purse, and that brick now had his name on it.

Hopefully, for Enoch's sake, Lois would be too distracted by Jean Pierre's extended stay in Harvest to seek revenge. He seemed to be in no rush to return to the bright lights of New York City, and Lois was a big reason for that.

"Pleasc buckle your seat belts. The captain has put on the seat belt sign. We request your attention for the safety demonstration."

"I can't believe we are finally going on our honeymoon," I said. "It has been months since we got married."

He smiled. "We had to make sure *Maami* was all right before we left. I thank God every day that she's made a full recovery."

"Me, too," I whispered and took Aiden's hand in mine. "Here we go. I can't believe you are taking me to Switzerland for our honeymoon. I've never even been to Europe!"

"I told you I would make it up to you when I had to cancel our first honeymoon," he said. "And what better place is there to take a famous chocolatier than Switzerland? They do say Swiss chocolate is the best."

"They do say that." I leaned my head on his shoulder. "But I would say that just sitting here next to you is the very best."

"I've always thought that," he agreed.

Swissmen Candyworks Raspberry Truffles

Ingredients

- ¼ cup freeze-dried raspberries
- ¼ cup white-chocolate melting wafers
- ½ cup heavy cream
- 1 cup dark-chocolate melting wafers
- Handful of extra freeze-dried raspberries

Instructions

1. Crush freeze-dried raspberries in a food processor until they are a fine powder.
2. Add raspberry powder to the white-chocolate wafers in a heat-safe bowl.
3. Heat heavy cream in a small saucepan over medium heat, but do not boil.
4. Pour the hot cream over the white chocolate and raspberry powder and stir until fully incorporated.
5. Refrigerate for up to one hour, and then portion the truffle filling out with a teaspoon.
6. Roll each portion into a ball.
7. Place the balls on a parchment paper–lined cookie sheet and refrigerate for another hour.
8. Melt the dark chocolate in a double boiler.
9. Dip the bottom of a truffle into the melted chocolate on the tip of a fork and make sure it's completely covered.
10. Place the truffle back on the parchment paper–lined cookie sheet. Repeat for all truffles.

11. Drizzle excess melted chocolate over the tops of the truffles and sprinkle with crushed, freeze-dried raspberries for decoration.
12. Refrigerate for another hour.
13. Enjoy!